"A book for anyone interested in the human heart."
Catherine Simpson

"I can't explain what this book has meant to me at this time in my life. ... I've been so scared. But this beautiful book has helped me heal by exploring the acute heartache of abuse and broken family."
Jillian Halket

"Harrowing, tragic, yet ultimately uplifting, *The Broken Pane* breaks your heart then puts it back together."
Alistair Braidwood, *The Skinny*

"A delicate and moving debut, studded with moments of beauty."
Kirstin Innes

"Beautifully crafted – and that is exactly why I loved it!"
Partridge Pages

"An incredibly open book – I can't wait to read more from the author."
I'm Reading My Book

"A remarkable and beautiful debut novel."
Bookish Geeky

"This is a stunning debut – shining a much needed light on working class women's mental health."
Spooks Books

"*The Broken Pane* is a striking debut – in that no-man's land somewhere between hope and despair."
Bethany's Blog

The Broken Pane

Published in the UK in 2021
Paperback edition 2022
Leamington Books
Edinburgh, Scotland

leamingtonbooks.com

ISBN: 9781914090608

Production Editor: Peter Burnett
Typeset by Main Point Books, Edinburgh
Editorial: Ambrose Kelly
Cover Design: Cavan Convery
Author Photograph: Ryan McGoverne

Printed and bound by Imprint Academic, Devon.

For the ones I love

THE BROKEN PANE

CHARLIE ROY

LEAMINGTON BOOKS

1992

Early phone calls, the ones which drag you from sleep, are rarely good news.

We all know this.

I was dreaming I had left something important somewhere safe, but did not know what or where, I was running in and out of different houses, different lives, looking for it. I was pressing a doorbell; it rang and rang until it became the shrill ring of the phone in the hallway. I pulled myself out of bed, the sheets and blanket reluctantly letting me go, stumbling on autopilot to pick up the receiver.

"M'yeah?"

"Tam? Have you seen him?"

It was Lou. My brother Nicky, who I nicknamed Bugs, had not been home for several days.

It was not unusual for them to have quarrelled.

But this time was different.

Everything shattered.

Try as I might, I could not piece it back together.

Ж

"Bugs! It's me. Come on, let me in!"

Nothing.

It was both odd and familiar to stand at the front door again, keys in hand, pulled from my bag out of habit. I noticed the green paint was peeling, more so in the parts that had been damaged through the years and re-touched with varying shades that did not quite match. The old-fashioned lock and the brass letter box, matching the number on the door. Unchanged after all these years.

I raised my fist and knocked.

I listened.

Silence. I knocked more resolutely but no response came.

I started to turn away, but as my ear was now positioned towards the door, I heard something. The radio was on. He must be in then. It could be no one else. I knocked a final time.

"I've not got time for this, I need to see you and then I'm off to work, I'm coming in!"

I selected the Chubb lock key first for the top lock, and then the main skeleton key, inserted it and leant back to get a better prise. The lock was stiff, as it had always been, so I pulled back on the handle, giving it the exact wiggle that it needed, just as my Nana had done the first day that I was brought here. As the door unlocked, I pushed it forward, against a few envelopes that jammed up against the door. I grimaced and scooped them up, dumping them on the hall table along with my handbag.

"Nicky, it's me, Tam. Wake up! Lou called. C'mon, I need to get to work."

The hall was filled with the grey light of an unloved place. Ahead, I could see that the kitchen light was on, the yellow glow anaemic. I walked down the hall, passing the under-stair cupboard to my left, the sitting room to my right, all beige, brown and saggy.

The kitchen was an absolute tip. The table was

strewn with empty bottles, overflowing ashtrays. All the counters were covered too. Crumbs, crumpled empties, cigarette papers, filters, clumps of shredded tobacco, a half-litre vodka bottle, beer bottles. As though he had been out partying with his mates, had a late one and left the detritus for the morning.

Except there was only one chair, pushed back under the table.

Everything was positioned towards the chair, even a cigarette that had burnt down the most of its length and lay in the ashtray. Only one person had made use of all of this.

How long had this been going on?

The sound of the radio came back into focus. Where was it coming from? I tilted my head to work out which room. Somewhere upstairs. I thought he must have passed out drunk or high in his room. The memory of the time I found him lying in his vomit flashed in front of my eyes. I needed to get to the chemist to open the shop, and I certainly did not want to be scrubbing a carpet in my work clothes.

"Get up, Bugs! The place is a mess. I'm not cleaning this up again, you know! This is totally disgusting. For fuck's sake!"

I marched up the stairs, irritation rising fast. I had told him not to stay here unless he was prepared to keep it tidy. I had always cleaned up after him. I was fed up with it.

I pushed the bathroom door open. It had been years since the lock had been forced, never to work again.

There he was, in the bath. Asleep.

No. Not asleep.

I screamed.

I took a deep breath.

I think I screamed again. It was a strange guttural sound that exploded out of my ribcage.

I was on my knees.

Lying there in the bath was my brother. His blonde head flopped back against the edge, the pink-brown water, his arm rested on the side of the bath, and a brown trickle running from his wrist. The paring knife lay on the floor. The thought that he looked like some sort of morbid art installation flickered across my conscience.

I am not sure how long I sat there, on my knees. I was not even sobbing. I sat, staring at my little brother Nicky, until I noticed my feet and legs had gone numb beneath me.

I had not taken my eyes off him once.

I pulled myself up, out of the doorway, backwards, eyes locked on him as the door shut. I let my leaden feet guide me down the stairs, across the narrow hall into the living room to the telephone. I picked up the old-fashioned handset and rang 999, turning my finger three times around the dial, listening to it click back.

"Which service do you require?

Hello?

Is anyone there?"

I blinked. I took a deep breath.

"Hello. I, um, my brother, he's …"

I tried to swallow. My mouth was dry. The words choked in the back of my throat. The operator said something.

"My brother. I think he's dead. He's dead. Help. Please. Help."

"Ma'am, I'm dispatching someone to you right away. Was there an accident? How old is your brother? Can you tell me any more about what happened?"

The next fifteen, twenty minutes or thirty minutes were a blur. I spoke to the dispatcher, sinking to my knees again, on the floor. I could not move. The image. His body. Every blink. Nicky, Bugs. Why? How?

Beautiful baby brother.

But not a tear. Not even one. Dry. Immobilised. Chest tight. Throat locked. Brownpink water. Ears rushing. Shoulders tight.

The police and some medics arrived. I must have left the front door open. First they came to me in the living room, but I pointed up.

A policewoman helped me from the floor and led me to the sofa. Her black-and-white checkered necktie seemed to hover in front of my eyes. Evidently, I had not said a word since they had arrived, and a brown-haired police officer had taken the phone handset from my hand. He spoke into the phone and hung up. He nodded at his colleague and went to stand in the hall.

The policewoman started to ask some questions which I answered unthinkingly, but she stopped after a couple, and looked me in the eye. She put her hand reassuringly on my shoulder.

"I'll be right back."

A few minutes later, she re-appeared, putting a hot cup of sweet tea between my hands.

"There you go. Drink that. It will help a bit. I'm going to get the medic to take a quick look at you, OK?"

The medic earnestly informed me that it was shock, and I stared at his hands, the funny tuft of hair sticking out from under his wristwatch. He told me I might feel cold and shivery a bit later, and with that, he left.

I noticed my hands were clammy on the hot mug.

Looming above me, the police officer returned and pulled out a small flip notepad. I looked down and lifted the mug to my lips, closed my eyes, breathed the steam in through my nose before taking a big swig. It went down well even though I hate sweet tea. I looked up and I was able to start answering her questions – name, age, relationship to Nicky, his

13

name and age, when I last saw him and what his state of mind had been.

A man in a brown suit came and told me gently that Nicky was indeed dead, and his body would be taken to the mortuary. Did I want to see him again before he left the house? I glanced towards the stairs, which I could see through the doorway, and saw a black shape on a stretcher being carried out.

It stopped quite suddenly, the black shape seeming to hover diagonally behind the door frame. I blinked. Mrs Ranjeet's head, shrouded in bright pink and gold popped into focus, the most incongruous vision, her ordinarily cheery face set to high concern.

"Tam! What an awful – is it a robbery? You don't stay here much now, an empty house is always a, well the thieves, they know, you know. So many police! At least they came, they don't always, did I see an ambulance? Was someone hurt? Oh *chotu*, shall I put on the kettle? You can tell me ..."

She trailed off into the kitchen, still chattering, and my eyes focused back to the stairs, now empty.

That was it, Nicky had left our childhood home forever.

I hadn't been there when it happened.

I knew what "it" was.

I was supposed to always be there.

I was supposed to look after him.

Mrs Ranjeet bustled back in.

"Now, *chotu*, there was no milk or biscuits, and we can go to my flat if you like? You know, I thought I heard you calling out. How lovely to see you! You never stop by anymore. How are you? How's the job? Are you fine? Good, good!"

She swept me up into a warm embrace, the familiar scents of cumin and Pears soap enveloping me. She launched herself into a barrage of news.

They were off to India the next month to visit Old Mrs Ranjeet, who had moved back a few years before. I was so rarely around anymore, I was looking too skinny, and I should catch up with her properly.

I nodded and pulled a smile across my face, forcing my sore eyes to open wider. I loved Mrs Ranjeet, who had been a kind, warm and maternal presence next door all my life, I wanted her to make it alright.

I could not bring myself to say a single word.

She seized my hand firmly, kindly, and looked straight into my eyes, so that I would know that she had something important to say.

She had been worried about Nicky, he had not seemed right recently. He had turned up a few days before, and he had not been out of the flat at all, not even to say hello.

She had heard him shouting one night, though she could have sworn he was alone, and another he had played music extremely loud. She emphasised the "loud". What was more he'd been eating fast food, which was something she frowned upon greatly, as he should have invited himself round and joined them at mealtimes.

She added that it was good to see me here, that I was needed. I had no idea what she meant. She told me that she had tried to offer him help to clean the flat so that she could get in and properly check on him, but he had refused.

Nicky and I had always been glad to know she was next door, not that we ever did run to her in an emergency. I squeezed her hand back, and nodded, saying that I would see her soon, that I would come for dinner, and to send greetings to her husband, love to the boys.

Somehow, I thought, she had missed it. The obvious thing. How could she not have noticed the paramedics, the morticians, the stretcher carrying Nicky away.

I could not find the words to point it out to her. I did not say "Nicky is dead" to her. I could not say "Nicky has killed himself".

A throat cleared somewhere above my head and Mrs Ranjeet looked up over me. She smiled and bobbed her head.

"Of course, officer, you'll be wanting to get your statements. I'm along the hall, next door, you'll want to know if I heard anything. Terrible though, all these break-ins, I'll write to the Council, we need more Bobbies like you on the beat."

Her voice followed her and the officer out of the sitting room, right out of the front door.

"Let me know, Officer, if she needs me. I'm Mrs Ranjeet. No, j-e-e-t. That's right. I've known them since they were ..."

Eventually, only the policewoman and the tall brown-haired officer remained. She sat down beside me, and gently took a now-cold cup out of my hand. I must have been holding it for well over an hour. My hand felt cramped and stiff. Mrs Ranjeet's cups remained full on the chunky coffee table.

"And you're sure there's no one we can call? We can run you home. Or Mrs Ranjeet next door maybe?"

"I'm fine, thank you. I should be at work. I need to go to work. I'm opening the shop. I have the keys."

The police officers exchanged looks. They told me that it was past midday, that work had already been taken care of, and with reassuring noises, the sort you might use with an animal or young child, guided me out of the flat, down to their car, and away, towards my own home.

I stared out of the police car window.

"Bugs, it wasn't that bad. We were OK. The ogre was gone."

16

1973

I do not have a first memory of my little brother. I
do not remember my mother being pregnant, or her
telling me that a baby was coming to live with us.
There is an awareness of Nicky's presence in my life
that appears in my childhood recollections, like a
bright light. Can anyone honestly say they remember
it all accurately?

My mother, Ange, was pregnant again at the age
of twenty-one. Not an unusual age to be pregnant
in those days, though her contemporaries in the
maternity clinic were all anxiously patting their first
bumps, asking her for advice on cots and layettes.

Shortly after her twenty-second birthday and a
relatively quick labour that lasted under three hours,
she gave birth to a healthy baby boy, Nicholas James.

This time round, my father Mick waited at the
hospital, pacing the halls of the ward, grinding one
finished cigarette into the standing ashtrays before
immediately lighting the next, breaking only to refill
his coffee cup, seasoned with a top note from his
flask.

A young nurse came to find him in the late afternoon:
"Congratulations, Sir, it's a healthy baby boy."

To the nurse's surprise, he hugged her in delight.

Mick, I mean Dad, always said that she had looked flabbergasted. He only ever used the word when he told this anecdote, savouring the use of it. I suspect he was not entirely certain of the meaning and had picked it up at the time to use in this specific context. I could never use it without picturing my father, sodden in his cups, welling up over the tale of the birth of his son.

He told it well, the birth of his second child, there at his wife's bedside as soon as he was summoned, how tenderly they kissed, the baby nestling between them. The room was warm and clean, my mother's blonde hair gently cascading down a shoulder, glowing with her light of happiness, basking in the joy that he had bestowed on her, a perfect boy.

This vignette was often repeated, the beats familiar, and we, his audience, knew to sigh contentedly at the end of the telling.

Nana's dear friend George came to the hospital a few hours later with me clinging to his enormous hand. He held a camera in the other. With it, he took one of our very few family photos. They may have had an unconventional relationship, but he knew how to step up to the part of Grandpa, albeit unofficially.

In it, my father sits on my mother's left-hand side, half on the bed with a foot still on the floor, his right arm behind her, supporting himself. She is sitting up, with my brother wrapped in a puce pink blanket cradled in her right arm, and I am sitting in front of them all, by my mother's right knee, a grinning four-year-old, a mass of unruly black curls with my new blue teddy, Mr Blue, that Nana had given me on the day.

Photographic evidence that we could be a perfect family, no cracks on show.

Truth be told, I do not remember that day. The

image is imprinted in my mind, soundtracked by the tale of Nicky's birth.

I do have a few memories from the following year, the year of my fifth birthday. Like the time my friend from nursery school came round and we spread newspapers on the kitchen table and Mum got us paints and paper. It can't have been Becky. I didn't become friends with her until primary school. We daubed it all gleefully and laughed. I have incorporated details such as eating biscuits, and smearing paint on each other's faces. I am able to remember it clearly because there is a photograph of us, our blue, yellow and green hands waving at the camera. I like this memory.

Mick, I mean Dad, swept me up into his arms every morning, with a "be good, Duckling" and a kiss on the forehead. Then he set off to work, giving Mum a peck on the lips on the way out, and I would run to the window to wave, my hair set neatly in bunches.

It was a perfect snow globe time in our lives. I recall being held up so that I could look down into Nicky's crib at the sleeping baby, his farm mobile playing a tune as it cranked round, the bright pink pig somehow more incongruous than the blue sheep. I revisit myself sat playing with a rosy-cheeked infant. I paint it in my mind as a warm and happy time, all together. I know this because Mick has often told me the stories of how good it was back then, when my mother was a gentle angel, I was a good girl and Nicky was a precious gift.

One of Nicky's favourites from the *Book of 101 Jokes* which he carried about for weeks was "What is the opposite of a snow globe?". He would stare intently at the adult he quizzed for a moment before shouting "A lava lamp!" and bursting into peals of giggles. His audience would laugh too, relieved to be off the hook. I always thought that wasn't quite right as a lava lamp has the same mesmerising effect as a snow globe. The exact opposite would be disturbing to watch.

There are times in your life you can hold like a perfect snow globe, some memories are the exact opposite: lava lamps, made of real lava, too hot to hold in your mind.

1975

I sat, holding a book as a shield, in a corner of the playground. I was only seven, but I preferred to sit alone over running with the others. I watched the new girl. It was her second week, she seemed to be well liked so far. They were playing hopscotch. I looked back down at my book. The illustration on the cover showed four children walking through double yellow doors into a wintry pine forest.

"Why don't you play with the others?"

I looked up, straight into the face of the new girl. She was tall for our class and I felt like I was looking up at an adult. I didn't know what to say. I lifted the book. She smiled.

"I love to read too. I'm Becky."

"I know. I'm Tam."

She sat beside me, tucked her brown hair behind her ear and launched into telling a great long story about the Scotland Street School in Shields. The laughter of long dead children could still be heard along the corridors, their laughter rang out at night when they liked to come out and play. I was enthralled. The bell rang. Becky ran ahead to the classroom. I was barely back on my feet when she reached the door.

The next day, I peeked over the top of my book and

watched her playing at break time. She was skipping rope and waved at me. I waved back. She ran over.

"Want to skip?"

"I don't know how. Do you have any more stories?"

"Come. I'll show you."

I went over. She nodded at one of the other girls who handed me the skipping rope. Becky flicked hers behind her. She hopped from one foot to the other, flicked her wrists and the rope arched above her, swooped down. She skipped over it. She swung it over again. She made it look easy.

As she had, I hopped on my feet. I flicked my wrists. The rope pulled up the back of my skirt. I felt my cheeks go red. I wanted to run across the playground. Becky was watching me. I tried again, swung the rope. It caught on my hair, hit my shins. I could feel the blood rise to my ears. The other girls were watching me.

"Don't worry, my arms are a bit longer, I can get the rope going better. Next time. Do you want to be the clapper and make a rhythm?"

When break time finished, Becky ran ahead again, but after school, she waited by the gate.

"Want to walk home together? I know a great story about Cathedral House. It was a halfway house for women prisoners. One woman had been away from her two children for so long that she didn't recognise them and drowned them in a bathtub. You can still here them giggling and playing on the top floor."

I listened to her all the way home, committing the tales to memory. From that day onwards I spent every break time with Becky. I tried to sit beside her for milk time if the teacher was not paying attention. I walked home with her. Somehow the other kids still liked her even though I tagged along. With Becky at my side, they smiled and said hello.

Her birthday was soon after that. A group of us

went to the park. She told me afterwards that I was her best friend. I was a dark-haired scrawny thing. She was tall, with a big grin and the confidence to go with it. Everyone noticed her. I was hidden in plain sight by her side. A perfect friendship.

1983

The light from the big street window in the waiting room at the Funeral Director's filtered through, past large display boards advertising their services to passers-by. The carpet was striped grey, beige, and black. The wallpaper had a coral sheen to the brown geometric pattern. The effect of the contrast with the pale green motif on the chairs was making my eyes swim. The scent from an immense bouquet of lilies cloyed at the back of my throat.

I was clutching a bag of clothes for my little brother Nicky. A pair of smart jeans, a jumper, a shirt. I brought socks, shoes, and pants too. The sympathetic lady on the phone had not mentioned those, but it seemed wrong to send him off without them. I had tried to find his *Star Wars* t-shirt, only to remember he had outgrown it years before.

The funeral parlour was on the route to the Odeon cinema, which is why I thought of the t-shirt. We only went there once all together, to see *Return of the Jedi*. Nicky had wanted to go on the Clockwork Orange, Glasgow's underground light rail service. It wouldn't have made sense though to walk down from Buchanan Street so we got the bus. George promised him they would go all the way round the circular together another time. I don't know if they ever did.

Waiting outside, under the enormous marquee, George told us that both The Beatles and The Rolling Stones had played there in the 1960s. Mick said all he remembered from the '60s were endless nappies. Nicky was not listening. He was bouncing on his toes, banging on about Boba Fett and something called a Sarlacc. I rolled my eyes. *Star Wars* had been everywhere. The actors were on *Blue Peter*. The school playground was a trading hub of cards. There was a column in *Just Seventeen* on the dos & don'ts of dating Mark Hamill, whether he was a better brother or boyfriend. We hadn't seen the first two films, but Nicky knew everything about the stories. He would draw landspeeders and storm troopers to swap for the comics with his friends. His pictures were so good that even the older kids sought him out.

He was working on a large hand-drawn version of the film poster which he hoped to swap for an AT-AT from the Jolly Giant. I didn't think anyone would go for that deal, but Nicky had a way of charming people into giving him what he wanted. That was why we were all there, Nana, George, Mick, Nicky and I, even though Bugs was the only one interested in the space films.

We were inside and he was yammering about the AT-AT when Nana strode across the foyer brandishing the tickets. Nicky squealed and did a victory dance in front of everyone, pulling his *Star Wars* t-shirt over his head and drumming on his tummy. There had been queues around the block for weeks, so I had warned him that we might not get in at all. He knew well enough this might be his only chance. Mick laughed. He half joined in before stretching his arms out, like a circus master, and took a bow.

"The Great Nicky, Ladies and Gents. World-famous clown."

There was a thin, indulgent applause. Folding back, Mick started up a conversation with another father in front of us. He had a gift for banter. I retreated behind George's robust frame. I hated when Dad was silly and flamboyant like this. It was a warning sign.

"Boys, eh? Love to be the centre of attention, don't they?"

By the time the line started to move, Nicky was like a dog straining at a lead. We walked countless steps until we found our seats in the cavernous auditorium. The room was packed with over a thousand people. I hoped I would not need the toilet as it would be impossible to find my way back through the steep bank of seats.

I don't remember the film. Science fiction was never of great interest to me. I had not got on with Jules Verne when the librarian had suggested his books. I liked *Little Women* and *The Secret Garden*. It was nice to all be together for a change. Mick, I mean Dad, rarely did anything fun with us. Nana sometimes took us to the big park in the summer. Of course, George always came too. Everyone assumed he was our grandfather, though he didn't live with Nana. No one expected older folk to be unconventional in that way. There were mornings when I could not understand how George was at Nana's house quite so early.

The curtains drew across the wee stage at the front for the intermission. Mick and George got up, and I sat there staring at the ceiling while Nana and Nicky chatted about the space barge, whether Boba Fett had survived. I didn't want to barge in on their chat. I wondered if Ange, my mother, would have liked it, or if she was like me. I couldn't imagine her going to see this silly stuff without having to take a young boy. I pulled my mind back from the thought she might have another boy by now. Nana said she thought

Leia's gold bikini would suit her, and we both groaned loudly.

"I didn't know what you wanted, so I got a bit of everything. Scoot over, Tam."

George came back from the concessions with so much they had given him a box to carry it in. There were sodas, popcorn, sweets, two tubs of vanilla and strawberry ice-cream and two choc ices. He handed them out just before the curtains closed again, and he put the box down on our fifth seat.

Mick didn't come back for the second half. None of us mentioned it.

1992

Nana and Mrs Ranjeet both offered to come and sort the flat out with me. I did not want them there. I knew they wanted to help me, to be there when the sadness hit. I knew that I would not cry and they expected me to. They needed to be of comfort to me. Comfort was the last thing I wanted.

I wanted the flat to be back in order.

I started by putting the sheets on for a boil wash, grateful for the washing machine. I picked his clothes off the floor, ready for their turn in the suds. Straightened out the room and ran the hoover over the carpet. My room and Mick's smelt dusty, and I set to them with polish and vacuum. The bathroom next. Someone had been in and given it a wipe down, there were no obvious blood marks. I doubted they would have done a thorough bleach clean.

Once I was satisfied that all was back in its place upstairs, I gave the hall and sitting room the same treatment. Having worked my way round the flat, enveloped in silence, I finished in the kitchen, clearing the debris of Nicky's last days, scrubbing every surface, lining the bin bags out on the walkway.

The afternoon light fractured through the broken lower pane in the glass kitchen door, casting tiny rainbows and dark lines on the linoleum, as it had for as long as I could recall. Nana relented from insisting she come with me by making me promise that I would take a moment to myself.

At the kitchen table of my childhood home, I began the work of unpicking the threads which had led me back here, alone.

)⦅(

It was Lou, worked up and speaking fast. Half asleep as I was, I struggled to tune in, drowsily trying to get my voice to ask him to slow down.

Tucking the receiver under my chin, I picked up the kettle and filled it with water. It was not a great stretch of the imagination to think that he had probably been up all night. No doubt even for a couple of nights, aided by one substance or another. I pictured Lou, his lanky frame moving in anxious cacophony, face taught, brown eyes red-rimmed.

I needed coffee to deal with his quick-fire monologue, a familiar manic hint to it. The loaded teaspoon of freeze-dried coffee dropped a few granules on the counter, I immediately wiped them up so they would not leave those thin damp brownblack trails.

Lou paused, listening for my response.

"I'm sorry, I've not taken in a word you've said, go again. Nicky is what?"

"Missing, Tam, missing!"

"OK, run it past me again."

Lou had not heard from Nicky for days, since Thursday, when he had lost track of him at some after show event or another. Nicky had seemed happy enough, not his usual sparkling and witty self, though not rutted in one of his "deep moods", as Lou called them.

"You've checked the Factory?"

Usually when those "deep moods" struck, Nicky took refuge in one of the artist crash-pad beds at their Sugar Factory Studios, curled up and quiet, allowing visitors to pet him, to be cared for, nursed, as it were, by everyone there, and by Lou especially. They had set up Sugar Factory Studios as an "artist's stable", a term I didn't really understand, and with it a lifestyle far beyond the parameters of my ordinary existence. Nonetheless, I knew enough to see there was a special connection between them.

"I've checked the bloody Factory, Tam."

I let his curt response slide. No point in stirring things. Lou had been there on Friday evening, and could not find any sign of Nicky having been there at all.

It was true that once or twice Nicky had maybe gone to see someone else for comfort, one of the others, and maybe he had bumped into one of the girls or boys of the Factory. I suspected that Nicky, my handsome, charming brother, had gone off on a bender with someone that Lou objected to. Someone that he was jealous of.

Nonetheless, he had called round, personally or on the phone, to every person he could think of, from the most likely to the absurdly improbable. Nicky was nowhere to be found. I poured the steaming water into my cup, stirring as the granules of cheap freeze-dried coffee dissolved, and rolled my eyes at their interminable drama.

Finally, he had come to me. I was the last on his list, an early phone call for me, though from the sound of it, an extremely late call for him. At this point, he practically demanded to speak to Nicky, as though, by virtue of his days of searching, he had earned the right for me to conjure up my brother.

"Lou, I don't know. I am sure he's fine. In fact, he

did come by last week. Erm, the day before the show, maybe? Anyway, he was in a great mood, better than I've seen him in a long time. You know what he's like. He is probably hooked up with someone, or he's woken up on the vomit comet at Polmont and not got the train back, gone for a wander, met some random and gone off with them on a bender."

"Please, Tam, I am really worried this time. Something isn't right, can you think of anywhere?"

There was a real edge of desperation in Lou's begging.

A wave of angst crashed against me.

The black coffee on my tongue went from full and rich to deeply bitter as my body flooded with adrenaline and my brain slammed into gear.

I put the mug down in the sink, automatically turning the tap to rinse it out. Still holding the phone with my head in the crook of my neck, I slowly recapped the facts. My brother was missing, when he was last seen he was not in one of his "deep moods", as Lou called them, but he had not gone to any of his usual or even any of his more unusual haunts. The cogs in my mind whirred. A longer absence this time, no other indications of distress.

"What's really troubling you, Lou?"

"I had a message on my answerphone. Well, I didn't have a message. It was a long empty nothing, but I could hear breathing, and at the very end I thought I could hear Nicky mumbling 'well fuck it', but I don't know. It was weird."

The only other possible place to look for him clicked into focus.

"Lou, there is somewhere you've probably not checked yet. Mick, I mean Dad's place."

"Would he go there?"

"He has the key. I know it's odd, but he does go

there sometimes. I know he does because I go once a month to keep it dust free, check any post, you know, and Nicky's not exactly tidy, is he? OK, look, I'll go up there now. It's close enough and sort of on my way to work anyway. I'll let you know if he's there. I'll call you from the shop."

There was a pause.

"I'll kill him if he's been on the lash for five days!"

"Come on, Lou. You've worked yourself up into a right state. I'm going to check, for you. He'll have probably met some pals and been out with them, for days, he could be in Edinburgh ... or Inverness, who knows? You know what he's like. Now, go and get some rest, you sound exhausted. Sleep, and I'll call you later."

"You're right, I'm sure, thank you. Good night, Tam-tam."

"Good day, Lou-bear!"

We used Nicky's nicknames for each other when we hung up, not intentionally. I could hear in the crack of his voice that the last few days of worry and nights of sleeplessness were about to wash over my brother's best friend, business partner, lover maybe.

I showered, the morning news on the radio, thinking about two weekends earlier when Nicky and I had gone to the pub, then found ourselves crazydancing in a nearby club till late. We had sat with a poke of chips chatting into the small hours. It had been great to see him so genuinely happy. At peace with himself for a change. Usually, there was an undercurrent, a sadness, anger lurking under the surface. This time, he was not high. He was happy with a nice beer buzz, genuine joy emanating from his smile.

As I got ready, I was slightly annoyed I had promised to check Mick's place before work. I pulled on my black work trousers, noticing one of the hems was falling out. I still had the spare keys, not that Nicky or I went there too often. Tricky memories crowded the rooms, but we had agreed between us to keep it in case Ange ever decided to come back to find us. While I stopped by to clean it, Nicky needed to go off into his own space every so often. He used it as a bolthole.

Dressed and organised for work, I pushed niggles of sisterly worry to the back of my mind. I told myself that Nicky was probably with one of the others, someone that Lou had forgotten about. It would not be much of a detour to our old home, though I very much doubted he would be there.

My little brother Nicky was flamboyant and charismatic from his very first gummy smile. Nonetheless, he had phases in which he turned quieter. His eyes would have a distance to them, as though he were an old man, even though he was only nineteen. It would build up over a few weeks, even months, and he would go off for a few days alone. When he was younger, he would be very mean at that time. Then he bounced back, reset somehow. I had been on the wrong side of his irascible outbursts over the years. Once he had opened the door, said "Not today", and closed it in my face. Without any sort of justification. He had never said anything about it afterwards. He wanted any intruders, like me, to know that they were unwanted. Lou did not see these sulky self-centred days because they mostly happened when he was away in Edinburgh, London or even Berlin on one of his many promotion trips.

I was certain that this episode was not one of his big sulks, or "deep moods" as Lou called them, as though their artistic personalities justified their erratic behaviour.

Rushing out of my flat early to squeeze in this visit, I resolved that if Nicky were in our old home, he could do with a sermon. Turning it all over, I pulled myself right back from the worry and decided that Lou was probably overreacting in an exhausted drug-addled panic. Nicky was being selfish and inconsiderate. I was fed up of being called in to sort out their dramas.

The morning air had a nip to it, and I pulled my scarf higher up my neck, over my ears and nose, thinking about how well things had been going for Nicky. I was proud of him even if I did not understand what he did. His latest show had been welcomed in a firework display of rapturous reviews. The child-prodigy had come of age and fulfilled all the promise of the previous meteoric few years. I let my mind's eye wander, imagining him hooking up with some arts journo and holing up in a gentrified croft somewhere off the A9.

Further down the road, I crossed at a three-way junction before making my way through the whole park towards the old block. As I did so, the usual thoughts arose, pondering why I had never left this place, this town. Walking this familiar route always sent me off on that line of thought. Our old nursery school and primary backed on to the park.

As I walked, I turned to my preferred line of thought, turning over the well-trodden ideas. I should go, I thought. Move away. I had always wanted to live off the Great Western Road. I pondered my favourite areas. All the places I liked to go were all on the other side of town. I promised myself that I would move there as soon as I could. There was no reason for me to stay local anymore.

Every time I reached this curb, I seemed to be making that same promise to myself. I had yet to do anything about it. I should travel. See some more of the world, before I meet a nice guy and properly settled down. After all, lots of people did go off on big adventures, to Africa, to South America, to the Far East. I had been saving up carefully since I was fifteen. I pictured myself on safari, in a soft khaki shirt, binoculars hanging from my neck. Then on a hike in the Andes drinking from a round canteen. I could disappear off, by myself, to see the world. I would go backpacking across the outback with Crocodile Dundee.

It was a bright, breezy autumn morning filled with gold and copper hues. I moved briskly, it was a nice walk, pondering a variety of futures, ways in which to spend my earnings.

The hedges changed to short walls and black iron railings as I walked and reality crept back in. A week in France would be enough, in a straw hat on a push-bike, a fresh baguette jauntily sticking out of the basket. I could settle for a weekend in the Lake District, walk the Fells. Who was I kidding? I was not the sort who lived great adventures. I was a good quiet girl. I had looked after Mick, now I looked out for Nicky, kept the flat ready for Ange to return to. I was there to listen to Becky, my best friend. I was the one who was never late for Sunday lunch at Nana's. I always washed up after and helped her to straighten up the place, do any jobs which needed attended to, her Charleston and Lindy Bop records scratching a soundtrack. I could not just leave her. Perhaps, though, a night away, even a day out with a couple of friends. That could be enough adventure for me, I supposed.

I opened the gate on the other side of the park and crossed the road, to the entrance of the estate. I made my way along the left-hand wall, to the third entrance and up six switch-back flights of stairs for the three levels, because the lift was broken, as it had always been. My musings did not come upstairs with me, they never did. The idea of spending my financial security could not withstand the reality of the tenement.

As soon as I started up the steps, I was grounded by the knowledge that I would not ever leave this part of town or sell the flat. I would always come back to the home that I grew up in, back to our prickly memories, even as it mouldered through the years, just in case Ange, my mother, did decide to return.

Reaching our floor, I automatically pulled the keys from my handbag. I paused before opening. If Nicky were there, he would not appreciate me barging in. Knocking was less intrusive, and I had always hated confrontation.

1992

The day after I found Nicky, I lay in bed all day. The chemist had told me to take compassionate leave until a week or two after the funeral. I would have preferred to stay busy and go in, but I could not bear to contradict the manager and thanked him for his consideration. I did not know what else to say. Becky took the day off and kept checking on me. I told her I was perfectly fine enjoying my book, that she should enjoy the skive and go up town to the shops.

About half an hour later, she poked her head around the door.

"Just popping out for a bit, OK? I'll be back soon."

She knew not to ask if I needed anything. I never asked for anything. I heard the door latch click. All the air gushed out of my lungs. I did not think that I had been holding my breath. My eyes prickled and before I could stop myself, I was sobbing. My chest felt as though someone had punched me, right in the middle of my ribcage. Visceral and raw.

Eventually, I pulled myself back together. My hands clawing into the tops of my thighs, I focused on the feeling of my nails in my own flesh, the heartbeat in my fingertips from squeezing so hard. My body and mind rejoined. I pulled the duvet over my head and sunk into a heavy sleep.

I woke up to distant laughter. The television was on low in the sitting room. Becky smiled at me when I walked in.

"Will I make us something to eat? It's past 8pm."

"Don't be silly, I'll do it. Mac n' Cheese?"

"Are you sure, Tam?"

"Absolutely. I think we're out of beans anyway!"

She snorted in amusement. Cooking was not Becky's forte. In fact, she was in no way a homemaker. It was why she needed me.

Later, I lay in bed, unable to sleep. I knew I had to go back to my childhood home. I wanted to tidy up the mess that Nicky had made. It was all that I had left of him. I was picking at the scab. I needed to do it. To touch these things myself. I dug my nails into my forearms and pictured the chaos Nicky had left behind.

A memory flashed up like neon. The kitchen door had two glass panes, one in the top half, and one in the bottom. The bottom one had a long crack through it, running from a circle of smaller circular ones, like a spider web in the lower right-hand corner. The night the crack had first appeared in the lower glass pane, Dad had come home late, the smell of whisky and stale cigarettes on his breath, laughing about Jim's story down the pub. He had hung his coat in the hall and walked towards the kitchen, where Mum sat at the table with a book. Mum had looked up, smiled, and asked him to tell her, to share the story.

He stopped laughing, suddenly, his shoulders stiffened. He screamed that she was always asking about Jim, and if she cared so much why did she not go and ask him herself. She would, she would go now, she replied. Their eyes locked briefly, a lull. Then Dad raised his fist and smashed it down on to the right of her face. It made a dull meaty sound. She did not even scream, she let herself drop off the chair with the force of the impact, and lay unmoving on the floor, holding back a breath, a sob perhaps.

She noticed me then. She looked up, straight in the eye. I stood there, sucking the corner of my nightdress, steadied myself on the bannister. I was about four at the time, I think, too young to understand what I was seeing.

Yet I knew that something had happened that I should not have seen, something private and not for my eyes.

I turned as quietly as I could, ran back up the steps. My dad slammed the door so hard that the bottom pane cracked, and sat down at the kitchen table. He lit a cigarette, chuckled again about Jim's story. Perhaps even deciding to tell it to his wife after all, who gingerly pulled herself onto a chair.

Strange how your own mind surprises you with what you remember. How easy it is to slip into those cracks and gaps of memory.

1974

One of my favourite memories is a day we went to the coast.

It is one of the few memories with both of my parents that I have regularly revisited, polished, nourished every detail. As a teenager, there were nights that I reconstructed every detail, and sat in the memory, wrapped in the warmsunyellow tinge.

We travelled in George's car. It was a big car because I remember that we were all in it – George and Mick, I mean Dad, rode up front. I was in the middle of the back between Nana and Mummy, who had Nicky on her lap. I held Mr Blue on my lap, with the same care as my mother did my brother, mimicking her hold. Best of all, Nana had brought a tin of boiled barley sweets with her.

Whenever I visit the memory of that day, I make sure to include the sweets. They were square, and orange coloured after the fine floury sugary coating was sucked away. I knew this because I made Nana stick her tongue out with her sweet on the end of it. She giggled when she did that, so I made her do it more than once on the way to the seaside.

At the time, I was quite obsessed with knock-knock jokes, and told as many as I could between barley sweets, asking George, Daddy, Mummy and Nana the same joke in turn. The front windows were open. Dad blew smoke out of his. Nana and George sang some old songs, clapping out a beat. They always did harmonise well together.

I recollect I was wearing a yellow sundress with a green and pink flower pattern on it. It had a broderie anglaise trim, which on the way home I poked at with a blade of grass until I drifted off to salty seaside-lulled sleep clutching Mr Blue, upside down now in my arms. But that was the end of the day.

The light seemed to become green tinged as we reached our destination. That could be real memory or an adjustment I made later believing that, on approaching the beach, the road narrows to near enough one lane between tall trees.

As we drew closer, we had to slow down. Without the breeze coming in, it grew hot in the car, and we quickly became quite sticky. This did not bother our happy anticipation, as Nana and George sang a cheerful rendition of the Chattanooga Choo Choo, with George singing the trombone and piano parts. We were all full of anticipation for the day ahead. I remember getting out the car, and feeling the sea breeze on my legs, it was cool and fresh. I hoped there might be donkeys to ride. George uttered those magic words:

"Well then toots, let's get you an ice-cream."

In my excitement, I left Mr Blue in the car, along with my knock-knock jokes, and ran after George's enormous steps to the ice-cream parlour by the beach. Nana followed with my parents who were pushing my little brother in a navy-blue pram, and George had bought them each an ice-cream. He was able to hold the four cones in his hands, like some sort of benevolent giant.

That day, I paddled in the sea for the first time ever, clinging on to George, and he taught me how to skip over the edge of the waves, landing with a big splash. Mummy lay Nicky in his pram with a white cotton parasol above his head, and she stretched out on a towel to take in the sunshine, and Nana and Daddy sat side by side on deckchairs, sipping ginger beer. They both loved fiery cold ginger beer.

George had brought his camera, and took three shots, one of me squinting at the camera with a melting ice-cream cone in hand, one of Mick and Nana in their stripy deckchairs, and one of Ange holding Nicky on her knees, his toddler face a blur.

Nana told me that that was the day that Daddy first recited to me the poem about a young boy called Albert being eaten by a lion in Blackpool Zoo, and about his mother not wanting to raise any more children to feed to the lions. I was enthralled, Mick knew the whole poem. I made him recite it at least three times.

On the way home, beachsticky and sandfooted, I made my father, Mick, promise that we would go to the zoo someday soon to see the lions. He smiled and agreed. I settled down to pick at the hem of my skirt as quietly and unobtrusively as possible for the rest of the journey.

1992

I was back at the flat, again. Since Nicky had passed, I kept finding myself there, looking at the old photo albums, unable to shed a single tear, numb through.

The photos made us look happy, each with their own well revisited tales to tell. In the quiet of dust motes and my own breath, not even a ticking clock to mark this time alone I knew we never were.

I turned another page in the album. One of Bugs' favourite snaps from our childhood.

Our day out at the zoo did not happen until a couple of years later. I think this one was probably Nicky's first true memory, we shared it often, spoke of it, pulled it apart, stuck it back together, recited it with honey and with salt.

It was just us: Dad, Mum, Nicky and me. We were so excited and spent the entire journey on the bus roaring at each other like lions, making "oo-oo-aa-aa" monkey noises, and trying to picture how big the elephant would be, and how tall the giraffe would be. Bigger than a bus! Taller than a house! I suppose we must have caught the train too. I do not remember that part of the day.

They were Dad and Mum to me at this point, still, not Mick and Ange yet. Maybe even Mummy and

Daddy. The big black Victorian gate had the words 'Zoological Park' in wrought iron over the entrance. It was a steep climb past the enclosures to the top of the hillside zoo with our picnic, the city sprawled in front of us, Nicky a sturdy toddler wobbling on his footing.

The sun beamed, and we walked happily from amazing beast to incredible creature, with our hands made sticky with lollipops. As we left the park, we walked past a man selling helium filled rubber balloons. I chose a big blue one almost the same colour as Mr Blue. Dad held Mum around the waist as I ran ahead of Nicky's pram towards the bus stop.
It was a wonderful day.

The balloon deflated eventually. I hung on to the memory. Becky teased me about it when we were teenagers. Kicking our heels off a wall, passing the time, I told her about the zoo trip.

"No one likes the zoo that much, Tam. All the sad animals in their cages. They never do anything interesting."

By then, I knew well enough that families are different. Becky had lots of happy day out memories to pick from. I didn't want to upset her, so I added a flourish about being given some spending money. We both knew that wasn't true.

I believe Dad was different back then. While I only remembered a few days here and there, I could not see that I might have made them represent all the days. In memory, he was different from the man I would later grow to know. Mum seemed happy, and solid to the seven-year-old me.

I thumbed the photo of us, Nicky on Ange's left hip, me standing in front and between her and Dad. I wondered about the stranger that took this photo. Did they ever think about that day too or was it lost to them, a leaf on the tree of their memories?

I closed the album. I had resolved to clear out some of Mick and Bugs' old clothes as an excuse for being back there. It would be good to have at least part of the flat sorted out before I went back to my place. Lou had moved in with me. I knew that we were treading water together, holding each other in grief, neither ready to make any decisions as to what came next.

I found myself going up to the bathroom. I climbed into the dry bathtub, fully clothed. I rested my head on the side, ran my hand along the edge. I needed to talk to Nana.

X

I walked round to Nana's house dragging an old suitcase the entire way. It was full of the clothes I had taken out of the flat. George put it straight in the car and drove off to dispose of them. I put the photo album on the table, opened it to the zoo pic.

"Nana, were they happy then? Together? We haven't really talked about it. I thought maybe now ..."

I let my voice trail off. I had not asked Nana about Ange, my mother, when I was young, so I had not thought to over the years.

She looked at the album, stroked the page. She was weighing up her answers.

"I don't suppose so."

Ange was young when I was born. It had been tricky for them. Nana had tried to help. She knew Mick found it hard to deal with the sleepless nights, but he had got himself a good job, he had stepped up to the role. At first, Ange had seemed withdrawn, but she had gone round often. After all, my maternal grandparents had left. When Nicky came along, Nana had tried to keep a close eye on her daughter-in-law in case she found the newborn days difficult again.

She had seemed to cope well, but Nana was looking out for cracks, she knew there were cracks. The girl had struggled with the babies. All women do. Some more than others.

"Nana, how about between them? Dad, well you know, sometimes he got a bit angry."

I could see Nana did not want to talk about this. I didn't either on a surface level. I felt the need to get this conversation over and done with. I was going to need to ask Nana so much more if I was going to understand what Nicky had done.

"Nana, did she have bruises back then?"

There had been the time that Ange kept wincing whenever she had to move her side. A few times, she wore her hair over one side of her face. She bought round glasses, which Nicky called her "owl eyes". One time she limped for over ten days. Mostly there were the times that she disappeared to the kitchen when Nana came over to play with us grandchildren. Nana would find her later, staring into blank space by the sink.

She noticed that Ange never wanted to speak to the children about the outing to the zoo which they raved about for weeks. The day after it, Ange had dropped Bugs and I off at Nana's. She said she had fallen on the stairs, burst her lip and brow and was going to the doctor to get it cleaned up.

"I think it was a week before she came back for you."

1977

Around the time of my ninth birthday, I had taken to reading fairy tales. Odd, dark, filled with monsters and strangely comforting to me.

At my local library, I had found a book of Hungarian fairy tales. It was not kept in the children's section, where most of the books were big with brightly coloured pictures. I had started to wander away from that part of the library regularly by then, but I'm not sure in which section I picked up this particular book.

There was one of the stories that I liked especially, it was called something like 'Lovely Ilonka', though I have mostly forgotten what it was about. I think there was a beautiful maiden who sprang from a well and ended up in conjugal subjugation to the prince who kidnapped her and swapped her for a swineheard's daughter. I read the whole book cover to cover twice before taking it back.

I told the librarian as much, and she suggested that I read some of the Greek and Roman legends. So that summer, I was Aphrodite, Athena and Diane in knee-high socks, dreaming of being championed by Jason or Hercules. I escaped into sun-drenched fantasy everywhere I went. Rarely was I the hero, the Grecian Wonder Woman. I pictured my mother as the perfect nymph or sylph who disappeared into her natural environment after being tricked into leaving a human child on the earth. The Gorgons and Arachne were my imaginary foes as I made my way home from school, from the public swimming pool, from the park to the real monster that I could only hide from.

More than anything, I was fascinated by the oracles and soothsayers who could read a person's future, the idea that I was predestined. That someone could tell me what that destiny might be. I became obsessed with the notion that my fate was written and perhaps always had been. Was I genuinely meant to be here, with this life, in this place?

When I was by myself, I never imagined that I was a princess to be rescued, like so many of my friends. I was always a changeling.

I knew that no one in my immediate circle was going to be able to inform me about my destiny, whether I was living out the right one. The closest to an oracle in our tenement was Old Mrs Pollock upstairs who fed the pigeons on the walkway, had several cats, and often spoke about things as though they were going to happen:

"You're going to get hurt if you keep playing here."

"Your parents will be disappointed in you."

"Reading won't get you nowhere."

Even at that age, I knew that she had no powers to tell the future or read my destiny. Looking back, I desperately wanted some magic in my life, a bit of sparkle, some sort of mysticism. Not that I had come across that word then.

Mrs Pollock was the closest to an oracle that I could find in the area, and though I was afraid of her, I tried to see her every week. I almost believed that what she said was true. I wanted her to say that one day something good would come of me.

In the evenings, when Mick was out, which was most evenings in those days, I would tell these stories to Nicky. We would lie in bed together, take a torch under the covers. We would make a sort of nest and I would tell him what I had read. I embroidered details with my own imagination. I told him of the Argonauts, the twelve tasks of Hercules, and of all gods and demigods of Olympus. His round face would light up, fascinated by the heroes of old, destined to greatness from birth. He especially loved hearing about the oracles. Eventually his breath would change and he would be asleep. I always stroked his head and kissed his cheek before going back to my own room. It was the two of us, alone in the flat, in the world, a tiny team of two.

By day, things were different. We left for school together, joining our friends as we walked along. We might have seen each other briefly at lunch time, and ignored each other as siblings do. On the way home, Nicky played football in the park and I stopped at the library. It wasn't until he sat down to eat whatever I had cobbled together for our tea that we would speak to each other. We never asked if we had seen Dad.

My ninth birthday rolled around. It had been a warm morning, but by late afternoon, dull clouds had started to gather. Nicky was wearing navy blue shorts, and a brown wool sweater over his shirt, one sock pulled up to his knee, the other had slipped all the way down to the top of his plimsoll. He looked dirty, he had been out all day, which was usual at the weekend, it was better than being at home, as Mick, I mean Dad, was out of work yet again. He would not have had lunch either, but then being at home was no guarantee of that when Mick was there.

"Tam, Tam, come quick, I've got something for you."

He had found something, that little brother of mine,

thought of me, and come straight to find me. I was sitting in my usual spot, at the top of the stairs in our building, where the sunlight often pooled in the mornings and warmed the walls, and that day it had stayed warm. It was a great spot to sit and read quietly, and by that point I was probably reading yet another version of the Roman myths which I already knew so well.

I stood up and patted the dust off my bottom.

"I don't know, Nicky, is this thing far?"

"Yes, no, not really, just behind the park, in the bushes at the back."

"Nicky, what is it?"

"It's a surprise."

I sighed. My concentration had taken wing and flown from the pages of my book anyway.

"Alright then, let's go."

I followed him as he walked down the stairs, turning left at the bottom, along the pavement, across the small car park, the tiny patch of grass. We waited at the edge of the road for a moment, waiting for a space in the traffic, and ran across, fast as we could. We were on the pavement close to the edge of the park, and we ran on, without stopping, pausing only to crawl under the park fence. Well, I would call it a fence, though it was not much of a barrier. It was more of a series of wooden pillars joined by a single metal bar at what is now my mid-thigh height, but was about waist-height then, I think. The grass was always longer at the edge and felt cool against my bare legs. I have nursed some memories more than others, and this detail stroking my limbs brings it back with such vividity.

My knees were damp and green, below the hem of my shorts. I scrabbled upright, and kept on running with Nicky, for no reason. There was no urgency. He ran because he was excited. I ran because he did. We ran because we could.

We raced right across the park, edging the football game that was in progress at one end, going around the jumper goal posts. On the other side of the green, there was a copse that ran alongside a track that edged the park towards a canal. As we got towards the trees, Nicky slowed down. He came to a halt, bent forward to put his hands on his knees and took a few big gulps of air. I staggered about dramatically pretending to catch my breath, gently mocking him. He looked up at me and grinned through his big blond mop of hair, blue eyes twinkling.

"It's here, Tam, it's here."

"What's here? Where?"

I grinned back at him, and suddenly he was on the go again, dashing into the undergrowth. He emerged with a triumphant grin and a stick and darted a couple of steps ahead. I was out of breath and hung back a bit before straightening out and walking up to him. He was poking towards something on the ground.

"Look, it's a *norackel*, Tam! I found a *norackel*."

As I got closer, I wondered what it was that he could possibly have found and taken to be an oracle. I looked down towards what he had been prodding with the stick. It was a dead pigeon. It was lying face up on the ground, wings stretched open on either side as though it had hoped to take flight one last time. An animal had ripped open the stomach cavity, and a few entrails, like pink spaghetti, had spilt out. There were small wriggly white things in with this gruesome spaghetti: maggots like living grated cheese.

Nicky prodded the pigeon again. The maggots wriggled as the entrails were moved.

"Will it tell us the future? Tam, can you ask it the future?"

Prod.

"I asked it the future, I tried, but it wouldn't tell me anything. How do you ask it the future? Can you ask it the future? Maybe the Norackel will listen to you Tam. In Greece they asked pigeons' stomachs the future, didn't they Tam? Tam ... Tam? Come back Tam! We need to ask it the future. We can ask it for Mummy. We can ask where she is."

Prod. A string of pigeon gut got hooked on a splinter at the end of the stick.

I felt my mouth go dry.

Prod. He shook it off.

Bile started to rise.

Prod. Some maggots spilt on to the ground.

"The future, Tam, it's your birthday. It's a special day and I found the Norackel. It will tell you!"

Nicky was calling after me, still prodding at the dead bird. I had started to stagger away, retching.

"Tam ..."

I could hear in his voice that he was upset at me walking away.

"Tam, look, let's ask it."

I turned around. Nicky had managed to somehow prod through the pigeon and impaled it on his stick.

He was running towards me, waving it in front of him, like some sort of dreadful flag.

The wings were flapping in an awkward rhythm with each of his steps.

Jerking open.

Sagging closed again.

I felt my chest heave.

A pinkish lump dropped from the pigeon.

Splat.

The bile was in my mouth.

Turning away from my brother, I bent forward, hands on my knees and I vomited.

A wet splatter.

I had not had any lunch. It was a bitterly acid liquid that found its way up from the depths of my stomach. I felt my stomach clench, and vomited once again, legs apart as I tried to avoid my shoes.

I spluttered, trying to catch my breath again.

I could feel some loose hair in my eyes, though most of it was tied back in an untidy and unkempt ponytail.

I heard a thud, and a shriek, and Nicky started to cry.

I noticed a tiny fleck of vomit on my left navy buckleshoe.

It was almost a lime green shade.

At the edge of my eyesight, I could see Nicky, wailing, the pain and distress clear in his cries.

I tried to gather some saliva and spat out what I could from my mouth.

I took a deep breath, my hands still on my knees, an unhappy imitation of my brother's exhilarated pose a few moments before.

Tears had sprung to my eyes, my face was wet, and felt warm. The blood had rushed to my cheeks. I stood up, aware of Nicky's sobs to my right. I looked up ahead, wiped my eyes with the heel of my hand, and then wiped my mouth with sleeve.

I turned to look at him.

He was lying on his back, fists pumping in the air, crying. As I moved towards him, I saw that he had pink smeared down his right side, beside which lay the now crushed pigeon. He had fallen hands first into the dead bird, maggots everywhere.

I retched again.

"Bugs, Bugs, Nicky, you are covered in the bugs."

"Help, Tam, help."

I looked at my little brother.

I took a step backwards.

It was disgusting.

He was disgusting.

"Tam."

He whimpered.

"Bugs."

I gulped and looked him in the eyes.

They were red and full.

Every fibre in my body wanted me to run away.

I took a step towards him.

"Come on, get up. You're not really hurt, you're covered in stinky dead pigeon and bugs. It'll wash off, but we need to go home straightaway."

I closed the space between us.

I held out my hand.

"Do you think Dad will be angry?"

"I don't know, Nicky, you know what he's like, but we need to get you clean, now. Give me your hand … no, not that one. BUGS!"

I took his left hand in my right one, and did my best to smile down at him, and we started our walk back across the park.

"Hey, Tam, you called me Bugs."

"What?"

"Now, after you threw up, you called me Bugs. I like it."

"Bugs? Well, you're bugging me. That's what, so I think you are Bugs."

With his bony hand in my hand, we walked back across the green. He was still sniffling as we went, trying unsuccessfully to wipe his nose on his right shoulder, obviously avoiding his regular back of the left-hand wipe, as it was covered in pigeon goo and mud. He held his offending hand at a strange angle, out from his sides, as though he was trying to leave it behind.

I looked across the park, towards home.

The football match was more energised now, one team well into the other side's half, and that team was working well together to defend the goal. We skirted around the empty side that only had a goalie yelling animated instructions at his teammates. I noticed that it was Beardy Stuart in that goal. He happened to look around at us, we had probably caught the edge of his vision, and he called out and waved, so I waved back, automatically, and awkwardly.

We got all the way back to the fence without speaking another word. Nicky crawled under the bar and paused to wipe his dirty right hand on the damp grass as I crawled under. I looked at him and smiled.

"Come on, Bugs, let's cross."

I emphasised the fact that I called him Bugs, and he grinned widely. From that day on, Bugs stuck as a nickname.

There was no time to stand there grinning at each other like a pair of loons. Nicky was covered in mud and guts, and we needed to hurry, back along the road, up the stairs, into the flat, before Mick saw him covered in mess and gave us a telling off about it. You never knew what you might get from Dad. He could turn on a penny, laughing one minute, screaming the next. We got to the door and put the key in the door as I pulled my weight on the handle and opened it. I dropped my bag in the corridor, about to sprint upstairs to the bathroom with Nicky, when we heard a voice from the sitting room.

"Happy birthday, Tammy!"

We froze on the spot and looked at each other. We knew exactly what the other was thinking and looked towards the staircase. Nicky might still have time to get upstairs before Dad saw us, and I could probably spin something about him needing to go to the toilet. He called out again, his voice sing-songy and thick with alcohol and smoke.

"Happy birthday, Tammy!"

It was too late, we weren't fast enough. He was standing in the living room doorway, looking down on both of us. I know that I took a deep breath and gave my best smile, hoping that he wouldn't start. He didn't shout. No, he laughed heartily at us.

"Well, look at the two of you! What a pair of scruffians I have here. What have you been up to?"

Still laughing, he bent down and took Nicky's hand, the one that had been clinging in terror to mine.

"We'd better get you scrubbed up for your sisters' birthday tea, hadn't we, wee man?"

And with that, we headed upstairs. In the bathroom, he turned on the bath taps, running it quite hot, and asked what we had been up to. We told him about the Norackel. We did not tell him everything, carefully picking out our secrets. We said that we had been for a walk in the park, and that Nicky had tripped and landed on a dead pigeon. I sat on the closed loo seat, Dad sat on the floor, Nicky in the bath. The windows and mirrors steamed up.

Soon we found ourselves giggling, the three of us together. Nicky was funny in describing his fall, all his earlier distress melting away, carrying with it the fear of his own father for this precious moment. He had been thoroughly scrubbed with a soapy flannel and was glowing pink, like a freshly shorn lamb.

More than once I have returned to this moment, gifted to us on my birthday.

It was precious, and rare.

I still cherish how heartily Dad laughed as we progressed onto jokes, and he even told a few of his own – we did not understand the one about the two bald scientists putting their heads together and making an arse of themselves but laughed anyway because Dad had said "arse". Nicky put on some clean pyjamas, then followed our father downstairs to "set things up". I let out the bath, gave the tub a quick clean out and had a quick bird bath myself in shallow water. I put on a fresh pair of jeans and pulled my stripy jumper over my head without a blouse.

I made my way back downstairs and into the kitchen. The kettle was letting off steam, and Dad had bought a small cake from the bakery on the high street. On the table was a pot of tea, three mugs, the sugar pot, a cold bottle of milk, three side plates and a big kitchen knife. We sat ourselves around the kitchen table. In front of me was a Victoria Sponge with a single candle in the middle. Nicky and Dad sang 'Happy Birthday' and I blew out the candle, without bothering to make a wish.

I picked up the big knife and cut into the cake. It was a small cake, but it divided comfortably into six generous slices for the three of us. I dealt them out onto the small side plates – one each for now and kept one each back for later. We had a cake tin that I could put them in. Nicky and I had a cup of juice each and Dad had something tea-coloured, but cold and alcoholic in a mug. It was dark outside the kitchen window above the sink, and I could see the reflection of our family in the darkness, hovering ghostly pale when I looked at it. My dark hair the image of my father's, Nicky's a beacon of golden light between us.

It was warm in the kitchen and Dad told us more funny stories and did voices and characters. His favourite one was a potato-picking Irishman, referred to as Paddy. When we were young, we found the character enormously funny with his lucky charms and pots of gold, but by this birthday, the joke was wearing thin. That said, it was so nice when Dad was trying to make us laugh that we laughed back.

We loved him, and he loved us back, then.

"Off to bed with you two scamps, Bugs and the Norackel." He chuckled, opened his arms wide, and we both knew to go into one arm each. He hugged us into his chest and kissed my cheek and the top of Nicky's head. He smelt bitter and acrid.

We went upstairs, leaving Dad in the kitchen to sip his bitter tea-coloured drink and smoke. We climbed into Nicky's bed together, and I read him a story as usual. We heard clattering movement downstairs. The front door opened, closed, and the key was turned in the lock.

Mick had gone out. The two of us curled upstairs in one bed were content and tired, and we soon dozed off.

)(

I was still there, asleep, with Nick's blonde head in the crook of my arm, his breathing soft and light when I was startled awake by a loud crash.

Mick was home. From the sounds in the kitchen, he was very drunk.

There was a much bigger thud and the sound of breaking glass. Nicky started in my arms, I stroked his head and made soothing sounds. He settled down again, snuggling deeper into the crook of my arm. I, on the other hand, held my breath, straining my ears for any tell-tale sounds. Footsteps in the kitchen below us – he was pacing up and down. The tap going on. The tap going off. The scrape of the chair on the kitchen floor. And then quiet, only the sound of Nicky's breath.

And then again, a loud slam, waking Nicky this time.

Angry shouts ricocheted up the stairs.

"What the fuck is this mess? I'm sick, sick to the teeth of living in this goddam pigsty, this is not a hotel you little shits!"

Nicky froze in my arms, his breath caught in his throat, his arms tightened around me. He was wide awake. I squeezed him back, his skinny shoulder bones digging into my ribcage. Our father's footsteps started to thud up the steps. Nicky's hand gripped around the top of my arm, his nails pressing deep into my skin.

A long breath of thick silence.

Then with a great roar, the monster outside our bedroom door punched into the wall. A whimper rose from Nicky's throat beside me, and then the spreading awareness of warmth against my thigh. A liquid warmth that lost heat almost as soon as I felt it.

Nicky had wet himself with fear.

I stroked his hair back and kissed his forehead, and started to inch out of the bed, taking him with me. As quietly as possible, we lay down on the floor and shimmied under the bed, skinny runts that we were. Nicky was pressed up against the wall, and I lay beside him, on the open side of the underbed.

The door opened, the light was flicked on and I watched feet stumble in, black shoes against the light. Mick, the ogre in the room, made a growling sound, and then, he must have swayed, as his heels went up, and then his toes. I know that he must have been truly drunk because he did not even bend down to look under the bed. He turned around, skulked out, slamming the door. Nicky trembled beside me. I reached up and pulled the pillow and then the covers off the bed. That was the first night that we slept under the bed. It would not be the last.

In the morning, I tiptoed out of Nicky's room and crept along to the bathroom. There was a hole in the wall beside Nicky's bedroom door, where Mick had punched it. Heading downstairs, I found the result of the previous nights' bangs and crashes. The kitchen table was lying on its side, broken glass on the floor, from brown beer bottles and a glass. There was ash and cigarette ends strewn across the floor too, though the ashtray itself had been picked up, and sat on the sideboard with half a dozen butts in it beside a half-drunk glass.

I hefted the table up, and set to cleaning up the mess, taking care to sweep up all the glass so that Nicky would not cut himself if he came into the kitchen barefoot. I remember that morning so clearly, carefully tidying, avoiding any noise, and I recall the growl in my stomach with clarity. All I had eaten the day before had been toast at breakfast time and the slice of birthday cake.

As I worked, I became aware of a presence. My little brother was standing there, watching me clean. I picked a jay cloth up out of the soapy warm water in the kitchen sink, rung it out and started to scrub the sideboard. He stood there, his hair flat on one side with a tuft of blond fluff sticking out of the other. His yellow and green stripy jumper was half tucked into his brown corduroy trousers. He seemed to shuffle between one foot and the other.

There was a sudden noise from upstairs.

The look on Nicky's face has stayed with me as though I had taken a photograph and looked at it regularly year after year. His eyes wide with fear. His lips tight. He turned, fled down the corridor, threw the front door open and ran out.

The sleeping ogre upstairs did not materialise at that point, not that day. Nicky was gone and would not be back until after tea time. I ate a slice of birthday cake for breakfast, sat in the sunny patch in the stairwell, while I read about Jason and the Argonauts yet another time.

Ж

Over the years, a couple of letters came from the school asking to meet with my father. Mick rarely acknowledged any post, so it was easy to smuggle them out in the rubbish. He never took the rubbish out anyway.

One time, they asked for a home visit.

I was sure it was after Nicky had his drawing jotter confiscated. I was not surprised. I had seen the drawings. I had tried to ignore them. Nicky had always been talented at drawing, even aged nine or ten. His *Star Wars* characters were terrific. These pictures were different.

At least two were quite detailed drawings of a woman lying on the ground, wounded and bleeding, and three were of my father's face covered in wounds and bruises. They were styled as a seventeenth century lady and gent, but the resemblance was obvious. It was particularly surprising given how long it was since my mother had left us, though there were still photos of her in the flat. They were detailed and intense.

The school never came to see us.

1992

What a circus, what a charade.

I sat in the front row at the crematorium, holding Nana's hand. Becky was beside me, gently rocking back and forth, and George was on the other side of Nana. He had not shed a tear, though he had blown his nose at least twice, very loudly, into his red spotty handkerchief. He was holding Nana's other hand, but he looked lost and small in his sturdy frame. George, who was always so solid. I closed my eyes a moment fighting back the tears. I could not bear to see him crumble.

The coffin was a black oblong, with a bright blue trim. It reminded me of that film, *Tron*. One of the Sugar Factory artists had made it, apparently for a show just over a year before, and had donated it for Nicky's funeral to "complete the circle of life and art". At least, that was according to some article in the morning's paper. The artist was pictured beside it, wearing a tee-shirt bearing the words "death is a joke". Lou had insisted, saying that Nicky would have wanted it that way.

Nana had agreed, of course. She had understood this side of my brother better than me. I could see her taking the scene in. Her face was set. There was steel in her.

I looked around. Every detail etched itself into my mind but I could not let myself care in that moment. Nicky had decided to leave us. I tried to set my face to neutral. I felt my jaw clench, betraying me. I dug my fingernails into the side of my wrist.

I wanted it over and done with.

George blew his nose loudly again.

Behind us were some of the 'Lost Boys', as I called Nicky's childhood friends. I saw John hugging Dev and Seumas. Dave must have been somewhere nearby, though I could not see his bright red hair anywhere. I smiled in their direction. Behind them, various families from the scheme, Mr & Mrs Ranjeet and their kids heading them up. I nodded at them but turned my head before Mrs Ranjeet saw it as a call to come and embrace me. Agnes, her husband Alistair and Davy had travelled in from the countryside and were staying with Nana. I saw old Mr Trencher who used to own the toy shop sat beside Ange's erstwhile boss's widow, Mrs McIntyre.

The family side of the cremation room aisle.

On the other side of the aisle was Lou, surrounded by some faces I recognised from the Sugar Factory, many I did not know. The full coterie was out in force.

The side we were sitting on was reserved, clad in black. The other side looked like a carnival, in bright colours, feathered hats, knee-high PVC boots and shredded jeans. Everyone had their position; they knew their role.

Lou was dishevelled and looked like he had not slept or eaten for days. He had stopped sobbing into the lime-green shoulder on his left and stared dead ahead, unshaven, bags under his eyes, his hair hung limply to his shoulders.

I believed him.

So many of these parakeets were sobbing wholeheartedly without a drop of sincerity, relishing in the collective outpouring of grief, the pathos of it all. They looked like the guests at a hyper-surreal rave wedding. Such a contrast to the family in black. The groom's side is always the rowdiest.

At the back, a swathe of press-types, journos, and photographers clogged around the door. They scribbled away and snapped photographs. The man officiating the service was speaking about friendship outlasting death, the importance of creating support networks and dark hours of the soul, and the curtains started to open behind the coffin. Somebody on the carnival side wailed.

Nana's hand was crushing my hand, her shoulders shaking.

How could he do this to Nana? To us?

The crematorium conveyor belt whirred into action, and I watched the coffin shudder. The plain white delphiniums and lilies on the top trembled in response. George blew his nose again. He was annoying me.

I focused on my nails digging into my wrist. There was something soothing in the pure whiteness of the feeling.

The top, head end of the coffin was slipping through the old orangey-brown curtains. As I looked up, I noticed that the flowers were too high for the door. Should they have been taken off the top to put by the memorial stone or something?

I glanced around the room, no one else had noticed, too busy in their shiny bubbles of perfect misery. I wondered whether I should get up and take them off the top of the coffin.

I had always sorted things out for Bugs, so I would, one last time.

Before I could move, the delphinium that shot out from the central arrangement at a slight angle hit the top of the oven door hatch and started to bend.

I watched it happen.

It snapped, unable to cope with the tension. I noticed that Lou was watching too.

The shudder of the snap caused the main flower arrangement to slip off the top of the coffin, towards my side of the gathering. Lou and I moved in time to stand up, leaning forward, rising, stepping towards the conveyor belt, towards the altar.

The assembled mourners gasped. It could wedge the door to the oven.

The man leading the proceedings noticed it too. In a couple of swift and graceful steps he moved to the coffin, lifted the flowers off and placed them in the middle of the front area, with only the one floppy delphinium evidencing the averted disaster.

He had somehow made it look intentional and perfectly timed. But in this, Lou and I found ourselves side by side in front of the lectern, at the top of the central aisle.

Lou slumped onto my side and sobbed once heavily on my shoulder. He straightened himself up, looked me straight in the eye, leant back in towards me, and kissed me firmly on the lips.

We were standing at the front of this room, of this farce, like some sort of grotesque newlywed couple in a first embrace. As Nicky's coffin was swallowed up by the oven, we were engulfed by the nauseously colourful side of the room, who started humming and singing around us.

What a spectacle.

It was not until about a month later, curled up in bed

together that we even mentioned the moment at all.

"Remember when I kissed you in front of everyone at Nicky's ..." he trailed off.

I did not reply. He knew well enough that I did. He spoke softly.

"That day, I felt so numb. Everyone was moving around me, grabbing my hands, hugging me. I let them. They needed to do it. They needed to believe that they were helping. I hated it. I should have found Nicky sooner. I should have been there."

His voice caught. I could see his chin wobble, lips thin. I looked up to the ceiling, an iota of privacy. He let out a single sob. He lifted his hands to his face and rubbed his eyes.

"Tam, I pushed him away. I told him he had to sober up. To choose. I made him feel like he wasn't enough. He was mine. I was his. That should have been enough. All those people, they thought they were hurting. Like fuck they were. I was the last one to speak to him. I should have said something. You and me, the only ones who should have been there. Who should have made sure we loved him just as he was."

He seemed to look out from himself for a moment.

At the funeral he had not even known if he could stand up any longer. He had looked over at me rocking on my heels, clutching my left wrist, like he was unaware of it. He noticed that the fingers on my right hand were going white. I had looked lost and out of place too. He had wanted to walk over and sit with me, but in that moment I had been flanked by Becky and Nana and he was being steered to a seat on the other side of he aisle by the man leading the service. After the delphinium snapped, he needed to make a connection.

I had felt it.

I had needed it too.

I needed to move on from whatever Lou and I were. Hiding together in our grief. Going through the motions of a relationship so that the world outside would leave us to it. Trying to prove to ourselves we were still alive. We knew it did not make sense.

I did not know what could ever again.

1982

"Nicky! Don't go. Please come back!"

"Fuck's sake, Tam. You're such a whiny bitch. I'm fucking going!"

The door slammed behind him.

I stood there, holding the mop, stunned, staring at the space where he had detonated in anger.

I had not tried to stop him.

During the week, I preferred the days when Nicky came straight back from school. I hoped for rain. I loved it when he sat at home, engrossed in his drawing. He sketched faces that stared intensely off the page. He had been looking up pictures in the library. I loved the pictures he had drawn of old tribesmen and women, from the pages of a *National Geographic* magazine, their wrinkled skin looked vivid and real. I was so proud of his skill. They looked sad but strong, resilience in their faces. He was also selling some of his fan art to his friends for posters.

On good days, Nicky had taken to meeting up with some of the boys after school. He had seemed happier, and I could read quietly before making our tea. They would play football in the park, ride their bikes, and do whatever it was that boys got up to, up to their ears in mud.

When he came home, after eating we would go to the sitting room and put the news on. His head bent over his pictures of *Superman*, *Star Wars* and *Tron* characters while I watched the story about Mark Thatcher disappearing in the desert, news of high unemployment. The Queen's Pearl Jubilee and the sinking of the Belgrano. When corporal punishment was banned in schools without parental consent, Nicky, without even looking up said:

"I don't think Mick even knows where school is."

"We're meant to call him Dad," I answered.

We could go up to bed when we felt like it. We'd hear a thud or crash in the middle of the night when our father came home. Mostly we ignored them, though occasionally Nicky would sneak through into my bed if something was off. We would leave in the morning without disturbing the sleeping ogre, and he was always gone when we came back.

As the weather got better, Nicky was home less and less, until at weekends he was out from when he got up until he came in to eat after all the others had gone in for the night. I missed him, but I never minded that he was out. I understood his need to be away from the flat. His mean spirited outburst, laden with swear words had cut deep. He was like a different person.

The previous week, I had been doing the laundry when I noticed that only one pair of Nicky's trousers was at all muddy around the ankles or on the knees, and it dawned on me that this was not the first time that neither his shorts nor his trousers had mud or grass stains.

It seemed peculiar.

I stopped and stared at them, smoothing them with the flat of my hand. I winced as the realisation dawned on me that it had been several weeks, at least, since Nicky had played football more than once in any given week.

I wrinkled my nose at the smell of cigarette that came from the laundry pile, and picked out one of Nicky's t-shirts, held it to my nose and sniffed. His clothes were starting to smell more like Mick, I mean Dad's. I let it fall back on the pile, standing there, stroking the clothes, disappointed. My brother was only nine years old, and he had already given up on games.

That morning, I had asked him to spend the afternoon with me and suggested that we could maybe go for a walk by the river, like we used to do sometimes earlier in the year. Or maybe we could go to the library together. There was a book I needed to take back anyway, and Nicky had always enjoyed a good read, or maybe he could look for some other pictures to copy. That was when he had screamed at me.

It was so sudden and unexpected that I stared gormlessly at him.

He swore at me.

It was the first time he had ever used those words at me.

I stood, broom in hand, wondering why it was that those words had ever been invented in the first place. Who would invent such unpleasant words to hurt someone?

It was not like it was the very first time I heard someone swear like that. I had heard it so many times and so much worse in my life at home. Coming from my brother's mouth to attack me they sounded wrong and more offensive than they ever had.

My eyes started to prickle.

We had fought before. All siblings do but this was different. The instinct to curl up into a tiny ball was strong.

I realised I was gripping the mop handle excessively tight, the nails on my fingers digging into the heel of my hand. I shoved the mop into the bucket and it fell over, water sploshing all over the floor. I threw the mop at the wall. It left a tiny brown dent, but given all the bump marks and scuffs, neither my father or my brother would notice or suspect it was mine. I would always know. For years after, I would give the dink a rub with my index finger, a reminder that I too could leave a mark if I chose to.

I knew I could race out of the flat, tears streaming down my face and hurl myself into Nana's arms, but I did not want to alarm her, she did not need to worry any more about us than she already did. I had read her face more than once – she frowned in a way when Dad came around to hers, or when we turned up at odd times, or when the two of us went around to hers and ate our tea too desperately. I wanted her to be happy, from the bottom of my heart, she was unhappy so often, I did not want to be the one to make her unhappy again, I did not want her to worry about us.

I decided not to do anything about Nicky at all, this time, or again. I reminded myself that I was his sister, not his mother. It was safer not to act.

I rubbed the red crescent fingernail marks on my hands, wiped my eyes and went to fetch a towel to sop up the spilt water, getting down on my hands and knees. I fought back the tears. It was Saturday morning, and I would clean the flat, top to bottom, as thoroughly as I always did.

I went upstairs and put the bucket outside the bathroom and leaned the mop against the door frame. I had put the cleaning products in the bucket to carry them up and would take them out as I needed them. Once they'd all been used and neatly lined up, I'd refill the bucket with hot water to wash the floor.

I went into Mick's room, changed the sheets, and picked up the heaps of dirty clothes, and repeated my actions in Nicky's. I took the sheets off my bed too and put the lot in the laundry basket at the top of the staircase. My clothes were there already, I was the only one who ever used it. I took out clean sheets from the cupboard on the landing and made up the beds in the three rooms.

The rooms were starting to look a bit better. I hated the way the sunlight cut in through the windows and showed the dust that always seemed to hang in the air. If only I could clean the air in the flat, that would have been good. Pure, clean, unaffected air. I could open the windows however, and I did so, every week regardless of the weather.

On to the bathroom next, though I would change the towels and bath mat the following weekend. I took the bottle of bleach, the cleaning cloth and the marigolds out of the bucket, pulled them on, and I filled the bucket with the hottest water possible and added a cupful of bleach. With the cleaning cloth in hand, I scrubbed the sink and tap first, then the tiles, the bath and tap, and finally the toilet. When that was done, I mopped the floor, and let it dry. I took my socks off so that my bare feet did not mark the pristine floor. I carefully emptied the bucket into the toilet, and then refilled it with fresh hot water and more bleach. I swept the hall floor next, moving backwards towards the top of the stairs, and then mopped it too. I worked my way backwards down the stairs, first with the broom and then with the mop.

I focused on every detail, mopping back and forth, dunking the mop in the water, wringing it out, getting right into the corners, and then pulling it across the floor, trying extremely hard not to let other thoughts sneak in. The trick was to focus on the task at hand. Then it was time to clean the living room. Today was a kitchen day, so I would only try to plump the tired sofa and armchair, wipe the windowsill, and do the floor, the knickknacks on the shelves would wait their turn.

In the hall, I straightened the shoes out, wiped the shelf above the radiator, shook the old worn doormat out of the front door, swept and mopped the hall. I pushed the fact that the shelf was wobblier than a few weeks ago to the back of my mind, no need to keep going over the night my father had thumped the shelf with all his might. Back and forth with the mop, dunk, wring, all the way to the kitchen.

I always liked to tidy the kitchen. It was one of my favourite parts of my Saturday morning cleaning routine. I did not like doing the bedrooms very much, and I hated scrubbing the toilet. The living room was acceptable to me, but I did like the kitchen. It had become my room in some ways. I enjoyed cooking, I liked to do my homework at the big table, I preferred to sit in the warm patch of sunlight that came through the kitchen window and read there over anywhere in the house other than my bed. Quiet, tucked away, inconspicuous.

I had been cleaning for about two and a half hours, methodically. I felt lighter, like my mind was more organised when the house was straight. Nana always said, "Tidy home, tidy mind."

The door burst open. Nicky called out to me as he headed up the stairs.

"Still scrubbing, Cinderella?"

I tried to ignore the sarcastic tone in his voice but could not help wondering what was wrong with him, and why he had run straight upstairs to the bathroom. I answered, bright as I could muster, a greeting which I hoped was submissive enough to avoid further conflict.

"Hey, Bugs. Did you have a nice morning?"

No answer came from upstairs. I went back to

mopping the kitchen floor, dunk, wring, mop. It was not long before I was done. I put the bucket down in the corner of the room beside the door and surveyed the kitchen. Ideally, I would have liked to get the brown ring out of the kitchen top where Dad had put a scalding hot pan one day a few years ago, and I always wished that the table didn't have the funny orangey-brown marks, small rectangles from where cigarettes had rolled out of the ashtray.

Nicky was still in his room. I stood for a moment and pondered whether I should go upstairs to see him. Instead, I stared at the kitchen floor for a while, rubbing my hands together. My nails were short and stubby, and the skin of my hands was dry. There were minute skin tags peeling off beside my nails. The edges were red and sore, though the latest red crescent marks on my wrists were gone.

It was coming up to lunch time, and I realised that I was hungry. I called up the stairs to Nicky to see if he wanted a sandwich. There was some bread, a little cheese and half a big beef tomato that would do nicely. He did not answer, but as the kitchen floor now looked dry, I decided to make one each anyway.

Carefully I laid out the bread, the cheese and the tomato in a line to one side of the chopping board, put two plates on the other, and got two knives out from the drawer. I used the blunt table knife to spread on two slices of bread which I had placed on each of the plates. The sharper chopping knife I used to sliver off some cheese, and I put that on the bread. I wrapped up the rest of the cheese in the wax paper and put it back in the fridge. It was the sharp knife's job again to slice the tomato, and I added the slices to the top of the cheese. Finally, I topped the stack with another slice of bread. Placing a hand on top of each, I squished them down a bit and put them on the plates. I washed the wooden board, the knives, dried them and put them away. I put the plates on the table and wiped the kitchen top that I had worked on and put the plates with the sandwiches on the table. Then, I got two glasses from the cupboard, and the jug, which I filled and set down on the table.

I sat and waited for Bugs.

It was a good twenty minutes before I started to nibble at my sandwich. There had been something about Nicky's tone that stopped me from going up or calling up to him.

I pondered the issue I'd been avoiding as I ruminated at my lunch, first pulling the crust off the sliced white bread, putting it in my mouth and chewing as a cow chewing the cud.

Nicky had certainly been less playful recently, and he wasn't as chatty at mealtimes anymore. I brought up a mental image of him from a few months before coming home, dropping his school bag in the hall, and climbing up onto a kitchen chair, reaching for a slice of toast and telling me happily about school. I compared it to the brother that had slammed the front and stomped up the stairs.

I considered the evidence, and concluded that my little brother Nicky, aged nine, was loitering in the back stairwell with his friends. He had stopped playing. They behaved like wannabe gangsters, but it was all for show. They weren't the type who'd qualify for the Barlinnie YTS. They lacked the real mean streak. I looked down at my half-eaten lunch. I decided to put it in the fridge for later. I knew I would be hungry as I'd had no breakfast, and that my appetite had not been sated, it had only vanished because of the realisation I'd had.

Nana would be so disappointed if she knew. Fortunately, we no longer went around so often, but

I would need to make sure that she never found out. The first give away was the smell. Mick smoked all the time in the kitchen, so the main thing would be to ensure that Nicky always had a change of clothes that was untainted. I considered keeping a pair of his trousers, a t-shirt and a jumper in the cupboard in my room, and then realised that it would not work. Word would get around that he was spending time with Seumas, John, Dev and Dave soon enough, and Nana would hear all about it. I called them the 'Lost Boys' with good reason.

That said, it was worth considering that she had not yet found out about what had happened last weekend, when Nicky had in fact been playing football, or at least enjoying a rowdy kickabout. One of them, John, I think, had kicked the ball into a front garden a few streets down. It had bounced off one of the house's front windows – not quite as dramatic as it is having gone through it, but enough to startle the house-owner into dropping his cup of hot tea onto his lap. He got up to see what the cause of the sound had been, only to see Bugs clambering over the fence and landing on his carefully tended flowerbed. He had been irritated by the time he had opened his front door to holler at the weedy blonde boy now standing on his patch of lawn, ball under his arm.

"What the hell do you think you are doing?"

He launched into a tirade. As he was starting to build up some steam, and berate Nicky for careless ball play. Nicky dropped the ball, and in three quick steps, launched himself up the man's front, and wrapped his legs around the man's waist. Clinging to the man's neck with one arm, started hitting him on the head with the other and shrieking obscenities into his ear.

At this point, John and Dev managed to open the

gate, run into the front garden. Dev grabbed Nicky under the arms and started to pull back, prising him off. Dev lost his balance and fell back with Nicky, against John. The impetus knocked the house owner back through his front door into his own hall. They had all stared at each other in shock, the man lying on the ground, trousers wet from the tea, aghast at these three young boys, and the extreme reaction of the blonde one.

They ran all the way back to our building, up the stairs. They almost ran past me, reading in the patch of sunlight that pooled at the top of stairwell. They would have kept going, clattering past Old Mrs Pollock's place to the end of the walkway if I had not been there.

They stopped in their tracks to report the incident to me, excited and speaking machine-gun fast. Nicky had been "fierce and monstrous" and had "given the man what for."

I sat there and listened, refusing to believe that my little brother would have reacted like that. I told them that they should not tell anyone what had happened. They were buzzing. Full of their own bravado. I was appalled. What if the poor man called the police? Mick would give Nicky absolute hell.

That evening when Nicky came home, I did not mention it at all. I had made carrot soup. We ate a bowlful in silence, but then Nicky grinned, declared that it was delicious and asked for more. We fell back into chatting, studiously ignoring the event.

As I pictured us sitting together over our bowls of soup, a wave of sadness came over me, his uneaten sandwich on the table. I knew those days were numbered even then.

I tried to remember him coming to eat it with me, his feet bunched up on the chair seat, knees poking up above the table, but it never sticks. The memory has shifted to sadness and grief, the uneaten sandwich destined to go stale, the tomato watery, its skin curling and the cheese waxy. The thought of me, alone in the kitchen putting my brother's sandwich in the bin was a punch of anguish to the chest.

1973

At the time of Nicky's birth, my father was twenty-four years old. At work, he received a promotion from labouring to planning. Mick was moving up in the world. So was I: he bought me a shiny red bicycle to replace my wooden trike. Red because that would be suitable for both a girl and, far more importantly, for a little boy later on.

That year, we went to the park often. Mick was the only Dad who always came, chest puffed out in pride. The same park where years later Nicky found the Norackel. Where later still, Nicky hung out with his mates and learnt some of the darker arts of socialising. I have a photo that their friend Jim took around that time. Dad wearing a thick black donkey jacket, and flared burgundy corduroys. His hair was shaggier than I remember him ever having. He was crouched behind me. I was a pale and skinny dark-haired girl on a red bicycle. From the perspective, I have started pedalling forwards, away from him, scraped knee and determined grin. Blurred in the background, a thin blonde woman almost lost in a large brown duffel coat pushing a pram, a knitted blue blanket hanging over the edge. Mum and Nicky. Her face was a blur.

Nana always told me how happy Mick was then. I revisited those days with great care, sticking to the script, panning out and zooming in on details.

I tune in, studying every aspect, fight off the hiss and crackle of degrading memory. There's Mum in the kitchen patting her beehive, radiant, as I come in, a knee-high sock adorably crumpled around my ankle. My hair is long, a pair of Anne of Green Gables plaits, bright bows on each. She frowns, adjusts the ribbons. I need help to be neat. Breakfast is boiled eggs and toast. Sometimes I make the mistake of imagining a stack of pancakes like in old sitcoms. Everything is neat and pristine. Ange, Mum, left nothing behind save these replays. Clean-shaven, a stylish parting through his hair, Mick sets off to work in the site office in a smart brown wool, whistling a tune

If I could give those childhood days a live studio soundtrack, I would. A collective "aww" every time the adorable baby is on screen. Encouraging applause for me, the quiet girl. When the doorbell rings, Mum swishes her full skirt down the bottle green hall to welcome Mrs Ranjeet, rapturous applause for the nosy neighbour on our set.

The screen wipes left to right as I set off to school with Mrs Ranjeet's boys. I rarely revisit my class days. It was a time when I wrote careful letter shapes, tongue poking out between my lips. Puzzled over maths. A grey reality, chalk dust and damp coats on pegs. One day our milk was left by a hot radiator instead of on the sill. The corner of the classroom smelt for days so instead of hiding there with a picture book I ventured into the playground and shivered by the door alone. School life before Becky joined the cast.

I prefer to nourish the memory of us all together.

I would trot home from school, maybe stop to play, let my imagination free, constructing careful worlds down rabbit holes, forests in wardrobes, friends to play with. A place of clear expectations and well laid plots. Then home to Ange kissing me on my forehead, a jam sandwich on the table and singing my multiplication tables with me while she made the evening meal. Perhaps I have corrected the dark circles under her eyes. I don't remember those. I have chosen to remember her eyes lighting up when Mick came home in the evening.

He would scoop me up in his arms, kiss Nicky in his crib. Then he would greet his beautiful young wife Ange. He would wrap his arms around her waist, stroke the nape of her neck. She would lean into his body, smile, and giggle. He asked about her day, if she'd been to the shops, the ladies at her mum's group. He told her about his day, about the lads at the site, retell an anecdote. He laid the table, she served up, he held Nicky in his arms. I sat at the table half-eating, half-pushing my food about, being difficult, though not unbearable back then. After our bedtime, they would sit beside each other on the sofa, comfortable, relaxed.

Over the years, I composed these scenes and edited them. I could never write myself out. I belonged in them.

I have always been certain that this was a golden time, the blurry shapes of memory polished. How could it have been anything else? Mick was finally becoming the man he had always known he should be, Ange was settling into the role of mother so much better with Nicky.

On Sundays, I was trusted to stay tidy. I could wear my favourite green dress and my black patent leather shoes with the buckles. Nicky would be put in a white or cream gown, a fluffy blanket over him in his pram. Once we were all out of the front door, on our walkway in the sky, Mick, I mean Dad, pulled his weight against the green front door shut and jiggled the key to lock it.

Picture perfect, our family would set off for Sunday lunch at Nana's. Dad carrying the pram, complete with baby in it, down the stairs, across the landings, all the way down to the bottom until the wheels could be set down. Neighbours would smile at us walking along the street.

Of course, after Nicky passed, I asked Nana if she remembered this happy time well. No matter what Nana answered, I did not remember Ange crying. She did not stare listlessly into mid-space. She did not look at Nicky with confusion. She did not stand in Nicky's room, gazing at a bawling baby. Or sit in another room, boobs painfully leaking, humming a drone to herself. I have revisited this time in memory. Ange was able to breastfeed. She glowed and cooed, and smiled, and sang made up ditties. I remember it was a few years later that the neighbours would frown seeing Nicky and I scurrying to Nana's alone.

1991

The tidiness was soothing, the freshly mown grass, bright flowers and sparkling new headstones. At my feet, a tidy rectangular mound lined up beside another, more settled pile of earth, a row stretching away from me. I stood there a moment. This one was probably closed this morning, the gravestone fresh from the box. I had a fondness for the older part, the crumbling tombstones, motifs weather beaten. Unlike most people who say they like cemeteries, however, I preferred the newer ones.

I made my way down the row to the more settled graves with footstones, curbs, rails, the occasional slabs. All we leave is this bland summary, a tiny facet in this place, reborn as memory. No other creatures make such ado about their dead.

The crash of the front door had awakened me in pitch black night.

Dad was home.

A cabinet door slammed, a tap gushing, the noises a drunk man makes in the kitchen. He would no doubt eat the pasta bake I had put aside to take to work the next day. I was annoyed, I had made an excellent one, with lots of vegetables and tomato sauce. Relieved also, better he ate something than come roaring up the stairs to find us.

I huddled the covers around me and squeezed my fists tight. I didn't live here anymore. Regret swept over me. I had come to stay out of duty. We barely shared news over a cup of tea then both my father and brother had gone out. I did not protest. Instead, I cleaned and cooked as I had always done. I didn't like staying overnight in the flat. I only stayed because I hadn't told Nicky that I might leave. He might not even come home for a few days. I dragged my nails down the side of my wrist. I could have been safely tucked in my own bed.

The noises stopped abruptly.

Perhaps he would fall asleep at the kitchen table? I needed to know he was done and I would be left alone.

My breath was fast, senses alert in the dark. Eyes open, I could almost see the shadows thicken and dance. The scraping of the kitchen chair told me he was on the move again.

Footsteps in the hall. Heavy. Uneven.

A bump off the wall.

A thick thud.

I knew that sound. Mick, my father, had passed out drunk in the hall. I felt myself relax. He wouldn't move until dawn at least.

I fell back into uneasy sleep.

Waking to complete silence, I took a moment to enjoy the bedwarm calm before I tiptoed on the cold floor to the bathroom. Mick, I mean Dad's, movements of last night crept back into my thoughts.

I guessed he would still be lying there as I had not heard him move around onto the sofa. He hadn't dragged himself up the stairs or thrown up in the toilet. I knew exactly what that sounded like. I decided to shower while the bathroom was still clean and smelt good. I knew that once he used it, it would be deeply unpleasant for hours, even with the window open.

As I got dressed, skin goosebumped from the chill, I realised that Mick was not snoring. It was unlikely that he had slipped out. I scraped my hair back into a ponytail. It helped me to feel prepared to face him if he was up, waiting to pounce.

From the top of the steps, I could see his coat was still hanging up, his shoes lying haphazardly on the floor. Still home.

I paused to listen.

Not a sound.

He would be prone on the sofa, no doubt. I hovered, weighing my options. Leaving was the best, but I would need to get my stuff from the room. That could alert him. Best to be as passive as possible before making a deft exit.

I took another couple of steps down. I glanced towards the sitting room, but my line of sight snagged.

Feet.

In the hall. At odd angles. Legs. Uncomfortably bent. Stained trousers. Crumpled shirt untucked.

Reaching the bottom of the stairs, I could see my father lying on his front, along the hall. His head was turned on his cheek, away from me, his black hair sticky looking. He was facing the broken pane in the lower half of the kitchen door. I walked around him, careful not to disturb. I could see his face now. His eyes were half open. Skin grey. He would never get round to fixing that pane after all.

Mick, I mean Dad, was dead.

A gaudy false tomb adorned with angels on columns brought me back from my pondering. Nana was waiting on an exedra, an ornate stone bench. Mick's stone was within her line of sight. The gravel crunched under my feet. She stood and together we walked over. The weeds had not grown back from my previous visit. It would be at least another six months until the depression formed. She placed the flowers. He never seemed to take any interest in blooms when he was alive. That did not matter now. So much easier to keep up appearances. The dead could not hurt you anymore.

It had been six months already. Nana was completely silent at the graveside. I looked at her in the fresh morning light. I noticed for the first time that she looked old. Less vivacious. She seemed more translucent, like the moment when you realise that something was made of rice paper.

She had never been like the other grannies. She knitted and made jam, that was true. She knew what to say at the market too. Folks were taken in by that. Nana was a sweet lady. There was no denying that. She was no soft marshmallow or powdery tablet. She was an aniseed ball, a liquorice shoelace. She had held the family together over the years. Patched things up more than once. After Ange left, she was there for us. With Mick gone, she was all the family Nicky and I had.

We turned out of the gates. Nana was wearing her fur lined suede zip up boots, and her thick beige tights were baggy around the back of her knees. Her skirt skimmed them so that only I could have noticed. Her smart brown fedora with the black band, silver hair curling under the jaunty angle she had always worn it. The brim did not hide that the rings under her eyes were darker, her lips thinner, the red lipstick bleeding up thin lines.

As we walked from the section with the newer graves through to the old gravestones, she started to chat. I had never heard her speak like this. The words tumbled out and I was listening as hard as I could, scooping up every detail to fit into my careful collage of childhood memories, the story of me, this was 1973 and I needed all the elements I could gather.

1973

I started school, Mick enrolled at college part-time to study for an architectural engineering qualification. I never knew what exactly. A diploma of some sort. In his first term at college, Mick, I mean Dad, was friendly with a couple of the lads on the course, though they were a bit younger than him. Being a part-time course, they worked too, but they did not have families of their own yet.

They were young, and looked up to Mick, with all the six years he had on them. He would let them cadge cigarettes off him, and they would chat about what was in that day's news. Increasingly they spoke about politics, the IRA, pit closures and the price of oil.

Mick revelled in their veneration. Back in school, he had been the one with a job and cash, the good looks. Self-assured and a bit cheeky, everyone wanted to be his pal. He knew most of the pub landlords and could hold his drink. His peers looked up to him.

After leaving school, they had all vanished into their own lives, just as he fell into the pit of domesticity. It was all laid out for him. His own mother's boyfriend, George, had got him the job. Dad's pride was wounded by the help, no matter how much he liked the older man. Out of respect for George the men were polite to him, the foreman's pet, amongst the real working men. He learnt to stop cracking jokes, to keep his head down, to eat his sandwiches alone. George kept an eye out for him. Nonetheless Mick spent his days alone for years. His promotion to the managerial side of the business did nothing to increase his popularity. After four years as a young hardworking father, making friends at college quenched a thirst he had ignored too long.

At college, he could pull on his old self again, exuberantly inhabiting the knowledgeable bon-vivant. To escape a chill October wind, the lads suggested that he join them for a drink down at the Hawk and Hare. It had been a long day on site but the lecture that evening had been interesting. No one could throw a double twenty like him. Soon the pints were flowing and everyone knew his name. It was a warm embrace away from Ange's tears, the enforced quiet to let us children sleep.

All Ange asked of him the next morning was to let her know if he was going out. Within the fortnight, he left every morning with a "don't expect me home for tea." The first time I came down the stairs to find him snoring on the sofa, I curled up in the crook of his knees. He was warm though he smelt bitter.

Evenings were calmer. I wanted Daddy cracking jokes at bath-time, telling stories, though since the promotion he was grumpy when he was home, and Ange was on edge. A gentle rhythm set in. I ate alone but Ange sat by me, holding Nicky. On bath night, she held him in the water with me, and I washed him with the flannel. I loved bath time together. Mum stroked my hair and mumbled, "Your Dad obviously enjoys being the working-class man more than being a working family man." There was no bitterness. I loved the power cut evenings by candlelight most.

I remember them like I was Jo in *Little Women*.

Mornings changed gradually. I no longer cuddled into Dad's sleeping form, he stopped drowsily stroking my hair. He pushed me away more than once. Rolled over and groaned. Staggered to his feet and threw up in the kitchen sink. Mum stopped acknowledging he was there at all. He changed clothes and left in the morning. He did not always come home. At night, I became aware of raised voices. Words like "money", "afford", "priorities" and "frigid bitch" came up the stairs. On occasion, tender loving words too, regular thuds I didn't understand. Giggles. Rarely.

Ange became panicky in the evenings. At home, Dad never smiled. They snipped at each other. On the 23rd of December, Mick went out, slamming the door behind him and leaving Mum sobbing as she wrapped the presents in the living room. I had heard them shouting and had snuck out of my bedroom, carefully tucking my nightdress around me as I sat down on the landing at the top of the stairs. There was a cold draft on my ankles when the front door was opened.

I watched her crying through the bannister from the top of the staircase. She was pale and thin. I thought her arms looked like the branches on the trees outside, as though they might snap in a sudden gust of wintry wind. She rubbed the top of her arm as though it was hurt.

The next day Nicky was gurgling on his back on the rug in the middle of the room, Mum and I tackled a wooden jigsaw puzzle of a train. The Christmas tree was in the corner of the room, sparkling cheerfully in the fading mid-afternoon light. No one mentioned Dad, but his absence was everywhere. He had never stayed away for two nights before.

In the evening, after fish fingers and chips, we went

to the local Watchnight service. George and Nana liked us all to go together. Even then I wondered why this was one of the few conventions they upheld. It struck me as out of character, and I was too young to register the importance of George shaking all the right hands on that evening, Nana's lipstick matching that of the properly married wives. Folk forget in time to question appearances they have grown accustomed to.

We went home for hot cocoa, a veritable treat, and Mum tucked us in. I tried to stay awake for Santa, but it was morning before I knew it. It was Christmas Day at last. I got up early and ran down the stairs, barefoot in my cotton nightdress. I knew that we would be happy, the four of us, because it was a magical day. Mick, I mean Dad, was surely home, and Mum would smile right up to her eyes. We would go to Nana's for a turkey roast with all the trimmings.

I ran down the stairs, and practically vaulted the hallway as I dashed into the living room. My Christmas stocking did not look right. It was not bulging in any way. It was hanging limply, as was Nicky's beside it. I unhooked it. I felt the length of it, and peered in. It was empty. Nicky's stocking was empty. That night, for the first time in my life, Father Christmas had not come to deliver presents for Nicky and me.

I stood in the middle of the room, an empty Christmas stocking in each hand. I knew that even if I maybe had not been as good as I could have been through the whole of the year, Nicky had. He was only a baby. He could not do anything wrong, not completely wrong anyway. How could Father Christmas not bring him anything? Mum would only cry if I told her, and I did not want to confess to her about the bonbons that I had taken from the corner shop last summer. Mum had been crying so much recently.

I knew which drawer the wrapping paper was kept

in and I took some out. I crumpled some up on the floor so that it would look as though I had opened my presents and collected a few of my pencils and one of the library books and a doll into a pile in the corner.

I looked under the sofa, behind the chair and in the nooks and crannies and found some of Nicky's toys, a wooden truck and a stuffed toy that was a round yellow velvety egg shape with an orange beak, twisted them into some wrapping paper and stuffed them into Nicky's stocking.

A sound. A soft "oh", behind me. I turned around and there was Mum, in her dressing gown.

Her chin started to tremble, and she dashed into the kitchen. I could hear her start to cry even though she had put the kettle on. I had not been fast enough. She knew now that we had been naughty. I would have to confess about the sweets. I simply had no idea what it was that Nicky had done wrong. Perhaps he was being punished for my failings. I was not ready to tell her straight away though.

I went upstairs and got Nicky washed up from the night's dribble with a warm damp flannel, changed his nappy, dressed him in a baby grow, and carried him down the stairs, his head on my shoulder and his bottom on one forearm, the other arm wrapped around his back, gingerly taking one step at a time, to Mum. He was getting heavier. She was sitting at the kitchen table.

For a moment, we stared at each other across the table, and then Nicky started to cry. I put him in her arms for her to feed and she simply stared at him blankly. I told her that I would have some toast for breakfast in a bit and went upstairs to have a quick birdbath of my own in the tub and get dressed.

By the time I got back down to the kitchen, Mum was breastfeeding my brother, and had made me toast, with strawberry jam and a weak cup of tea. She looked sad. Mimicking Nana and in my brightest voice, I said:

"Let's tidy up. It will make us all feel better!"

I nodded at her. Activity was certainly better than sitting around. We tidied the bedrooms, cleaned the bathroom and the kitchen together. I put on the radio, but quickly switched it back off. The Christmas service had brought Ange to a standstill. Every speck of dust, every last mark was dealt with. As the morning came to an end, we got ready to go to Nana's. My best green velvet dress and black patent leather shoes. They were barely broken in and already tight. Mum was about to tuck Nicky into the pram just as the front door burst open.

Mick.

He was wearing a novelty red hat with a white fur trim, had a scratchy two-day stubble and carried a bag of presents in one hand, and a half-empty bottle of cheap whisky in the other.

"Ho ho ho! Merry Christmas! Tam, Nicky! My little cherubs. Here are your presents!"

He stumbled in and sat on the floor in the hall, pulling me down onto his knee and into his body. The now familiar bitter smell of him, sweaty, unwashed, enveloped me. His chin scratched my cheek as he kissed me, crushing my arms. He reached up towards Nicky, whose face had gone bright red. I thought my little brother would burst into tears, but he looked up to my mother. Mick, I mean Dad, let his grip on me ease and pulled out a present for each of us. I adjusted myself more comfortably on his knees. I had to get this exactly right.

My Daddy was home. I would be happy. I ignored the nasty smell on his breath. I threw my arms around his neck.

"Daddy, my Daddy! Merry Christmas!"

Christmas had kept its magical promise because we were all together. I looked down at the present, it was a book of the Grimm's fairy tales. It was not new, the front page was ripped out and there was a library code on the spine. Doubtless my name had already been on the card. I looked up at him. I loved fairy tales. It meant that my father knew that I loved them too.

I held it up to show to Mum. She was backed up against the wall, beside the doorway, squashed against it, staring at my father, baby in her arms, her eyes still red, chin wobbling. He looked up at her, and pushed me off his knee, and swayed towards her, with a low voice, almost a growl.

"Well, a merry Christmas to you too, Ange."

For a moment, we froze, me on the floor with my book, Mum holding Nicky, Dad leering towards her. She held Nicky out to me, told me to get upstairs. The edge in her voice rang clear. I took Nicky and made my way upstairs as fast as I could with none of my earlier care, squeezing my brother too tight. On to the landing, to my room and crawled into my bed, shuffling Nicky in with me while the screams and crashes rose towards us through the floor.

I held Nicky, his head in the crook of my elbow. I tried to think of a lullaby to keep him quiet. All I could muster up was the alphabet song.

The front door slammed.

Nicky was crying in a strangely quiet way for a baby and I could smell that he had soiled his nappy. We wriggled back out from our blanket nest. Mum was sitting in absolute silence at the kitchen table, the bottle Dad had carried in was smashed on the floor. I tiptoed around the broken glass to ask her to change Nicky. I could have done it, but it was difficult for me when he wasn't in a simple sleepsuit, and poo made me retch.

She looked at me.

Her face was swollen, and her lip was bleeding. Mummy was hurt. Daddy was gone. Reluctantly I took my brother back upstairs, and sat on my bed holding him, trying to rock him to sleep, knowing full well his bottom would become sore and red but unable to face dealing with his dirty nappy.

After that, Mum mostly stayed at home, sometimes unable to even leave the kitchen table. For a few months she worked in the corner shop, and then part-time as a secretary for a local accountant. She started to wear her hair with a chunky fringe, and dark tinted glasses. There were days of calm and quiet togetherness with Mum. Days out to the park with both of them. They would joke and laugh, for our sakes. Mum was distant, and Dad too enthusiastic.

Nights of screaming and shouting, crashing, and slamming. The words "money", "afford", "provide" found my ears in the night. I cried and balled my fists. Occasionally the thuds were rhythmic, fleshy. Beyond my comprehension. "Trapped with the bloody children" made me squeeze my eyes tight. It was my fault. I had trapped them together.

I turned six that year.

1992

I could not sit still. I could not clean.

I was going round the flat, picking things up, putting them down. I must have had about eight or nine cups of coffee that morning. I had told Becky I would go through the joint bills, go down to the post office with our electricity and gas money.

Like I used to when it was Mick, Nicky and me. The three of us. Only one of us now. I broke Mum, I drove Mick to drink, I could not even look out for Nicky. I was the rust that ate them away. I looked at the knife in the kitchen drawer. The paring knife. The special one. I thought about the release it could bring.

I had promised Becky I wouldn't. She would check my wrists. My thighs too since the last time she found me.

It had been the three of us for so long, our spiky triangle holding on to each other. It was less complicated when Mick died. I had cried. I had missed him. The flat was so weird without him. I still jumped at loud noise, no matter that I knew he was gone, but it was easier, not bracing for it all the time.

Nicky was hardly ever at the flat. There was always a painting, a gig, a launch. I was alone with my books, the memory of Mick in the smoke in the kitchen when I allowed myself a cigarette. I would throw the windows open but I couldn't get him out. I should get things fixed now the flat was my responsibility, the old shelf in the hall and the broken pane in the kitchen door. The burn marks in the lino.

A fat envelope with a claim form revealed that Mick had life insurance. We never had expected him to, and the truth is he did not set it up himself. A little investigation revealed that Mr McIntyre, the accountant Ange had worked for, had set it all up after she left. He never contacted us directly. I went to thank him one day. He seemed embarrassed as he handed over various documents and asked me not to tell anyone. We owned the flat and had some money over. I moved in with Becky and put money aside, Nicky paid down the lease on the Sugar Factory where he set up a studio flat with Lou in the old foreman's office.

We kept the flat on because of Ange.

In case she decided to come back one day to look for us. Maybe with Mick gone, somehow she'd know it was safe to return.

I should have sold it. Nicky had wanted to. Maybe hanging on to the hope and pain was too much. It kept Nicky coming back, kept him from flying away. I kept him from flying away.

I was so lost in thought, I hadn't even realised I had picked up the paring knife.

The damned flat. It was always waiting for us, for her, for him to come and never leave. I was left behind, still waiting, always waiting, waiting for what? For Nicky to be older, but he will never be older, and Ange will never come back to find him. Why would she come back for me? It was time to stop waiting, to do something. Speak to Nana, see if she knew anything. I realised I had never asked her if she knew where Ange went.

Yes. That was what came next. I put the knife back and slammed the drawer closed. Ran out of the kitchen.

I fell on the sofa and let out a deep breath.

I was tired. My arms felt heavy, my legs leaden.

I flicked the TV on.

I lay down, wedged a cushion under my head, just as Mick, I mean Dad, used to lie, and dozed off as the lunchtime news came on.

The theme tune from *Countdown* seeped into my awareness. I pulled myself to seated, groggy on the sofa.

Enough.

I decided it was time to get back to work. The manager had given me extended leave, but I never liked being off work, not being needed, not being useful. Anything was better than hours alone at Mick's flat, or my flat.

I needed my Nana. She was in the garden with George, in silent companionship. I tried to join in the weeding. It was too uncomfortable. Nana followed me into her kitchen. I lit a cigarette.

She frowned at me but pulled one out of the packet for herself. I raised an eyebrow at her. She rarely ever smoked. She picked the blue lighter off the table and tried to light it, but her right thumb let her down. Her joints were starting to stiffen with age. She sighed in disappointment and rubbed her hands.

Once, twice, and then she took the lighter in her left hand and used her right forefinger to roll the spark wheel. A flame sprung out, and she took a deep drag before putting it back on the table. She always found a way to make things work. She blew out the smoke, she took my free hand in hers.

"Tam, some people are meant to burn bright. They don't burn for long."

I nodded. It was little comfort.

"It's in their bones, there's nothing you can do. It seeps in like damp and they can't shift it."

"He could have spoken to me."

"He knew that. He made his choice."

This was not the conversation I had been hoping for. I had meant to ask about Ange.

I smiled at her, sighed deeply, tears threatening to spill from my eyes. That would never do. I pulled my hand from hers, curled it around my cup.

Nana stood up. She was never one to wallow over anything.

"First time I smoked was at a dance, to impress a tall GI. I coughed so hard I spilt my drink all over him!"

"Oh no! Nana! What did you do?"

"Elspeth came over and batted her eyelids and offered to take him somewhere to dry him off. They were dance partners for a few weeks until he was posted somewhere else. Never heard from him again! It was the war!"

Her eyes were bright with memory as she described dancing the Lindy Bop and learning to Jitterbug with the GIs. It was not the day to ask about Ange. I needed to find the moment. Wait for the right time to bring the subject of my mother with her. I was in no mood for the thrill of war time adventures.

Instead, I asked Nana about that Christmas disappearance. Her face settled hard. She assured me that I had remembered it all wrong. He had only been gone a few hours the day before Christmas Eve to do his Christmas shopping. This was not open for discussion either.

"Shall we put on some of your records, Nana? You can teach me a step or two."

My docile peace offering was accepted.

1984

I constructed the scene.

Nana and George sat silently across from each other at the kitchen table. He was waiting for her to formulate an answer. The table was square, with a speckled Formica top and a metal edge to hide the chip board. In between them, on the gleaming surface, was a plate of biscuits, the pink wafer ones. He leant in on his elbows, a large hand wrapped around the mug of tea that was slowly growing cold. Nana was twiddling her teaspoon.

George was not Nana's husband, and though he had been part of her life since Mick was ten, he had chosen the role of silent supporter. The day had come to say something. He knew she wanted it too.

He had asked her to move Nicky and I in with her.

Mick had been increasingly erratic, and we had sought refuge more frequently. Nana was worried that Mick would take an even worse turn if he thought we were being taken off him. Being a young woman afforded me some protection. A rapidly maturing boy of eleven was at risk. Though she hated admitting that it was her own son who was at the root of the problem, she could no longer make do with patching up the kids whenever they appeared.

Nicky had appeared at their front door late the night before. Nana had already switched the television off after the ten o'clock news had finished and was "shutting up" the house. The right side of his face was dark red and clearly painful, and there was a bloodied scratch above his eye. They had let him in to the house without asking any questions. He would sleep in the spare room as usual. They didn't ask where I was.

She and George resolved that we would live with them on weeknights, staying at the flat on Fridays and Saturdays only. Maybe we could all find a better routine in our lives and Nicky might even settle into schoolwork. Conceivably Mick might even go home more if there were no children to remind him of his failings.

I had always tried to be anything but a burden to anyone. I had always known that I was a difficult child to look after. I was too much from the moment I was conceived. Or maybe not enough. I never did work that out.

I took it as my job to keep the flat clean and tidy when Ange left, to provide food, to study, to help Nicky with his homework. It wasn't enough. Not for Nicky. Nana knew I could not cope. I was exhausted. At fifteen, my exams were just around the corner.

She smiled weakly at him and nodded.

He let go of her hands, which he had reached across the table to take, and automatically picked up a biscuit. It crumbled pink onto his jumper when he took a bite.

$\rtimes$

Nicky was not happy about the arrangement. I remember, clear as day.

"I'm not moving in with Nana. If we live with her, we will never see our friends. It will be straight home from school every day. I'd rather stay in the flat with Mick."

"You mean Dad. We can't keep turning up like that, unexpected. Nana and George need to know what we are doing. It's not fair to go barging in all the time. They want us to be there, with them. Away from Dad."

"It's not like Dad is ever here. If he is, he's asleep on the sofa."

"Or ready to have a go at one of us."

I could see Nicky switching off to me, his eyes disconnecting. He was the determined one. He would dig his heels in. I acquiesced. I wasn't going to go without him.

He rolled his eyes at me, but he knew that was it. We never spoke about it after that. We stopped running to Nana's when Mick got angry with us. She never asked how he was when we went round for Sunday roast, and she ignored the bruises.

We were a team, deep down, and when the going got tough, Nicky and I looked out for each other.

I was almost certain.

1986

Nicky had a new group of friends, all older than him. They were not like the 'Lost Boys'. This new lot, they were different. At first, I was glad that Nicky was not hanging out on the street corner anymore, throwing stones at passing car wheels, being a boisterous nuisance, getting into trouble with the neighbours. They spoke of us enough already, surely, thanks to Mick.

One night, coming back from the cinema with Becky, I changed my mind about his new friends. We had been to see *Top Gun* for the third time. We were both obsessed with Tom Cruise and had posters of him in our room, though, truthfully, at that time I had more of a thing for Morten Harket of AHA.

As we came around the corner by the old corner shop, I saw the Cureheads lingering by the old bakery. They were not true Cureheads anymore, to be honest, but they had been the previous summer so that is what we still called them. None of them had Robert Smith hair now, though they were still wearing the clumpy boots.

One of them was in our year. He called out to us. He had always had a thing for Becky, even when we were in primary school.

We answered in unison as we slowed to a halt and

stood at the edge of the group. Nicky was hanging on every word the tall one was saying. He spoke in a low voice. His name was Lou. He was talking about some album release, saying it was the event of the year.

It was all posturing.

I yawned, not out of boredom, but genuinely tired. My brother's voice rose from the other side of the group. He was leaning, unnoticed by me, against the shop window.

"What, Tam, you think AHA have more musical integrity? Or maybe you think Madonna's new album is going to be a future 'classic'?"

He was surprisingly good at sarcasm for a thirteen-year-old. The older boys laughed softly in approval, egging him on.

"My sister is such a pop tart. If Top of the Pops likes it, she buys it. If it's the movie to see, she's seen it twice. And fallen in love with the lead actor, of course. Or dreaming to marry the lead singer."

He stood up, walked towards me, and flicked the big black bow on the side of my head.

"Crimped hair, black leggings and bows won't make you Madonna. They won't make you pretty. They sure as fuck won't make anyone want you. They won't make you anything. They just show what you are. You imitate, and you're nothing. Nothing but frills. Nothing original. All you can do is clean, Cinder-fucking-ella. No Prince Charming is coming for you."

Humiliated, I took a step back from the group, and mumbled at him not to be late, and that I was cooking fish fingers.

Becky directed a "see you later" straight at the lad who had called us over. He had taken quite the beamer.

She sped to catch up with me. I was walking fast, my eyes prickling. It wasn't the first time Nicky had spoken harshly to me. Becky said something about the lads. I clenched my jaw. Nicky had never done it in front of others before. Becky said it was only two weeks since her break up. I balled my fists. Nicky had been intent on humiliating me. She wasn't sure if she was ready to go out with someone else. Nicky had attacked me. My nails were digging into the palm of my hands. Nicky had gone in for the kill. I felt my chest tighten. Becky was still talking about the lad outside the old corner shop. She had pulled a face at Nicky. It was not a big deal to her. She was from the sort of family where everyone knew they loved each other, no matter what was said. I knew otherwise.

When I got home, I ran up to Nicky's room. It was a tip. I took a deep breath. I may not be wanted. He still needed me. I tidied his room. Then Mick's. I got out the cleaning bucket. The bathroom, the sitting room. I got down on my knees and scrubbed the kitchen floor. The water was too hot. The bleach too strong. My eyes stung. Nicky's words were on repeat in my mind.

I pulled off the marigolds. Scraped my nails down my forearms. The clarity of white pain was just out of reach. Nicky had crossed the line. I dug harder, ripping skin. Nicky had marched up to the line. It hurt, but I could not get the control back. Nicky had broken our pact. I needed something more. I stood up and opened the kitchen drawer. The paring knife. I dunked it in the bleach bucket. I ran the tap and washed it thoroughly. I had snapped onto a point of focus. I held the blade to my skin. It was cold. Sharp.

Nicky's voice had gone quiet. I took a juddering breath. I held the flat of the knife on the scratched skin. Soothing. A steady breath now.

I put the knife back in the drawer. I already knew that next time, that would not be enough.

X

The school sent a letter to say that they were concerned Nicky's work was slipping. They noted that his drawing and painting was advanced for his age and suggested that this might be a good interest to encourage. I kept some of the housekeeping money aside, a couple of weeks of beans on toast and baked potatoes and bought him a sketchbook and two nice pencils.

He drew a picture of George Michael and gave it to me. He drew Morten Harket. He drew lots of young male pop stars for me. I was never surprised to find magazines open to their faces lying in his room.

I found an empty blister of paracetamol in his bedroom. That did surprise me. I had only bought it the day before. I could not think of what he had done with it all. He was sick though and complained that his right side ached. Why he would take paracetamol for a sore tummy was beyond me.

I suggested we go to the doctor, but he refused.

Looking back, it is clear he had taken the whole pack of tablets intentionally. He was terribly ill after.

I missed all the signs.

1992

Like cleaning cobwebs from the corners, I have brushed away many conversations over the years. The spiders always come back.

Becky and I went to The Keys often. It was by the bus stop on the way home from work. The regulars knew us well enough to nod in greeting, had offered condolences when Nicky passed but never asked for details. Mick, I mean Dad, hadn't liked this pub. The previous landlord had barred him.

I stood at the bar, reminded of the Friday after a football match when some guy had come over with whisky flavoured condoms from the vending machine in the men's and offered us "a shot". Becky had retorted with "I don't go for men with whisky-dick" and everyone had laughed. I was glad to have such a self-assured friend.

The pint in my left hand spilled as I sat without putting them down first. I wiped the back of my hand on my trousers.

"I'm not going to sail away into the sunset forever, but I might take some of the money and go travelling, get away from all this."

"Great idea. I'll come with you, we can get our courses done and spend the summer going around

Europe together, like get an interrail pass thing. You know I've always wanted to go to Paris, Vienna."

"Becky?"

"Madrid, Rome, it will be fun, we could stay in hostels ..."

"Becky! We could but ..."

"But what, Tam?"

I didn't know how to tell her I wanted to go alone. To try and find my own feet. Her eyes were a bit puffy from long workdays and late nights, sparkling in the smoky pub light. Strands of her chestnut hair had started to escape her work bun. Soon she would pull it out and let it tumble over her shoulders. She was grinning with enthusiasm for her travel plan.

"I think I might leave sooner than that."

"What? No, Tam, what about me? Who will make me bacon, egg and tomato sarnies on Sunday mornings if you're not there?"

Her tone was light, yet I promised to stay. I didn't want to risk falling out. It would become Becky's trip. I would book it and organise it. She would live it, with me as sidekick and witness. In the meantime, she needed me for rent after all. There was Nana and George too. I was needed here.

"Nana would hate it if I left now, I guess."

"She'd be lost without you. She'd do anything to keep you here, you know that."

"I was thinking I might ask her more about Ange. We've never really spoken about her."

"Like what?"

"I don't know, Becky! I don't remember her well. What would I ask? Everything, nothing."

Becky looked at me steadily.

Funny how moods and memories can dilute and mix into each other. She had been there through the years, the good and the bad, picked up the pieces, literal and figurative. The times I'd cried over school grades, sometimes mine, mostly Nicky's. Over boys, crushed lipstick and badly timed periods, and dancing in each other's bedrooms with the radio on loud. She had taken me to all the parties. Made sure I did not waste my teen years with my head in a book. I had been her faithful observer, analysing what each person said, how the schoolboys moved around her, lending her my notes before exams.

She raised an eyebrow at me, nothing else needed. I shook my head. Becky was funny about Nana, always had been. I did not want to go down that road with her. I trusted Nana, no matter that Becky thought she was a bit controlling. I didn't want to have that discussion again, torn between my loyalties to them both. I laid down a conciliatory end to the conversation.

"Fish 'n' chips on the way home?"

1966

Nana didn't want to say much at first. I had decided to start by asking her about how my parents met. I played the movie of it in mind.

It was an autumn Saturday morning. Babs and Ange had gone out to the corner shop, to buy their weekly *Jackie* magazine, with its pin up posters and below the waist issues that made them blush. Babs was my mother's best friend. She stopped by the flat once or twice after Ange was gone. She had puffed blonde hair and blue eyeliner when I last saw her, her body soft when she had hugged us. I tried to overwrite that mental image of her and picture her as a teenager. I struggled to think of her as anything other than a Glaswegian Farah Fawcett.

When they had finished browsing, bought the magazine and left the corner shop, they snuck down the back street. Ange pulled her right hand out of her coat pocket, bringing out the cigarettes. She slipped one out of the packet and passed it to Babs. They exchanged a look. Sometimes they shared the cigarettes they'd been able to get hold of, to eke them out, but Ange smiled as she popped another one between her lips.

"Ooh, good work, Ange!"

"Some parishioner left Dad a whole carton, but he didn't even notice them."

She tilted her head back and let out a cloud of smoke.

They didn't linger long over their cigarettes. Leaning into each other shivering and giggling, as teenage girls do, they made their way back up the alley. Ange pulled her gloves out of her left pocket and back on to her cold hands. She looked up towards the top of the alley.

There he was. Dark hair flicked across his forehead, framing his brown eyes. He had heavy eyelashes, full lips, and a three-day stubble. He was wearing flared jeans and a brown leather jacket. Arms linked, the girls held their breath as they walked past him.

Babs whispered to Ange.

"That's Mick. I was telling you about him. Isn't he dreamy? We should go to that new club, La Strada. I think he goes there. It could be fun."

Ange peeked back over her shoulder. It certainly could be.

It was only a few days later that Ange saw Mick again, this time outside her school. He was obviously waiting for someone and nonchalantly assessing the girls as they walked past.

As she walked out of the school gates, the extra weight of her coat caused her bag to pop off her shoulder. She grabbed the bag to stop it hitting the ground. She was thrown off-balance. She straightened herself, looking up towards his side of the road, and noticed him, dressed in sharp shirt and black trousers, like a dark shadow on the red brick wall under the gold and brown hues of the trees around the school.

He was looking at her. She could feel the thud of her bag against her hip match the beat of her heart as it quickened, up her throat and into her cheeks. She felt herself flush. She crossed the road, eyes down, and did her best to scuttle past him unnoticed. Though she tried to keep her eyes down, she could not help but glance towards his face and gasped when she realised that he was looking right back at her, straight into her eyes.

Babs had no trouble in talking her into going dancing at La Strada the following Saturday. Jane, who made up their trio at school, fizzed with excitement the entire week. They spoke of nothing else at break and lunch time.

Saturday finally rolled around. The girls spent the afternoon in a haze of make-up, nail varnish, powder puffs and hair rollers. They tried on all the possible combinations of all the clothes that they owned and that could be deemed suitable for dancing. It was a good hour before they finally agreed on their outfits. I pictured Babs wearing a green dress with a daring low décolletage, a full skirt and a bodice that hugged her curves, Jane in high-waisted wide-leg red trousers and a pale cream blouse, and Ange wearing a purple slip dress with floaty sleeves.

They arrived at La Strada full of excitement and glee, a cloud of cheap perfume. The place was jumping. The four-person booths along the window each housed at least six people, and others stood around chatting. The windows were always misted up. Although it was packed, the girls made their way easily enough to the bar. Jane and Babs bought lemonades, but Ange opted for a ginger beer. They were served promptly, the barman popping a straw into each of the three bottles.

"Cheers!"

They tapped their bottles together, and the three of them turned to walk further into the bar. They found themselves face to face with the tall dark-haired man. Ange froze on the spot, feeling her heart rush to her skin. Him again. He gave her a sort of half smile and pushed between them. Her friends giggled, but she could not move. It was as though a jolt of electricity had seared through her. Babs grinned as she grabbed her immobilised friends' arm.

"Don't stand there gawping!"

Ange rocked on her feet, smiled back. Babs was pulling her towards the back, where she had seen some of their school friends. That night would be the first of many through that autumn and winter that the three girls organised sleepovers at Babs'. Ange's parents, my grandparents, insisted she was home in time for church. The girls always followed the same routine. They tried on countless outfits, doing each other's hair and make-up before going out to La Strada. Once there, they always went to the booth at the back, to join the group they knew from school, mostly lads. They would chat, flirt, and rock to the beat of the latest hits.

Mick had been there every week from the start, and her breath would catch in her throat whenever she saw him. At first, she could barely look, but after a couple of Saturdays, she smiled shyly at him. He gave a crooked half-smile back. The following week, she was dismayed when she had looked over to see him talking to a girl in an A-line knee length blue skirt and green polyester shirt.

He looked up and caught her eye. The crooked half-smile made its appearance and he leaned forward to whisper in the girl's ear, hand on her shoulder, pulling her close yet never breaking eye contact with Ange. She felt herself blush, embarrassed to witness this intimate moment. She forced herself to break the gaze and looked down at her hands, which she had knotted on her lap.

"Ange, isn't it?"

She started and looked up.

Her eyes widened in shock at the voice that came from above her left shoulder. Mick was standing at the end of her table. Babs and Jane looked as though their eyes might pop right out of their skulls.

He leaned forward and ground his cigarette out in the ashtray in the middle of their table.

"Evening, ladies, gents."

The girls looked down, and the lads frowned. Mick extended his hand to Ange.

"Dance?"

Ange nodded, and reached her hand up into his. He pulled her up from her seat and led her to what the group described as the "dance box". They danced to The Beatles' *Paperback Writer*, bumping into the other dancers as she avoided direct body contact with him. They didn't say a word to each other. Ange felt quite breathless with excitement by the time he returned her to the booth. She expected him to sit down but he walked away.

The next few weeks, he nodded and greeted her with a smile, and simply said her name, but only ever when she was away from her friends. He would catch her on the way back from a chat with Jane, or from dancing with one of the other boys. She felt bolder and looked him out, deliberately staring at him, challenging him to speak to her in front of them all.

One night, he stopped her on her way out of La Strada, separating her from her friends as they walked out of the door. He lent in and spoke into her ear: "Two o'clock by St Ninian's graveyard tomorrow." He let his lips graze her cheek as he pulled back, turned, and returned into the depths of the bar.

She walked away in a dream state that night, her

heart thumping through her ribcage. She didn't even tie up the scarf around her neck or remember to put on her gloves as she followed her friends home.

She did not tell Babs and Jane straight away about Mick's invitation. The unspoken rule was that they would analyse every detail of the evening together. If they noticed at all that she was detached and quiet that evening, they remained unaware of the turmoil raging inside her.

That night, she barely slept. As she lay in bed at Babs', she let herself picture how the meeting at the cemetery the next day might play out. She could not quite picture him walking up to her, just as she could not picture his face without getting lost in a wave of anticipation.

She could just about grasp his words from earlier, but not his voice, nor the feel of his lips on her cheek, though her skin still tingled. It was as though she had been stung there by a nettle. She was aware of every follicle that had been touched. Her body fizzed.

By the time Babs and Jane woke up on Sunday morning, Ange was sitting at the dresser brushing her long hair. She was already dressed and had packed up her overnight bag.

"Babs, I need to go. I'll be late for church."

With that she let herself out of the room, bolted down the stairs two at a time, called out in a single breath "good morning thank you for having me to stay see you next week" to Babs' parents who were sat at the kitchen table.

She shot out down the path through the front garden. Instead of taking the shortest route home, she turned right, past the top end of the alley. She sped down the street opposite La Strada, now quiet and closed, somehow grey despite the bright red window trimmings. She paused to look at it. Her haste diffused in the morning air.

The sight of the bar, the memory of his lips by her ear, the thought of seeing him that afternoon made her veins rush like she had eaten too much tablet. Later that morning, she spent the entire church service trying to keep her mind from thinking about kissing him. The contrast made her feel fluttery and she struggled to focus on what the Minister was saying.

She pulled every outfit from her cupboard. Too juvenile. Too matronly. Was Mick going to take her for a walk? That skirt would drag. Maybe they'd go into the cemetery. She'd heard that was a spot. Bulky jumper. He would kiss her, not a messy boy kiss. He would lean in and kiss her properly. This skirt, too short. He was nineteen. Practically a man. She settled on a figure-hugging polo neck and red cord skirt that sat just above the knee. Would he reach up her skirt? Maybe. She hoped he would try. The red skirt was inviting enough.

She finished her hair and make-up, straightened her room, checked her watch. Where had the time gone?

Back out, she adjusted her scarf, and smoothed her hair. Before stepping forward, she sort of bounced on her toes. She tried to ignore the nervous buzz as she walked down the road, her breath hanging in the air in front of her, the low sunlight cut in between the houses.

It was a twenty-minute walk before turning onto the wide street. The church was on the corner at the far end, with the cemetery curling up behind it, so she would have to walk down the hill alongside the graveyard's wall before she could turn into it. Her stomach lurched. Her throat tightened. Her hands felt warm and clammy in her mittens. Instinctively she felt like turning around and running as fast as she could. She stopped dead for a moment and took a breath. She looked at her watch. She was, despite her circuitous route, a good ten minutes early.

She leant back against the wall, focusing on every detail of her surroundings in the hope of settling her thoughts. It felt to Ange as though her heart was a caged bird, fluttering against her ribs. She realised she had crossed her arms and was holding her elbows across her body, her chin tucked down. She breathed out, stood up straight from the wall and shook her arms. Ange stomped her feet and brushed herself off. Once again, she smoothed down the front of her duffel coat.

She was ready to meet him.

1992

The song was wrong when it said "love is all you need".

Mick had loved her. On his slower days, he would sit ever so quietly and talk about the first time he'd seen Ange, coming out of school, wobbling on her platforms, legs like Bambi. She dropped her bag and looked up at him through thick eyelashes. He said she was breath-taking. He had wanted to catch her. The time she was dancing in a purple dress, arms in the air, her face smooth and soft, all the fellas' eyes on her. Somehow, she only had eyes for him. He did not deserve someone so lovely.

He missed her. They had been happy, the two of them, for a time. He was not worthy of her love.

Mick apologised to me for Ange leaving once, on his knees in the hall, a three-day stubble, his shirt untucked and the fire of cheap whisky on his breath. I had hugged his head against my belly, rubbed his hair, the smell of days in the pub clawing up, shushing him:

"I could never be enough. I didn't deserve her."

"There there, Daddy, you've got me. I won't leave you."

"I know, my girl. I'm sorry. You will look after me, I know."

I looked through the sitting room, clean, but threadbare. There was a tiled fireplace with a gas

125

fire, gleaming in the sunlight that shone through the lace curtains. There were flowers on the mantelpiece, carefully chosen silk artificial flowers, in a brown glass vase behind a framed picture of my parents' wedding day.

The couple were smiling, him with dark hair and broad shoulders, a glint in his eye. Handsome, with a sort of rockabilly edge. She svelte, her blonde hair silvery grey in the black & white photo, none of her ethereal beauty lost in the revelation process. He held her right hand in his left across the front of their bodies, slightly raised toward the camera, his other arm around her slender waist. They could have been dancing had they not been posing under a tree. She was only seventeen, and he was still nineteen. Impossible to see if she was showing yet. I am hidden.

He had sobbed and sobbed, and I felt my heart shatter with every heave, knowing how I had chased her away and broken him. I had been the impossible needy cuckoo that shattered the nest. I would have done almost anything to make it better, to step up into her place and make him happy.

It was the same spot where I found him lying dead years later, maybe because in that moment I stopped him from doing absolutely anything to try to make it all better, to make me take her place in every possible way. It was a flitting moment, a matter of a head turned and a step back. Perhaps he died there because a part of him never left that spot after that.

He heaved himself back to his feet, patted my head awkwardly, trying to reset the father-daughter dynamic. He was going out again. I would go to the kitchen. Squeeze my eyes tight. Clench my fists. Fingernails on my palm not enough. Fingernails on my wrists. Shuddering with tears. The kitchen drawer. The paring knife. The burning hot tap water. Clean.

126

A fresh tea-towel. Wrapped. Ready to take upstairs.

Control was creeping back.

I sat in the bath and cut two long perfect lines across the top of my forearms, and two on my thighs. Bright red.

Clean.

1968

I was born in the autumn, the first hint of winter hung crisp in the air. My mother was in labour for an endless and agonising forty-seven hours. The contractions would ramp up, only to die away again, before coming back.

Nana always said that labour was the only pain in the world worth enduring. Ange stared at the purple-tinged baby girl with fluffy hair on a soft skull.

"Congratulations, you have a daughter. Would you like to hold her?"

She was exhausted. Her hair, damp with sweat, clung to her forehead, but from deep down a euphoric energy seemed to bubble up through the pain and discomfort, as she reached and smiled to her new-born. I was warm, still damp, turning red under the yellowish vernix on my skin. Ange felt relief wash through her as she looked down at the blinking towel-wrapped infant in her arms. The labour was done. The tiny creature had made it to the world whole. She had done her part.

Before she knew what was happening, I was taken away from her again, to be checked up and checked over, whilst she was stitched up and tidied up, rebuilt for her husband to enjoy in four to six weeks. Every muscle, every bone, the very membranes of her ached from the last two days. She could not believe it possible to feel so very exhausted. Her eyeballs felt too big for eyelids. Jaw all too aware of teeth. Calves, thighs somehow rubbery and hardened at once, knees crunching, her heart too tired to beat, certainly too tired to feel much.

As for me, I was cleaned up and given a terry nappy, swaddling clothes, and the green light of being a normal baby, we were re-united and wheeled to the recovery ward, where a curtain ensured a degree of privacy.

She had settled down to follow how to feed me as per the nurses' matter of fact and rapid instruction to "put the infant to the breast". She didn't know what was meant, and held me tightly, afraid to drop me and smash me. I held my breath, going slightly blue, she stared at me fearfully, forcing her arms to relax. I screwed up my face, now red, angry, and screamed. Fists balled and pumping, every fibre of me poured into rage. Ange was frozen in fear. Perfect as she was, she had no response for this. She closed her eyes to it. To me.

It seemed like forever before Nana appeared by her side. She had been waiting in the reception area, the fathers' room being far too smoky. It was quickly obvious to my mother that her own mother-in-law had been in the hospital for several hours, probably for most of the labour. Nana looked unkempt and tired despite her natural composure.

Having inspected and briefly held her first grandchild, she instructed my mother to get her breast out and press my nose above the nipple. My toothless gums clamped on either side with relative ease, and with a tongue like a cheese grater to the soft end of the nipple, I suctioned the pre-milk, colostrum, hard from her body. I went quiet, and Ange looked at me properly for the first time. A fuzz of hair on cheeks and ears, squished eyes, piglet nose, translucent tiny fingers like a newt. No porcelain solidity. An ugly, squashed otherworldly thing, that had battered its way out of her body.

Nana went back to the ward reception, and phoned Dad at his work. It was, after all, the '60s, and men were not necessarily expected to be present at the birth of their child. They needed the money, and she had agreed with her son that it made sense. This was women's work anyway. She twirled the phone cable between her fingers as she listened to it ring, crackle, ring five or six times.

George picked up the site phone. George probably should have been my real Grandpa, but life isn't always built that way. He asked about my mother and I, and Nana told him that mother and babe were fine, if a little tired. It had been a long couple of days, and we all needed to rest. George told her that her Mick was not there again, after two days. They were both concerned for him. He was not the first young man to start a family this way. It was the making of some of them. They feared it would be Mick's undoing.

The first time that I heard this story, I was told that he had gone hunting wild geese in the hills, in celebration of my birth. I believed this until I questioned how killing a goose was a way to thank a stork. I have been able to picture Nana's face at that time, a younger version of the one I know. She walked up to Ange's bedside, smiling gently, with determined eyes, and laying a protective hand on my small, swaddled body, she leaned in and kissed her daughter-in-law's brow, saying "Mick will be here as soon as he is able, dear, you know how it is."

She saw that Ange had been crying, her tears still

131

wet on her cheeks. I was snuffling restlessly below her exposed nipple. Nana, realising that we had not found a good feeding latch yet having dropped the first successful one, sat down on the edge of the bed and patiently explained how to help me get started.

"Nose to teat, girl, nose to teat. Baby will smell the milk and open her mouth as wide as a yawn, you need to make sure you do not pull away. Draw her in, that's right, oh she's a fussy one, isn't she? Hand round the back of her head, there you go."

Ange gave a small yelp of pain when I found my way back, but a small sense of achievement settled on her. Nana sat down on the chair in our curtained-off section, picked up her sewing bag and pulled out a bib that she was making.

Our small section contained a bunch of flowers, a small bowl of grapes and three generations of women. Right then, in the warmth of the late afternoon sunshine coming through the window, my baby breaths somehow sweetening the air, Nana smiled serenely, proud of Ange, her daughter-in-law, and of me, her first grandchild. It was the happiest that we would ever be together.

Two days later, I was taken home.

George had come to pick us up at the hospital in his new Rover P5. It was dark blue, and he would wash and wax it every Sunday for the next fifteen years. It would be the favourite car in his lifetime, and he was enormously proud of it, just as he was immensely proud of "his" girls, Nana beside him, Ange and I in the back. He drove us slowly all the way home, pulling up at the bottom of our block.

George got out of the car first and opened the door for Nana. She then scooped me up out of Ange's arms, allowing her to stand up, clearly still feeling bruised and sore. She moved to hand me back, but Ange didn't lean in, so with me in the crook of one arm, she slung her handbag over her free shoulder, bent down and picked up the bunch of flowers and green baby cardigan which she had knitted in the hospital off the backseat, and led the way. Mum stepped behind her in a daze. George followed; hand ready to steady the new mother. We stepped into the lift and travelled up to the third floor.

When we got to the front door, Nana handed me to Ange. She needed to open the door, and the younger woman was standing there, arms hanging limply at her side. The front door was bright green, freshly painted, the doorknob and letter box shining proud. Nana leaned back to get a better prise with the key, stiff in the new lock, and pulled back on the handle, using the jiggle that was needed.

It was a modern flat for the time. There were three plants in simple earthen pots on the windowsill that looked out onto the walkway between the flats. Three happy healthy plants, as yet unburnt by the winter frost that loomed.

As the door unlocked, she pushed forward against the doormat, a few envelopes slowing down the swing of the door. She bent at her knees to pick them up and allow the door to open fully, and smiled at her daughter-in-law, who was holding me awkwardly in her arms.

The look between them acknowledged the significance of it.

Mick had obviously not been home for a few days, certainly not since Ange went to Nana's five days earlier, overdue, exhausted, and completely disconcerted by her waters breaking.

Nana first hung up her jacket on the rack behind the front door, reaching for me so that Mum could do the same, and then ushered Mum into the living room and onto an armchair before handing me back to her arms. My surroundings were humble, warm, someone had taken great care and attention to make it homely.

"You'll be after a cup of tea, put your feet up, dear, I'm sure, and the little lass will need to feed again too, I'll get the kettle on, make a pot and find us a biscuit or something nice..."

Her voice trailed off into the kitchen, and I'm sure I found my Nana's chatter comforting at the time and made that sigh that contented babies make. These days, I would recognise it as a sign, one of Nana's tells, I suppose. Nana was disappointed on Mum's behalf, and angry at her son, but she wouldn't say, she wouldn't rock the boat, she wouldn't want anyone to get upset, and so she filled the absence with tea and biscuits.

We settled down into the armchair, Ange's feet on a footstool as I slept in my mother's arms.

George switched on the gas fire. Nana put the pot of tea, a milk jug, a bowl of white sugar and three cups and saucers onto the side table. Nana poured the tea and passed them out. Mum took the cup off the saucer, smiling and looking down at me to indicate the impossibility of managing a baby, a saucer, and a cup.

For a long while, the three of them sat in the living room, in silence, until George declared that he was hungry. After a protracted to and fro, Ange agreed to let Nana come back with some food for her too. She knew that there wasn't much in the cupboards, and after all, it would be easier than having to cope alone in the flat by herself with a baby while still struggling to move about let alone walk to the shop.

Nana left with George, her house was not far down the road, around the block from his, though they often stayed together. They would always have their own houses and never acknowledged publicly that for years they were as husband and wife. I stirred again, gumming my fisted hands, and making strange squeaky grumble noises, so Mum carefully moved me into position, glad that I had latched on without as much difficulty as in the hospital.

Once the initial burn of breastfeeding pain had passed, Ange found herself enjoying the quiet warmth of her first real moment alone with me. She sighed as she stared down. Maybe this fuzzy pink bundle nuzzling contentedly was not so terrifying. She would not have the nice nurse to bring me to her in the night for feeding, but that couldn't be so hard.

There was a sudden and loud noise in the silence.

A hard bang against the front door. The first chip in the paint.

Ange started, almost letting my head flop back.

She tensed.

I bit then dropped the latch and let out a whine before snuffling back into position.

She heard the key in the lock, and her husband filled the doorway.

"I'm home, Ange."

He stepped into the room and observed his wife and baby girl for a long moment. They looked right, the perfect homecoming for him. A pretty pink baby, swaddled in a fluffy yellow blanket, cradled by his beautiful silvery blonde wife, in the eternal pose of motherhood. He leant forward and kissed his wife on her right temple, lingeringly, without noticing her complete lack of reaction. He kissed his baby girl on the forehead.

I sneezed.

To him, this was the funniest sound he had ever heard. The most precious sound ever. The purest and most true. He felt his heart contract and miss a beat. It was love. True love. He made a promise to himself there and then that he would always protect and never ever hurt this beautiful, warm baby girl, his little princess. He slurred this information to me more than once.

Unfortunately, he never was the type to keep promises.

"We'll call her Tam. From Tamara."

This was his decree, and that is who I would be. Even if it was a boy's name where we lived. That did not cross his mind.

Perched on the edge of the sofa, he put his arm around us and patted my mother's shoulder and kissed the top of her head again. I stopped and sneezed drowsily, before snuggling back in. And he stood up and went upstairs to their bedroom – that first sneeze a warm tickle in his mind. He did not stop to consider why I might have sneezed. He had been entertained by it. Perhaps I had sneezed because of the dust, though the flat was spotlessly clean. Or perhaps it was the smell of cigarettes, of whisky, of a man who left his work three days before only to wander the bars and pubs, sleeping where he could, if at all, and I had sneezed because my tiny brand-new nose had never before encountered these bitter smells.

This is how I have chosen to remember my homecoming.

1992

I believed that Nana was my safe harbour.

She wanted to be that person.

Thrived on being needed, cold when you managed by yourself. My paternal grandmother, she could never push her own son away, she never chose him over us. We needed her more. The dock leaf that grows near the nettle.

Before she was Nana, she had been Jenny. As a child, she wanted to be a primary school teacher. She worked hard in class at her sums and her letters, would go home and line up her three dolls and two teddy bears and teach them everything that she had learned at school. She smiled whenever she told me about it, eyes lighting up.

All through her secondary schooling, she continued to work hard. She enjoyed all the subjects, but History and English were her favourites. She could spend hours reading, and I have always said that it is from her that I get my love of books and stories. She told me that in English class she read stories of individual people, and that in history class she read the stories of all people. Once everything has been said and done, stories were all that were left.

As a young girl she had had the run of the small

town she lived in, and as she grew, she would walk further afield. I pictured her with her brown leather satchel of books. A favourite spot of hers to read was on the hillside overlooking the railway. In my mind, I imagined it to look like the spot by the tunnel in *The Railway Children*, but when I saw it, it was nothing like that. She liked to watch the trains as they headed to the big town and planned to leave on one.

The Second World War started when she was nineteen, and she immediately signed up as a 'Land Girl'. She was sent to work on a farm on the other side of the country and, despite her homesickness, she always spoke of it as a happy time in her life. It was close to a large market town, on the other side of which there was a military base.

I picture her as a pretty and self-assured young woman, popular with a 'can-do' attitude and quick humour. Her easy-going and practical manner made her popular with the other girls. On Saturday nights they would go to a local dancehall, where pilots and soldiers from the nearby base went to blow off steam. She enjoyed the sense of purpose in her job, meeting new people, her days off in the nearby market town, and the nights out at the dancehall.

I had seen pictures of Nana in her jumper and dungarees, standing by a fence with some of her friends, all six of them posing with spades and hoes. She looked happiest in the one of her and her roommate dressed up to go out, hoping to dance the Lindy Bop with any of the men from the nearby air base. Her hair was arranged into a victory roll, and her knee-length floral dress had obviously been pressed. She told me it was pale blue, with yellow flowers, and that it was hard to get it properly clean but had been her favourite, nonetheless.

When he was five, Nicky used to like me telling

him the Adventures of Young Nana. He loved them so much, I started to make things up to keep him entertained. It was easy to believe that Nana had delivered Spitfires across the country and invented a special double looper. Nana had been a spy in France, setting up a network of women masterminding the French Resistance. Nana singing in a smoky London club for the top generals. Before that, she was a plucky young woman solving local mysteries, like the Missing Cow or the Midnight Prowler. He never doubted her ability to do those things.

As Nicky got older, he got bored, lost interest, and then he questioned the details that I so carefully painted in. Like why she was no longer friends with any of the women from then. Or why the stories ended in 1943. Nana never spoke of the end of the war, or what happened after. She never spoke of Gerry, Mick's father who died not long after he was born. We had assumed that he had died in the war until we realised that the dates didn't match up. Dad was born in 1948.

1992

I walked straight through the house into the kitchen. I startled Nana, who looked up from the papers on the table. I knew immediately that I was not meant to see those papers. She seemed flustered and shuffled them into an untidy pile.

"Erm, Tam, hello, I'll, eh, just a moment …"

She picked up the papers and scuttled past me, clutching them tightly to her chest. The handwriting. Familiar. I stood there, my heart thudding. Trying to place the scrawl I had glimpsed.

It could not be.

Every sense tingled. I called after her.

"Everything all right, Nana?"

"Perfectly. I was just sorting some of Nicky's old paperwork. I'll give them to you next time, once they're sorted."

She was back at the doorway to the kitchen, serene, smile in place. She truly could have been a spy in the war. I started to doubt myself.

I had connected the dots wrong.

I told myself it was dealing with Nicky's paperwork that put her out of sorts, but as I walked home, I kept coming back to the bundle she had hidden. I chewed over the scene with every step.

It had not been a flat, neat pile.

There were fold lines. Handwritten pages folded and unfolded many a time.

Could Nicky have sent a note to Nana? No, that would be just one page, two at best, and certainly not as worn looking.

My gut knew that it wasn't. She would have told me, I was sure. Not his handwriting. I was skirting around what I knew to be true. The paper was too old. They were not Mick's old papers. It was a stack of letters. Ange's handwriting. I knew it in every fibre of my being.

A pile of letters from Ange.

I stopped dead. The realisation rippled through me. My handbag clunked off my shoulder into the crook of my elbow. Each thought was a blow. Nana was hiding post from my mother. Right hook. My mother Ange who had abandoned me seventeen years before. Left hook. Disappeared without a trace. The rabbit punches. I never knew if she was dead. I never knew if she was alive. Kidney punch. Ange had been writing to Nana. Bareknuckled. Writing.

Ange was alive.

Uppercut. Nana knew that Ange was alive. Ange was writing to her. I was on the ropes. I wondered if Nana was writing back. The suckerpunch. Ange alive, and Nicky dead. Knockdown.

Not out. Maybe Nana was protecting me. Just as she had wanted to protect Davy and Agnes. This would not be the first secret she had kept from me. Secrets did not make for happy families.

I turned on my heel and marched back.

George was still in the garden.

"She's gone out, right after you."

I stopped. I did not like conflict. Typically, I shied from confrontations. Surely George was innocent. I swallowed my hang-ups. In that moment, I needed to be certain of what he knew.

I strode up to him and asked straight away if he knew whether Nana had ever received a note or a letter from Nicky.

George was an open book, incapable of lying, so when he said no, I knew he was telling the truth.

"And Ange? What about from my mother?"

He grunted.

He didn't want to answer. He was torn. His loyalty to Nana. His love for me. Duty to the truth.

"It's alright, George. We don't have to talk about it."

He nodded and went back to digging the flower bed.

There was a time when I would have left the matter there, in the discarded plants and mud. Not this time. Nana was not going to tell me. I knew that. She would deny them. I had to confront her. The only way to get an answer was with the evidence. I would have to find the letters myself.

I did not know if I could do that.

1980

We were all at Nana's for Sunday roast. Dad was helping George to chop a branch off a tree that was looming over the house and would, like as not, fail to make it through the winter without smashing through the kitchen roof. Nicky was sat at the desk in the living room drawing, which he would spend hours doing, even though he was only seven. I was carefully drying up the big plates with the gilt edge that we used on Sundays with Nana. The kitchen was built on to the back of the house, a sort of annex extension, and the main window looked over the garden. On the left of the windowsill was a jar of rinsed milk bottle tops. There was also some rather overgrown cress growing on a flannel in a low dish. Nana passed me a serving dish, water still trickling off it. I could hear Dad and George's footsteps above me as they worked on the roof of the extension.

My twelfth birthday was coming up.

"Have you thought about what you would like for your birthday, Tam?"

"A telescope. There's one in Mr Trencher's shop. I want to look at the stars, and see if I can see Jupiter, and the rings of Saturn."

"Are you sure that it is what you want?"

"Oh yes, Nana, it's just a little telescope, but it works fine to see the Moon's mountains and Saturn's rings. Mr Trencher let me have a look at it."

She took the plate from my hands, turning her back on me as she reached up to put it in the cupboard. She never heard me say that what I most wanted was Mum to come back.

It was five years since she had gone.

The morning of my twelfth birthday Nicky dashed into my room and leapt onto my bed, straddling me and bouncing and shouting, "Happy birthday, Tam-tam," at the top of his voice. I think that he was mostly excited about going to the pool that morning, which was my birthday treat. My friend Becky and a couple of the new secondary school friends were going to be meeting us there, and I had told Nicky he could come. Even though he was five years younger than me, I enjoyed his company, and he could be good fun, especially at something like the pool. One of the girls had an inflatable mattress, a lilo, as she called it, which she said she was going to bring.

After the pool, we went to Wimpey's where we had burgers, chips, and milkshakes for lunch. Dad had given me the money for the outing, so we had gone alone, and I remember feeling very grown up. After lunch we said goodbye and agreed that it had been a fantastic birthday treat. Nicky and I, my hair still damp and clinging to my shoulders, headed to Nana's for birthday tea. I was hoping for triangle sandwiches with the crusts cut off, biscuits and even cake, though I knew that was maybe a bit much to set my hopes on.

We were almost halfway home when Nicky realised that he had left his bag with his towel and swimming trunks at Wimpey's. We stopped to decide whether it would be better to go on and be told off for being careless, or whether we should go back and get a row for being late. Since we had walked and still had change for the bus, we decided to turn back, pick up the bag and then catch a bus along the main street and on to the edge of the park near home. We reasoned that being late was probably not as bad as lost swimming trunks and towel.

Because of the setback, it was mid-afternoon by the time we had found the bag and waited for the bus. I pulled the front door key up from under my t-shirt by the shoelace on which it hung around my neck, over my head, and unlocked the door. As I opened it, Nana leapt out of the living room, wishing me a happy birthday, and telling us to hurry upstairs, wash and get changed. As we started up the stairs, I could hear my father saying to George:

"Is that the brats back then?"

From his tone, I knew that trouble was brewing, and hurried Nicky along as best I could. We wiped our faces with a warm flannel, I put on the blue dress Dad had bought for me the week before, it had a shirt-like bodice and a full skirt, both with white trim. I brushed my hair and pulled a comb through Nicky's bright blond mop, and he pulled a red jumper on over his t-shirt. I gave him a kiss on the forehead and whispered a warning "Fee, Fi, Fo, Fum, Bugs" in his ear so that he would know that we needed to be careful not to awaken the ogre inside our father.

Best smiles on, we ran down the stairs.

"Hello Nana, Hello George. Daddy!"

I threw my arms around his neck. His smile was frozen on, and there was no warmth in his arms as he hugged my back. The familiar bittersweet smell of whisky was on his breath.

"So sorry we're late, we had to wait for the bus, we had a lovely morning at the pool, Daddy, thank you so much! Mel was so funny, she was pretending to be a dolphin!"

"I'm glad you enjoyed yourself while we were waiting for you."

"I'm sorry, Daddy, it was the bus. I've had a lovely birthday outing. Thank you for letting us do it and for the money to go."

"Right, well you'd better open your bloody present. Your Nana tells me that's what you want, so I had to take my lunch break to go and get it last week. You'd better like it."

"Now, then, Mick dear, I told you that was what Tammy wanted, and you offered to go during your lunch break. Here you go."

She spoke firmly before softening her tone as she turned to me.

"Thank you, Daddy, Nana, George."

I sat down on the armchair and tugged up my left sock which had slipped down to my ankle. I rested the brightly wrapped box on my knees. I pulled the bow out of the green ribbon and started to pull the Sellotape carefully off the spotty paper, so that it could be put aside and kept to be re-used. I unfolded the ends.

As the paper fell away, I could make out the face of a smiling young boy, one eye scrunched up and the other pressed against the eye piece of the telescope. I opened the other side of paper, which revealed the boy's father, one arm around the child, the other pointed towards an overly starry sky, grinning happily. It was the telescope from Mr Trencher's Toy Shop.

I was so excited that I would be able to see the Rings of Saturn, and the dry mountains of the moon. I lifted the box off the paper, letting the colourful wrapping drop to the floor, and set about opening the box itself. The lid was snug to the bottom half, but with a gentle shake, it slipped off with a vacuum effect.

There it was, glinting in the card holdings. The length of Nana's forearm, it was red, with a small tripod attached to the middle that folded back along the main part. At the thin end there was a rubber circle to rest your eye on. The thick end had a silver edge around it. It was perfect.

With great care, I took the new telescope out of the box, where it lay diagonally alongside a booklet bearing the title "Discover the Night Skies". I propped the tripod legs on my own legs, and looked through the rubberised end towards Nicky, who was lying on the floor. Even without pulling it out, his head was certainly hugely magnified, and I could see each hair, but there was a great big black line across the middle. I twisted the end, and adjusted it, but I realised quickly that one of the internal lenses must have been broken. I knew immediately that I couldn't let Dad find out. There would be hell to pay, given the mood that he was in.

"It's perfect, Daddy, I'm going to keep it safely in the box for tonight so that we can look at the stars!"

"Look after it properly, now, Tam."

"Yes, of course, Dad. I love it."

"Right, that's me. I need to get back to work."

I looked up in time to catch Nana and George glance at each other. Even though I could not have given it a name, I knew that something had worried them. They looked back at me, and Nana smiled warmly, but no one said a word as Dad left the room, wrapped his scarf around his neck, took his heavy felt jacket off the hook, slipped his arms in through the sleeves, and did up the buttons one by one with slow fumbling fingers. I could swear that I remember him tip gently

149

forward and back on his toes as he concentrated to do them up. He walked straight out of the house without a backward glance. We all knew he was going to the pub. He would not be home until after bedtime.

Nana stood up from her armchair and did her sort of funny wipe with her hands down the top of her skirts, as though they were wet. She tucked her hair behind her ear, in a gesture that I would eventually recognise over the years as her setting her face to "best foot forward". She went into the kitchen, and within minutes switched off the living room light at the hall switch. There was a glow in the hall, and as she started to sing, I knew it was candlelight.

"Happy birthday to you! Happy birthday to you! Happy birthday, dear Tammy! Happy birthday to you!"

All three of them sang it twice over, and I blew out the twelve candles. We settled down together on the settee and the two armchairs to eat the moist chocolate cake. Nana was always so good at baking cakes. Afterwards, while George cleared up the plates, Nana announced a surprise "little something" from her personally. It was the latest three editions of *Bunty* magazine for me, and a bright red lollipop each.

The rest of the afternoon was spent flicking quietly through the magazines, Nicky and George playing with the train set that we kept at the house, while Nana sat listening to the radio. Shortly before night fell, we had fish fillets with peas, boiled potatoes, and ketchup. I remember it all with care, the same care Nana used to wrap us up in our jackets. It was time to go home. She and George were going to walk with us, they could use the air, she said, and anyway we now had the swim bags and the telescope to carry home.

When we got back, we both had a bath, as our skin had started to feel a bit itchy from the unrinsed chlorine from the pool. Nicky got into his pyjamas. I put on my pink nightie, and George and Nana stayed to tuck us in. Nana stroked my hair, kissed my forehead, and wished me a happy birthday one last time. After that, they both left us and went home. They knew that it would be better to leave us alone than for Dad to come home and find them there – he would take it as a criticism of his parenting, and his reaction would be painful for all of us. It must have been about half past eleven by the time he got home, staggered up the stairs, and burst into my room.

"Wakey wakey, Tam. Get up! Come on Tammy, get up! The stars are out! Where is that telescope? Come on! Let's go and look at the stars!"

He was in that exhilarated mood which set my adrenaline pumping, his eyes wide and bright, intense under his dishevelled hair. I knew that this was going to need me to react in exactly the right way. I had seen this before; his mood could spin on a penny. I sprung up with the brightest smile that I could muster.

"Daddy, I'm so glad you're back! I fell asleep waiting for you! Look, it's set up by the window for us!"

"You awake?"

"Well, yes, Daddy, so that we could look at the stars together."

"Oh, you don't know what that means to your old man, my little Princess. No wait, my little astronaut-ess."

"It came with a map of the stars too, so that we can find the ones we want to see, like Saturn. I really want to see the rings."

"Let's see."

He sat down heavily on the chair by the window, pushing aside my folded shirt and trousers, and pulled me onto his lap, his hand heavy on my left shoulder. His breath was like that of dragon, hot and bitter, and it made my eyes sting, but I found Saturn quite quickly on the map, and worked out where that may be in the sky. I had read the instructions three times before I went to bed and had used the telescope at school in the physics lab a few times, so I was able to point it in the right direction before he pawed at the map. He squinted at it, and then Dad unsteadily put his eye to the eyepiece.

"Can't see a fucking thing! Not a fucking thing!"

I had completely forgotten about the broken lens. I was on tenterhooks trying to keep the monster in my room from breaking loose. If I could keep him on an even keel a bit longer, he would soon feel tired, and head off to sleep. I stood up and looked up through the window. The moon was clear that night, about a quarter moon.

"Let's start with something big, like the moon? There are mountains on the moon!"

"Right-oh, "astroness", I mean ash-tro-not-ess. Astronautess."

He slurred and tripped over the words. He moved the telescope around, in exaggerated movements, looking for the moon in the sky.

"Why ... why is there a big black line across the moon?"

At first, he seemed to laugh.

He reached forward and tried to wipe the window, his fingers squeaked against the glass.

"There's a great big line across the moon. Like a meri ... meri ... equator."

He looked through the telescope again and frowned. Then, he wiped the end lenses, becoming increasingly agitated. He looked through the eyepiece again. He picked up the telescope, stared down one end, and then the other, inspecting it. He would find the cracked middle lens. And I could see by the change of colour in his face that the ogre was surfacing. I fumbled for an explanation.

"Maybe, maybe Daddy it's meant to be there to help us measure the moon?"

"You can't fucking look after anything, can you?"

He was unleashed. He pushed me off his knee, and I landed on my behind. My tail bone would ache for days. I tried to protest, to invent some sort of reason for a black line in the telescope.

He was brandishing it above his head, looming over me as I lay sprawled on the floor under the window.

"You stupid bitch, I am going to teach you a lesson that you won't forget!"

And that much was true, I certainly haven't forgotten that day, because that was the first time Nicky tried to protect me. My father's roaring must have woken him, but instead of hiding under his bed he had come quietly into my room and was suddenly between us, glowering at the fire-breathing drunk.

"Don't you dare hit her, Daddy, don't hurt Tammy, not on her birthday."

He stared down at the blonde boy, balled fists and resolute in his pyjamas.

He threw the telescope on the floor. I heard all the lenses shatter. He stormed out of the room and locked us in. I can only guess that he either fell into a drunken stupor or went out again.

Nicky and I spent the next twenty-four hours locked in that room. Fortunately, I had a bowl that could be used as chamber pot hidden under my bed and a small stash of biscuits and a full glass of water. This was not the first time we had been locked in, though it was one of the longest, and we knew not to use these resources too fast.

We slept, cuddled together in my bed, and in the morning, we got up, got dressed, and spent time reading, playing games, telling stories, half hoping that Dad may never come back, even though we were awfully hungry.

When he unlocked the door the next day, he did not speak to us or even show himself. We listened to his footsteps going down the stairs, to the front door opening and closing. We gingerly opened the bedroom door. No-one was there. We ran down to the kitchen and stuffed a couple of slices of stale bread in our mouths, washed down with water straight from the tap.

That evening, the two of us took ourselves to Nana's for our evening meal. That day we had a great pudding. There was some chocolate birthday cake left, and she put a slice each into a bowl. Then, she chopped up some fresh strawberries to put over them and added a good slurp of cream. She even let us eat it in front of the TV, cross-legged on the floor.

I kept that as another carefully polished memory, Nicky grinning at me, chocolate crumbs on his lips.

1992

"Hi Becks! I'm making chili!"

"Brilliant, the one with the roast peppers. Love that. Want a hand? I'll change out of my uniform."

By the time she came into our kitchen, I was almost done. She grated us a big pile of cheese while she told me about her day.

"Mr Stanhope came in again."

"No! Really? Did you hide?"

"Just in time, I ducked into the tampon aisle!"

"Ha! Great hiding spot. He'd never follow you there."

We both laughed and I headed to the fridge.

"Beer? Or cold water?"

"A beer thanks."

I paused. I needed to tell Becky about the letters from Ange.

"Speaking of hiding, Nana did something weird yesterday."

"I've always said she was a slippery one."

I raised my eyebrow at her. Becky was trying to get a rise. We had rowed a lot about Nana when we were younger. It was the only thing I ever stood my ground on. Becky felt that Nana should either have taken us in or made efforts to track down our mother, anything but leave us alone with Mick, I mean Dad. At the very least, allowed social services to be involved. She was not wrong. She was not right either. She had not lived it.

I dumped a large palmful of cheese on my chili and rice, and took my bowl through to the living room, automatically flicking the TV on. I could see Becky was expecting me to defend Nana. I took a swig of my beer. I fought the urge to fall back into the usual sparring over my family. It was not the time. The reflex wasn't as strong these days. Not with Nicky gone. Not with Nana's innocence in question.

I wanted to tell Becky about the letters. My mother, Ange, was alive. I poked at my bowl of food. Nana had been corresponding with her. My appetite had vanished. All my life. All of Nicky's life. He grew up not knowing. Becky glanced at me. I looked back at the TV. *Star Trek The Next Generation* was on. She knew I hated science fiction. I made a point of softening my face. I focused on Picard and my food. At least Patrick Stewart was a good actor. The rest of it, the makeup, the silly languages. Another forkful of food.

I knew once I told her, a whole sequence of events would be set in motion. The words would be the spell summoning a different future into existence. I wanted to savour the last moments of calm normality but I couldn't hold on much longer. I needed to find the words. Jordi LaForge with his hairband over his eyes was saying something to Data about the nacelles. It made as much sense to me as the words I was formulating. I let them out.

"I think Ange is alive. I think she's been writing to Nana. I saw her hide some letters."

"Letters from Ange? Are you sure?"

"No. I barely saw the handwriting, and then she went and put them away."

156

"Tam! We need to get those letters!"

"Don't be silly! I'm not going to snoop about her papers. Forget it. She'd tell me if it was something important."

"Sure. Of course she would."

This time I could hear the sarcasm dripping in her voice. I ignored it. After all, I was thinking it too.

That night, I lay awake, wondering about the letters. I recreated the note my mother had left in my mind. I could not be sure unless I saw them, but I knew they were from her. Nana must be hiding them for a reason. They must have an address. I would know what had happened. Where she had gone. What she had been doing. Where she was. I might see her again.

By dawn, I was resolved. I had to find the letters.

I had to find her.

1967

When my parents had married, they had moved into a modern '60s concept building, one of these city-in-the-sky pipe dreams of that era's dreaming architects. These days, trendy hipsters like to take black-and-white photographs of this type of building, while waxing lyrical about the ethos and spirit of them, their brutalist architecture. These types never had to grow up in one, surviving the '70s, the strikes, the power shortages, the unemployment, Thatcher and the '80s as the decay settled in whilst the go-getters moved out, pulling up the ladder behind them on their way up, burning all their bridges. It did not matter that the Queen Mother had opened them.

There were three large blocks set in a u-shape, originally around a small park, or green space. Each block consisted of a stacked house arrangement: several cube-shaped two-storey houses that were nestled side-by-side, on top of each other to form three "house levels", the whole being six storeys tall, and four houses across. These were linked by a walkway along the front of the building, a concrete walkway which looked over the public space, and across to the other buildings. The brochures promised benches, sunny days and picnics, balloons, and happy children. A community of streets in the sky and promises of idyllic family lives. In reality, damp concrete, stairwells that smelt of piss, grey sky and layabouts filled the space instead. Grassy parks were soon paved over to become a car-parking spaces, in which no ball games were allowed.

Not long before she left, Ange told me that her life was a kaleidoscope. Just as a pattern seemed to make sense with Mick, life had given them a shake, and all the pieces landed in a completely new pattern. I was about seven and thoroughly confused by these notions, so I painted a romantic picture of them in my mind, young and in love.

Years later, I revisited Mick's role in this movie I had made. I learnt he took out another girl, Pneumatic Pam from two streets over, on a date and drunken fumble. Pam wore the shortest skirts and was rumoured to own a bra that undid at the front. But then Ange, that is to say Mum, missed a period and this being 1967, he proposed and she accepted, as she had to.

They were married days after her seventeenth birthday, and as there would be no visible bump until relatively late in the pregnancy, and I was born on the small side, I was accepted by those not in their strictest confidence to be a premature honeymoon baby. For their honeymoon, they never made it further than a long weekend in Blackpool.

George helped my young parents find their first and only home together. He was working at a building company, lead foreman on the "village in the sky" project of duplex style flats, at the cutting edge of the era's housing ideals. He organised some sort of deal with them. It meant Mick had to take a job with the company to be entitled to it, but with a young pregnant wife, and the financial help package available, how could he turn it down?

Back in the spring of '67, the young newly-weds had moved in with Nana while they waited for their new dream family home. However piecemeal my information gathering has been through the years, I understood from an early age that even then, in those early months, it was not a marriage made in heaven. I played their story like a film.

※

"Good morning, Ange. Did you sleep well?"

"Thanks Nana, I slept really well. Snug as a bug."

Nana knew that Ange was lying. One look at the bags under her eyes, and the expression on her face as she slowly and mechanically moved around the kitchen and it was clear that the poor girl had been awake all night, crying, even if the sound had not dripped through the walls of the house in the dark of night. She would lose that baby if she wasn't careful. Why, she was well over five months now, and she was not showing at all around that slender waist of hers, she was still wearing her tight flared cords. She needed to sleep and to eat better, especially if she was going to recover from the first trimester morning sickness. She looked drained. The physical change in her was extreme given how quickly it had happened. A sort of anti-blooming, like she was being drained from the inside by her own child.

"Will I make you a slice of toast? I've got some strawberry jam. Milk's in the fridge ..."

Nana trailed off, she knew that Ange wasn't even taking the offer in.

"Did you hear the news, no, I suppose you didn't, you are only just up, well in Paris there have been some sort of riots, I wasn't listening properly, but anyway, it was on the radio ... maybe we could get the paper later today? Do you think you'll pop out love? You could perhaps pick up a few things?"

Nana knew that she was filling in the gaping silence as she fussed around the kitchen. She put some bread in the toaster anyway, and the butter dish and a pot of home-made strawberry jam on the table in the kitchen. She took a butter knife and a spoon for the jam from the drawer, and pulled a small plate from the cupboard, placing them alongside the butter and jam. Ange was sitting at the table, stirring her cup of tea in a languid absent-minded fashion, her big eyes staring at nothing. She looked dreadful, so pale. It was fair to say that Nana knew her boy Mick was no saint but now she had a nagging feeling that there was more to it.

Nana sighed deeply. Ange looked up. They stared at each other, straight into each other's eyes. In that moment, Nana knew that whatever was going on between her son and his young wife, it would be a great cruelty to be anything other than as kind as she could possibly be at every opportunity to the girl. Regardless of the cause, Ange was alone, pregnant, struggling to cope, miserable and did not have anyone to count on. And what would the neighbours say when they saw her like this?

Nana walked around the table, lent forward and awkwardly wrapped her arms around her, her lack of practice making her self-aware. Ange sat stiffly in her arms for a moment, and then Nana felt her body relax. A sudden muffled sob erupted from the weak creature. Minutes ticked by, and when Nana stood up, Ange looked less grey, as if she had been warmed up into Technicolor somehow. Nana did not know then, but to the lonely, scared, pregnant teenager, that awkward hug was the breath that rescued her drowning soul.

Ange took a swig of tea from the mug and pulled a cigarette out of the packet that was on the table. She did not light it, but started to tap it, filter end, on the table, a slow gentle tapping. Nana sat down opposite her. Ange put the cigarette away.

Ange could not think of anything to say. She felt grateful for Nana's caring fuss, but in a numb way, almost disconnected. It was like she was watching the scene in the kitchen through a fishbowl. She knew she should say something more than mumbled gratitude, make small talk. She could not. It was as though there was a voice in the back of her mind. A new, weak voice from within, that told her that she should respond, though it still lacked any power or will to make her act.

Ange could smell the strawberries in Nana's homemade jam on the warm toast.

Ange took a bite, chew, swallow, sip the tea, swallow, repeat until she had finished it. That was the best she could do, and better than she had thought she might when she had first sat down, feeling tired, dizzy, and clammy. Staring at the teacup, her jaw slack with the lethargy that in recent weeks had piled onto her, Ange realised that she was feeling better because she was actually feeling something, she was feeling gratitude, and glad that any feeling had replaced the absolute numbness.

When she was done, she cleared the plate, and took them to the kitchen sink where she washed them. Nana seemed to approve of this, and indeed she did, believing this action to be an improvement. As she walked out of the kitchen, she let her hand rest on Nana's left shoulder for a moment, and the older woman reached up with her right hand, across her body, to cover Ange's hand.

I can picture it. Over the years, I've carefully built

up the scene, directed it, edited it, even sound tracked it with birdsong through the window. I have lit it in an orange hued light.

Once she was dressed, she lay on her bed for a while, hands circling her still-flat stomach in an automatic fashion. She was going to do the right thing for her baby. She was going to eat well from now on, and she was going to look after herself. The baby would be along in a few months, and Mick would be the man she hoped he would be. He would step up to being a father. Maybe his behaviour, his way, would change once they were a family. After all, he was nineteen, his life plans had fallen away from him, in the space of a few months he had traded them in for a job, a wife, and fatherhood. That was it, he was scared. He was not ready. She was not ready. That was why, surely. Since they came back from Blackpool, maybe his foul temper had been because he had been running scared.

✖

"Blackpool? Oh, really? That's lovely! The two of us? I've never stayed away from Mum and Dad before!"

"Silly girl, of course, it's our honeymoon!"

"Our honeymoon! In Blackpool! How many nights?"

The warm April sunshine was spilling between the buildings, flooding in through her window, gently lapping at the edges of the yellow curtains and surrounding Ange, who was sitting on the single bed in her narrow room, reaching out to her fiancé. He held an open envelope and note in his hand.

"Three nights, three nights, you and me, sweetheart, in a B&B somewhere along the seafront, we'll go out to dinner, go out to some bars, go dancing, stay up late, walk on the beach under the stars, and then

164

we'll go back to our room, and ..."

"And?"

He dropped the envelope, the note, took her hand, and in two short steps crossed the room, dropped to his knees in front of her. He raised her hand to his lips, kissed her knuckles, turned it over, kissed the palm of her hand, her inner wrist, began to work his way up, his other hand sliding up the outside of her thigh to the hem of her miniskirt.

She giggled nervously – a surprisingly full sound for one so slight, her blonde hair tumbling around her face.

A short while later, they lay together on the narrow bed, her head resting in the pit of his arm, their legs entwined. He stroked her flat belly. It was so soft, smooth, like a fuzzy peach to his mind. She smiled, she knew he was thinking of the baby, of the wedding. She felt warm, safe, drowsy in the sunshine. Contentment.

Then a voice came up the stairs.

"Ange? Ange, come down here at once, please!"

Her parents. They would want her to pick up the school bag that she had left lying at the bottom of the staircase, and the coat lying on the hall floor. They would not be angry, simply expecting her to answer straightaway. She got up, pulled her mini skirt on and the light brown polo neck jumper, and kissing Mick on the lips, headed down.

)(

That weekend, they had been married by the vicar at the church her parents attended, after the regular Sunday service. The congregation had been made up of his mother, sniffing beside George, his best man, Jim, and her maid of honour, Babs. Ange's parents had no siblings, so they were the sum extent of her family, sitting straightbacked and hardfaced in the front pew.

On the bus to Blackpool, married that morning and exhausted, Ange curled up contentedly, her back against him, facing the window, watching the late afternoon scenery flicker past. The light had a gold haze to it. Through the road dirtied window, it made him squint. He stared down the bus aisle, gripping the armrest. His neck was stiff with tension, his eyes sore and heavy from tiredness, from the late night and booze the night before. Jim had made sure to see him off right and had organised a night with the lads at the Lions', making sure Pam had been there. He thought again how right he had been to choose Jim as his best man. He had definitely made the most of his last night of freedom.

Arriving in Blackpool, he stood up, stretched, handed Ange her jacket from the coat rack above the seats and reached for their suitcase. He made his way to the exit without even looking back at her. He was off the bus before Ange had sleepily finished wrapping herself up against the evening chill.

He stood on the pavement, rolled his shoulders back, tilted his head left then right, stretching out the muscles. The rush of fresh air cleared his foggy head somewhat. With a deep breath he looked up at the darkening twilight sky, a few stars beginning to twinkle though it was not late.

Then and there, Mick resolved to make the most of these few days. May as well. They could go out for a few drinks, a walk on the beach, maybe catch a show. Best of all, enjoy the relative privacy of the hotel. She did not yet look like a pregnant wife. He smiled at her and reached his hand out to her as she joined him on the pavement.

They walked down a gently sloping road towards

the sea, a strong breeze in their faces. Ange shivered, and Mick wrapped his arm around her shoulders. They turned right at the seafront and walked a few steps before stopping and turning to stare at the sea, taking in the enormity of it, a pier twinkling merrily to their left, the helter-skelter and pavilion barely outlined against the darkening sky, and to their right, the other pier outlined against the rapidly fading pink sky and glittering sea. Ange jumped and clapped her hands once, and together, they ran across the traffic, dodging a bicycle, and a car in each direction. They reached the barrier which ran alongside the promenade at the same time, gasping as they looked down to the shingle beach.

"Come on, darlin', let's go and check it out."

They were magical days, blissfully happy. A late-night fish and chips one night. Ange ignored the fish in favour of five pickled onions. A night in a cosy pub, enjoying a young curly-haired man singing while playing a battered guitar. Long afternoon walks, past the helter-skelter pier and the tramway. A morning at Madame Tussauds waxworks, and promising to come back once the new Dixieland Palace opened. Dreams of living in a house with a front porch and black railings around the balcony. Evenings holding hands on a promenade bench watching the sun set. Nights holding each other, discovering each other. Mumbled words of love.

Ж

Nana met them at the bus station and nodded in approval to see them rosy-cheeked, her son protective, his arm around his young bride. Now that Ange's parents had dropped off her belongings she would need the support. Mick spoke up:

"Good, we don't have to go and sort all that out then."

Ange followed Nana and Mick into the house, her entire life to date packed into four medium-sized boxes and one suitcase, now all stacked in the hall. It was not a surprise. Ange had packed them herself before the wedding. Her parents, my grandparents, were leaving for Australia before the end of the month.

Strange to think that just a year before, she had read the Easter Sunday lesson in their church.

She had loved seeing everyone in the congregation every week. She had grown up with them. It was a big family. She had once loved the stories. Loved the songs. Around her sixteenth birthday, something had changed. Ange no longer bought into the Scriptures. She declined to be confirmed. The Minister asked her to read in the hope she might change her mind, and decide to join the church officially. Everyone came up after and told her that she had read beautifully. She smiled and thanked them, answering "the word of the Lord is beautiful". She had practiced in the mirror and found every beat to it, knowing when to pause, when to look up at the congregation, hoping the light from the stained-glass windows would catch her cheekbones. She knew it was all her.

Ange continued to attend even as her faith evaporated. Her parents would never force her to go now that she was old enough to decide for herself, but she liked to see everyone. That was until she started going out on Saturday nights. Not long after she started dating Mick, she stopped going to church. It didn't feel right anymore. She could not keep her thoughts in line during the service. As she fixed her hat in the hall mirror, face set to disappointed, Grandmother said:

"You're sure you don't want to come? You will be missed."

Ange would say "next time" and dutifully clean the kitchen while they were out. Grandfather said nothing. A sharp exhalation through his nostrils was enough to convey his thoughts on the matter. She tried to avoid these awkward conversations altogether.

She felt like a stranger in their home, coming and going to the rhythm of her school days, seeing friends. Grandmother no longer commented on the length of Ange's skirts. Stopped insisting on good behaviour. She came home at the usual mealtimes, and they ate in silence. Not a smile. No "how was your day?" She cleaned up around the unspoken disappointment. She stopped having breakfast with them, leaving for school on an empty stomach. She came home late. They ceased to expect her home for dinner. She wondered if they put her plate on the table and said grace over it or if she was expected to say it herself. The after-dinner bible readings carried on in the sitting room, without her. She darted past the door so as not to interrupt them. Sometimes she leant on the wall by the door frame, wondering if they would ask her in.

Saturday lunch was the one family gathering of the week Ange had yet to find a tacit reason to avoid. She had started to notice just how much older than her friends' parents they were. Not just in age. They had been in their mid-thirties, surprising themselves and all their friends. A baby eight years into their marriage had been an even more baffling turn of events. Now in their late fifties, they were almost two decades older than any of the other parents, and it showed. She had never questioned their ways when she was young, but their moral codes, their ideas on manners, on a women's place in the world were markedly pre-war, and so distant from her that Ange found it easy to detach herself from every value they had tried to instil in her.

Grandfather was slicing off another forkful of a ham. His lips were still moving as he chewed the previous mouthful. Ange could see he had missed a few hairs in the folds of his skin when he had shaved that morning. Grandmother had set some fresh early spring flowers in the middle of the table. Ange focused on them a moment, trying to pull some of the brightness into her voice. She wanted to sound confident.

"Mother, Father. I am going to get married this weekend. Mick is coming for tea. He is going to ask you, Father. You must say yes."

Grandfather stopped chewing. He set his knife and fork down on the plate. The fork wobbled and settled by the carrots. He looked across at Grandmother. She slowly lowered her glass.

For a moment it was as though they had all frozen. No one moved. Ange was not even certain that any of them were breathing. Grandmother gulped. Choking back a sound. She stood up, excusing herself automatically. The ticking of the clock in the hall through the open kitchen door pushing time forward. Grandmother returned, placed her napkin on her knees, picked up her knife and fork, pushed a potato around. Grandfather nodded.

"I see. You are a woman now. We will wish you well."

He picked up his glass and drank the contents in its entirety, in one long draw. That was it. Ange hung her head. She didn't want to cry in front of them. Both her parents had stopped eating. Grandfather stood up.

"I will make some scones. He will be here at three."

Her parents left the room, the half-full plates for her to scrape, the leftover carrots and potatoes put in bowls, the ham wrapped in wax paper. She put it on the cold marble slab in the food cupboard. She washed up, wiped the table, swept the floor. Her last chore as their good daughter. She would make the scones for herself, and switched on the oven.

The next square in the patchwork of family memories is Mick telling me how he had been to ask for Ange's hand in marriage, wanting to do the right thing, and spent almost an hour in a silent sitting room alone with Ange and a plate of scones. Her parents did not think him worthy enough of her to even take a cup of tea with him. He had wanted to make it right. Ange's father had stopped in the doorway and said:

"You could take her to the Salvation Army. They will deal with the problem."

Mick stood up.

"We will be married on Sunday."

"Well, good luck to you both. Angela, your mother has packed a case for you."

Mick would only visit the house one more time, a few days later. He picked Ange up from school. Her parents would be out, and she needed a few items.

Mick stood behind her as she gazed into her parents' room. She had that look on her face. He wrapped his arms around her, his hand on her still flat belly.

"This baby of ours is not going to get in the way of our dreams. We will be a happy family."

I don't know if Ange ever saw Grandfather and Grandmother after the wedding.

I needed to ask Nana if she had ever heard from them since then.

1992

I sat in shock.

The whole room had seemed to blur. Turning sharply to Nana, the words tumbled out.

"You what?"

She looked across the room at Davy and Agnes, the last of the mourners at Mick's funeral. Not that there had been many, but these were family, my dad's cousins. Nana had drunk quite a bit more than her usual Sunday sherry and was loose-lipped.

She nodded towards them and repeated:

"They're my children, you know. They don't. Know I mean. They think they're here for a cousin. He was their brother. I'm going to tell them."

She stood up. I grabbed her arm quickly.

"No. Not here, Nana. Not now. It's not the time, it's not the place."

She stopped dead, wobbled, and fell back into her chair. Agnes bustled over.

"Aunty Jen, are you alright? Shall we get you a glass of water?"

I was still holding her arm to stop her from getting up again. The last thing my father's wake needed was a family revelation. I squeezed a warning, but I could see that Peg's condescension, the use of the special "shall we?" voice that was usually reserved for the elderly and infirm had got Nana's hackles up and her mood for revelations had evaporated. Thank goodness. The atmosphere had been weird enough with failed tributes on one side and a raucous group of odds and sods on the other, his pub and site friends, making up noisily for their low number.

Once everyone had left, I got Nana a biscuit, which she pushed aside in favour of a sherry someone had left on a side table. Even though it was a long and exhausting day, and I was feeling lightheaded from the drinks, I knew this was important. Nana was ready to share this secret with me.

She had met Harry in a dancehall. She described him to me as a kind, quiet and thoughtful man. For a few weeks they were regular dance partners. He brought flowers when he came to pick her up.

As Nana spoke of him, her green eyes went soft and sad. He had been shot down in an air-raid. She had been heartbroken, but rather than wallow, she had simply put her best face on, gone out more often and later than any of her friends. She stayed out mostly with Gerry, who had been Harry's friend in the RAF. Harry and Gerry had been the archetypal combination of the quiet and softly spoken man with a loud charismatic friend. Gerry made her laugh, and they found solace in each other's company.

It was more than solace that they found, given that she was already pregnant with Davy when they married in 1943.

For the first few years, as the war raged on, their marriage was fuelled by the fact they never knew if this was the last time they would see each other. Gerry was deployed to the Front, and the rare time that they spent together was filled with "last ever" moments.

Nana's eyes twinkled with the memory.

The war ended, Agnes was born, and they settled into a pattern of calm and uneventful domesticity which did not suit Gerry. After several frustrating months of not being able to find work anywhere, he finally found a job on the docks.

Nana's eyes were shining, with sherry and tears.

"I thought about bringing Wee Davy back from Ayr, from Great Aunt Nancy and Great Uncle Alfie. They never had children of their own. We visited every couple of weeks. But our wee flat in the tenement, the shared toilet, laundry and mould in the stairwell, Peggy was only just starting to toddle, it would have been so cramped. He was far happier there."

Nana assured me, and herself. She had clearly told herself this many times over.

Davy and Agnes were my uncle and aunt. I felt the room spin.

How could she have hidden this? All these years. My stomach rolled over. How could she have made such a cold decision? Why not find a way to make it work, for them to be together.

"Bears need space in their caves," she said ruefully.

I nodded.

Gerry was not easily suited to family life. One day, he came bounding in waking Agnes from her nap in his glee. Gerry had won a motorbike from one of the floor managers in a bet. He proceeded to race around on it as often as he could, blowing off the dust of boredom. He took Nana out on it a couple of times, but it was around then that she became pregnant for a third time, the perfect excuse not to have to go out on the motorbike.

During one of these mad-cap races around the countryside, Gerry smashed his bike into a tree. He had been drunk at the time. About three months later Mick, my father, was born.

She took a deep breath and knocked back her dram. I patted her arm, unsure of what to do. She had never spoken to me as a friend before. I wanted her to keep going.

"Gerry died. I had Agnes and baby Mick on my own. I knew Agnes would be happier in Ayr. I did what was best. Great Uncle Alfie never went to war. When he was teenager, he was climbing on a mechanical combine harvester kept in the barn and lost his leg. Great Aunt Nancy had a crush on him at school and visited him every day after the accident, helping him to recover and learn how to walk again. Even though he was missing a leg, he was always happy and kind. An excellent farmer too. Davy started to call them Ma and Da. We agreed never to correct that. After all, Davy and Agnes were the children they could not have. It was best for them to call me Auntie. After the war, lots of families got moved about, rebuilt. They were happy on the farm. I never corrected the assumptions. So, maybe I spoiled Mick a bit. Just the two of us. Of course, I was working, so Mick went with a neighbour after nursery or school. He played with his friends, in the street."

Her face shifted. I nodded, encouraging her to keep speaking.

"I should have been home more. He played until he wandered off down the street, away from his friends. He never liked the cold, you know, and he would go and get a heat in the pub. The landlord let him stay if he helped collect the glasses. It suited me because I knew where he was."

X

George and Nana went home, and I was alone in the flat. I wanted to talk to Nicky about it, but I hadn't seen him since he had slunk out of the back of the service.

I tidied the room and pondered this bombshell about Nana's life. About my father.

I thought about a school photograph of my father. His ears stuck out under an unruly mop of hair, scowling at the camera. I constructed a scene. A skinny boy, a jumper with a hole in the left elbow, shorts, and a grazed knee. I pictured him running a stick along the walls, clanging the bins, sneaking into The Crown, sipping the ends of pints left on tables. There he was chatting to workers, running errands for them. Learning the banter.

I picked up some empty glasses and took them to the kitchen, still piecing the information together. Mick was already a tearaway when George came into the shop where Nana worked. I had never really asked about his childhood before. I had assumed so much.

I knew that George made her giggle. She made him blush.

I knew that it was only about six weeks after they met in 1958 that George proposed and she said no, she had a son. They had joked about that once. I added this to the movie in my mind. I stopped drying the glasses for a moment. I had always thought I knew everything about Nana. I could not believe she had kept Davy and Agnes a secret from him all these years. When had she told George?

He had proposed again. There was a running joke I had never thought to question.

"I asked Nana twice, now I'm waiting for her to ask me!"

Maybe she had told him about Davy and Agnes then? I scoured my memory for a clue as I went back into the sitting room.

Nana never hid George. George was there for tea

most evenings, except Fridays when he went for a drink with "the boys" from work, and Mondays, when Nana set her hair and painted her nails. We never knew if he stayed the night, or if he went back home. He was there at the weekends to help with the garden, with the DIY, there with her. No matter how early.

But she did not speak the truth of their relationship to us. Neither did George. He went along with it. As with the truth about Davy and Agnes, I supposed.

I made myself sit down.

Mick loved George, but he had always had Nana to himself until George solidified into their life when he was ten. He stayed away. Playing out. He would stumble home, bruised, once with a black eye, burst lip, and missing tooth, brought home by the cuff from the pub by the landlord. The local beat policeman. George was there at Nana's side. Forever repairing the damage from Mick's tantrums. Punch marks in the doors. A broken chair. There to pick up the pieces.

George was not a weak man. I had assumed that he had never intervened with Mick because Nana and he were not married. I realised that had never been the heart of the matter. Nana had given up two babies. George would never have wanted to step in and make her feel like she failed her third child. She had worked hard to keep Mick and her as a family unit. That was why she had never married George.

My pulse quickened as anger flared at all these secrets over the years.

1981

Dear Nana,

Thank you for all your letters! A wee bundle of them, in one go, just a couple of weeks ago. I can't believe you sent me so many. You never stopped writing to me!

It was lovely to read all the stories of Tam and Nicky. I can't believe my girl is thirteen already and my little man is nine. I liked reading their adventures; it makes me feel closer to them. My heart always weeps when I think of them, I carry them with me every minute of every day. I am glad they are so happy now. I knew it would be easier for Mick with me gone. You don't say anything about him in any of the letters, but I would guess that he found a nice girl who suits him well, so much more than me, and is a good mum. A better mum than I could ever have been. I won't dwell on that. It is just guessing on my side, anyway. I will tell you what I have been doing.

I didn't stay in Goa long, a few years. It was happening, you know, but it wasn't the place for me. The very first place that I went to was the wee hotel. That is where you have been sending the letters to. It was fabulous, there were lots of interesting people. But

179

then after about a month I met a group of wonderful folks there. They were planning to set up a retreat about thirty miles away. It was sort of inland but along the coast.

So, I met this group of artists and freethinkers and I decided to join them! With them, I really found myself, it was such a journey for me. I am an artist! I have helped people find themselves by expressing themselves and their souls through art at the retreat. While I was there, I also learnt the ancient practice of yoga. It is such a wonderful strengthening and soul-cleansing practice.

Nana, India has such a beautiful and ancient culture, all the people are so wise and kind. It is so different. I think some of your letters must have started arriving at the hotel around then, but the guys there did not have any way of passing them on. It is so good that they saved them in case I should pass through one day.

I met Greg at the retreat. He was my second yogi (that's a yoga teacher). He was learning the art from Yogi Ravindra – such a beautiful soul. I mean Ravindra, but the same is true of Greg. He taught me how to love myself. About two years ago we left Goa – something about the spirit of the place had started to change, and we decided to move back towards Europe. We are on a Spanish island. It is always sunny and beautiful here. We have opened a yoga and spiritual centre together. We live above the studio – every morning the sunlight fills the room to wake us up. That is if Cleo doesn't wake us first! Cleo is our tabby cat and quite the madam. She does her stretches, and we do our sun salutations together. It is such a zen way to start the day.

Don't think that I don't miss my babies, Tam, my little bookworm, Nicky the adventurer. I have spent years wondering if I should have left them at all, whether it was the right thing. Of course, Nana, you and whoever Mick chose to raise them will have done a lovely job of it. Of course, I cried when I read about them, but dear Nana, thank you for being so wonderful to them. Don't worry, I won't spoil it all and tip their lives over by contacting them now. My heart is true to them, but we have different paths. I can live with that.

Anyway, it was Ralph who happened to make the link between Greg & I and Goa and sent us your letters – such a funny story. He was here to visit some mutual friends … anyway, he sent the bundle over. I loved receiving them, but there is no need to send any more.

Nana, your job with me is more than done. I know that you are looking out for Tam and Nicky, that you have got Mick back to being the man I knew he was without me hindering him.

Thank you,
peace, love,
Ange xxx

I copied it out word for word into my journal and headed home. There were half a dozen letters in total. This one had the most useful information. It had been sent six years after Ange left. The remainder were short and functional, other than a condolence note for Old Mrs Pollock's family and a letter that seemed to be intended for my grandparents. It was accompanied by a letter requesting that Nana take it to them.

I ruminated this on my way home. Why would Ange be asking Nana to hand deliver post for my maternal grandparents to a Glasgow address? Surely Nana would not have lied to us about where they were.

We had closed ranks that year. We didn't go round to Nana's as much. Is that why she hid Ange from us? It was around then that Nicky had given up on childhood games She had let Nicky assume that his mother was dead. I had always wanted to believe Ange had left, but I was never completely certain.

Of course, I had also let Nicky assume that our mother was dead. His whole life. I wanted to protect him from knowing that he had been abandoned. Nana was protecting him too. Ange's letter clearly stated that she did not want to hear any further.

I read Becky the letter the moment she came home.

"Tam. I've always said Nana was not as perfect as you thought. She let you think your mum was dead. That's worse than the secret Aunt and Uncle. And, Tam, come on, your other grandparents live up the road. What's that all about?"

Later I struggled to sleep, reviewing it all, trying to work through all the new facts, all the evidence. Why did Nana have a letter for my maternal grandparents? I wanted to read it, but it was sealed shut.

Grown and in my own bed, I wanted my Mummy to hold me. All these people in my life who had decided what I was allowed to know. Once, I was just a child, but why let me keep living with the lies? Was I not old enough to know the truth?

1982

I looked at my little brother.

He had tears streaming down his reddened face.

These were tears of laughter, and my own cheeks were hurting. Dad was guffawing too. All three of us laughed and giggled and roared until our sides ached.

We were halfway through our Saturday lunch and in a great mood. Instead of cleaning, that morning we had all gone for a walk, across the park and over to the canal. It was a warm cloudy spring morning, we had joked and chatted the whole time. By the time we got home, famished, and tucked into our lunch, the silly giggles took us over.

I can't even remember exactly what we were laughing about. I remember the laughter.

Dad could be funny sometimes.

※

Dad had been well for a couple of weeks, and life had settled into a rhythm. On the third Monday he came home with that odd look that was like clouds on a horizon. I was surprised on the Wednesday that he had come home sober at all, and though he didn't say a word, he ate the sausages and mash that I had made, with Nicky and I at the kitchen table, before sitting watching the television while I tidied up, and we did our homework. He didn't even mention that the peas were overcooked.

Then he did not come home on Thursday evening, and neither Nicky nor I mentioned it. This was not surprising to us. It happened so often, and all that we could do was hope that it would not be for too long – a shorter absence usually made for a smoother return to the tempo of our routines.

Friday rolled around, and I stopped at the library on my way home, as I usually did. At that time, I would take three books out per week. I often chose something serious, something funny and something based on real life. I didn't always, because sometimes I would take out a set, but I liked to have a method. Though I spent at least half an hour choosing my books, Nicky wasn't home from school by the time that I got there. It was a nice afternoon, so I hoped that he was playing football with the boys in the park.

The flat was quiet and calm, but I wasn't ready to sit after my walk, so I decided to get ahead on the weekend's cleaning. I started upstairs, and stripped Dad's bed, squeezing the sheets into the laundry bags. I opened the window to let some air in. I never liked that strong smell that always hung in his room. I picked up the underwear that was strewn across the floor and put it in the bag that was hooked onto my arm. I moved on to Nicky's room next, and I straightened it out, collecting the neat pile of dirty clothes from by the door. His sheets would have to wait until next week. I alternated our sheets and our father's sheets, week in, week out. Next, it was on to the bathroom. I cleaned the bath, the sink and then the toilet, opened the window, and threw the towels into the bag too. I washed my hands, and then went to the boiler cupboard. Half of it was shelved and in it we kept the fresh laundry. I got out fresh towels and hung them off the rack in the bathroom. Then I took the double sized sheets out and made up my father's bed. I took the laundry bags down and fetched up the cleaning bucket and mop from under the stairs and scrubbed away until I was done.

It was the kitchen's turn next. The living room was fairly tidy and it wouldn't matter if I didn't get to it that evening. It would be easy to do the next day. I was starting to feel pleased that I might be able to spend a good part of Saturday morning with my nose buried deep in a book. I washed up from breakfast, dried and put away the dishes, I washed the sink, I wiped the outside of the cupboard, the worktops, the table, and the cooker top. I had just finished scrubbing the inside of the oven when the front door opened and I felt a draft run up from my lower back. I pulled my jumper back down to the top of my trousers and looked up. Nicky was standing in the kitchen doorway, in a pose that was older than his nine years.

"Anything to eat, Tammy Tam?"

"Not yet, Nicky. I wanted to finish the oven first."

"Oh come on Tam, you're so bloody boring all you do is clean all the time. You're like Cinder-bloody-ella, but you'll never find a Prince Charming if all you do is stay home and fucking clean."

"Bugs, I told you not to swear, come on!"

"Bloody bloody bloody, Tam. Fuck fucking fuck!"

I didn't want us to start a fight. He could be quite stubborn when challenged, and I recognised that bullish look in his eyes, daring me to rise to it. Besides, he had a point. I backed down and half-smiled.

"Alright, I'm almost done here, and I'll get something organised now."

His face shifted and quick as mercury, a smile flashed up.

"Thank you, Tam. You're a great sister!"

"So, what did you do after school?"

"I was playing football with the guys, and we were winning when ..."

His mood had swung around to truly cheerful, and he chattered away about the game as I finished with the oven. He took a couple of glasses from the cupboard, put some squash in the bottom of both and went over to the sink to add the water. I knew all was calm again. As he started to pull the chair out to sit at the table, he was interrupted by the front door opening, and we both froze, holding our breath. It could only be him, though I am certain that we were both longing for Nana to call out. The door slammed, and we knew a storm had blown in.

Before we could react, Dad was in the kitchen, red-eyed and wild-haired. It was clear that he hadn't stopped at all over the past two days.

"I'm fucking hungry. Where's lunch?"

"Well, Dad, I've not had time to make tea yet."

I stressed the word tea. He didn't even know what time of day it was.

"What have you been doing, you slut? Running with the boys, like your whore mother?"

I was stunned by the sting in my father's words. Before I could react, Nicky swung around to square up to him, though he barely came up to Dad's shoulders.

"Don't you dare speak to Tam like that you bloody ... bloody ..."

"Bloody what? Spit it out. What are you going to do? Run and cry to your Nana, wah wah wah?"

Nicky pulled back his arm and with all his strength punched him in the stomach, and then kicked him in the shin.

Mick didn't flinch, numbed by the booze. He punched Nicky in the face. Hard.

186

I screamed.

My little brother fell to the floor, clutching his nose, blood oozing between his fingers.

My father looked at me, eyes unfocused. I tried to make myself shrink. He pulled his hand back and slapped me. I fell to the floor, against the cupboard.

"That'll teach you, bastards."

He stormed back out. I stared at my brother's bleeding nose. Red dripping on the freshly mopped kitchen floor.

)(

We didn't speak about what had happened.

Mick did not come home that weekend. I did my homework. Nicky sat and drew. I ate toast and curled up in bed with a book. Nicky made himself sandwiches and stayed up watching the TV. Mick stayed away. The week passed.

Nicky hovered. Slammed doors. Glanced up at me.

He wanted my attention.

I had none to give.

I had tried digging my nails into my palms. Numb.

Crescent shaped scars on my wrists. Tearing. Scraping. Not enough.

Mick's razor? I turned it over. Small hairs from his beard were trapped between the blades.

I cleaned the paring knife.

The following Saturday, Nicky came into the kitchen and cheerfully launched into some anecdote about the morning's football match and a spectacularly muddy patch of grass.

"Can we have pasta for lunch?"

That was it.

I ignored the bruises on his arms.

He ignored the neat cuts on mine.

1993

"To hell with it all, Becky, fuck it. I give up."

I leaned forward to retch again into the toilet. As I rarely drank alcohol it hadn't taken much of the cheap wine for me to end up sobbing and wrecked in the bathroom. I had gone home via the corner shop, and Becky had come back from work to find me starting the second bottle. That had been barely an hour before, and in that time I had filled her in on the letter.

"I'm going to take all the Sugar Factory money, and fuck off. After all, my mother ran away, so I'm going to do it too. Why the bloody hell not? I've had it with this mess."

I threw up again, partly on myself this time and that was as far that conversation went that night. Becky helped me out of my clothes, into the bath and turned on the tap to the shower setting. It was one of those white plastic tube connectors which mixed the water from both taps, and there was a shower rail with a curtain that hung into the bath though it was not possible to stand under the shower head anyway. I sat in the bath, and once Becky started pouring the water over my head, I was able to take over. She left me alone in the bathroom, and I sobbed in release under the hot water.

Clean and dry mouthed from the booze, eyes washed out, I headed to my bedroom and pulled on Nicky's old t-shirt that I'd been sleeping in. It smelled clean. Becky must have washed it that morning. I was so glad to have her back. She'd moved out while Lou was there. I think our wallowing had proven to be too much for her in her own grief. After all, she'd known Bugs most of her life. In some ways I was glad that she had left us to it. I'd needed that space. But now she was back and had quickly put the flat back to order, not that I'd even noticed that anything was out of place. She had done mountains of my laundry too. I'd resisted washing Bugs' t-shirt, somehow trying to preserve his smell. If she'd offered to wash it, I would have said no. However, if I'm honest, it only smelt of me by then and as I slipped between my clean bedsheets, in the clean t-shirt, tears howled out for now. I was empty. I held my wrist, sank into sleep.

After breakfast, I started to flesh out a plan. Nicky's share of the Sugar Factory sales and all the intellectual property belonging to him had passed to me, and with his death everything to do with the arthouse had shot up in value. He may have been only nineteen but the critical acclaim and buzz around his work was front page news. For the first time in my life, I had some money behind me, and more money still coming in.

I sat up on the sofa, knocking my plate off the cushion it was balanced on, crumbs gong everywhere.

"Oi! Watch the ketchup!"

"I'm going to go to the States, to LA. I've always wanted to go there. See Mann's Chinese Theatre, the big Hollywood sign, Rodeo Drive where Julia Roberts goes in Pretty Woman. A few months away will do me good. I'll pay my share of the rent for the time I'll be away, so that you don't have to worry about that or need to move my stuff out. In fact, I can leave now, I'll get a ticket today. I have a passport."

I paused and gulped, thinking of Nicky's grin when he announced we were off to Greece in the summer. I had told myself it was time I owned a passport but in truth I was excited to see the Parthenon and the Temple of the Oracles with him. It had never happened. Nicky had got too involved with his projects.

"We never did go."

Becky nodded at me, encouraging me to carry on, but I had run out of words. She knew me well enough to know where my mind had taken me.

Thinking about the passport and the trip that never happened, my face must have dropped and whatever excitement that had clung to it evaporated because Becky grabbed my hand.

"You need to get away. I know. Have an adventure, have fun, far away from here, from this."

I hugged her. We both knew I needed to do this alone.

Ж

I was twenty five when I first went to an airport. Twenty five when I first travelled abroad. Twenty five when I flew away, at last to the East Coast of the USA.

Twenty five when I left the lies behind.

I kept this press article cutting:

"The movers and shakers are lamenting the untimely death of "Sugar Factory" teen prodigy Nicholas Gerald Hall, known to most as Nicky Bugs.

Nicky Bugs was found dead in his childhood home, and a verdict of "death by suicide" has been given. I was lucky to have met him frequently at the seminal Divaz REV-oh-lushion night, and my verdict would be death by brilliance. This talented and precocious artist was tormented by his creativity. All of us who had the privilege to know him would agree that he was as skilled with a paintbrush or spray can as he was on the decks or in creating "concept nights". Who could forget his most famous event: a night when the club patrons were encouraged to use living human models as "free paintbrushes moving to the beat" on a wall made of canvas. This piece of work is on display in the entrance to the controversial "Sugar Factory". His co-founder and partner-in-crime, Lou TM, has said that he is "devastated" – this will be a huge creative and personal loss."

Beside is a picture of Nicky in a sort of lurid body suit.

Was that my brother?

Nicky, Bugs, I know it was hard. I know I was hard. Mum left. Mick cracked.

How could you leave me too?

You always wanted to fly, to soar, I thought I would get to watch. You burnt your wings. Will I ever find anyone else who understands? I can't be a team on my own.

How do I carry on alone?

1993

It was over four months since the morning that I found Nicky in the bath. Since the circus charade cremation. There were cards, flowers and tins of biscuits. Someone I had never seen before brought a stew. The Sugar Factory delivered some paint brushes arranged as a bouquet. There had also been a nice whisky, and a magnum of Perrier Jouët with the instruction to celebrate Bugs' life. It was an unusually decorated bottle, covered in flowers. I was perplexed by the notion. Late one night, I shared it with Lou.

There had been a series of specials on the local radio and in the paper about Nicky's "artistic output". Everyone spoke of his creative genius, described him as a shooting star. Those of us closest to him all declined, but some of the Sugar Factory crowd had spoken to the press. My world was too shattered. I heard that there was already a tell-all memoir underway.

I was alone, sitting by his memorial plaque. Black marble, with his name, date of birth, and date of death, an epitaph: "visionary". Well, I knew him all along, and I didn't think he was a visionary. Yet Nana and I agreed he would have liked being called that.

I didn't know where they came from, all these people. It was always us, just us.

Bugs and Tam and Orion's belt.

Bugs and Tam and the Norackel.

Bugs and Tam in the Secret Fort, behind the sofa.

Bugs and Tam against the Ogre.

And Bugs the knight in shining armour, as directed by Princess Tam.

Who was going to tell that?

He didn't know how it was going to play out. He had to trust Princess Tam knew what came next. He was a stupid cowardly boy. He was an annoying mean boy. He ran out. He left me here, alone. He didn't trust me to know what came next. He simply had to wait it out. Mick hadn't even been dead a year. The Ogre was slain. The knight didn't need to vanish. He could have been king.

Bugs and Tam. Tam and Bugs. Tam.

Tam.

All alone.

It had gone quiet. Everyone had gone back to their lives, to normality. Even Becky. I had pretended to. I needed to piece normality back together.

Perhaps it should have been raining in the cemetery. A middle-aged black-clad widow weeping into her white, lace-trimmed handkerchief a couple of plots away, with a pillbox hat and fishnet veil. There should have been an old man patting the gravestone of a long-lost brother in arms, and a forlorn dog sleeping on the tomb of a young man. All united under the patter of a soft rain, sounds deadened by the gentle rustle in the trees, and fine raindrops building into fat drops of water running down the petals of the flowers left by mourners at the gravestones.

From where I sat beside Nicky's memorial stone, I could hear the hum of the cars driving down the main road on the other side of the new wall. The occasional horn.

I was at the back of the cemetery, in the new cremation memorial plot. There were builders finishing off the wall to my right, and though I was sure they weren't meant to, they had the radio on, playing current singles, Snap's *Rhythm is a Dancer*. It was not loud, but enough for the tinny beat to carry out over the new, undug area to me. The memorial plaques, new and shiny spread to my left and ahead, down a slight slope, so that I could only see the top of the main gate. There was a back gate used only by the gravediggers here at the top. It was a non-descript cloudy day, one of those when you resort to discussing previous weather events to avoid the current blank page.

I took a deep breath.

I felt like I had been trapped underwater. In a bubble. As though I was seeing through distorting trick glass, hearing muffled conversations, reacting as I knew I should – smiling, frowning, thanking. Commiserating on cue. My mouth and body were puppets that I was controlling remotely, from the cabin of my brain. I did think that I should cry at some point, but I hadn't been able to remotely operate my tear-ducts. Not one tear since the day I walked in to the flat. I could make myself smile, but I could not fake a tear.

I had been off work, but there was the funeral, the distant relatives, the press and sorting out Lou.

Lou was a mess. After the cremation he stayed at mine and Becky's. He spent almost the entire wake without uttering a word, smoking cigarette after cigarette standing on the walkway outside the flat.

After everyone had left, he came back into the flat, and took my hand. Not to shake it, and not to hold it romantically. It was the way a toddler goes to take their mother's hand for comfort. I asked him if he wanted to come back to mine and Becky's for a drink. He nodded, so I sat him on the sofa, tidied the cups and plates, washed up and gave the kitchen a once over, before taking Lou's jacket off the hook and handing it to him.

Silently, he stood up, took my hand, and did not let it go until we got to my flat. Not when I closed and locked the front door of my childhood home, not when we went down the stairwell, not when we left the estate, nor when we were walking along the pavements, crossing streets, or climbing up my stairs, not when I unlocked my flat door. I remembered holding Nicky's hand like this all the way to Nana's too, for my own comfort as well as his, as we fled yet another storm. It was only once we were locked inside my flat, in the living room that he let go as he sagged down onto the sofa, still in his coat.

Once I had hung my coat and scarf on the hooks in the hall, I went into the kitchen, and made Lou a sandwich. I poured him a beer, which I put with the sandwich on the low table in front of him, and I sat down beside him.

We sat in silence as Lou chewed. We hadn't spoken since we left Nicky's funeral. Mechanically, we went about getting ready for bed, an unspoken methodical choreography between us, as though we had done this dance a million times before. I handed him a t-shirt to sleep in, pillows, sheets, and a blanket for the sofa.

I lay awake for about an hour, not thinking, lying there, drained. Lou opened the bedroom door and got into bed beside me. He did not say a word. I was lying there, wide awake, entombed in my own body. He wrapped his arms around me, his head against my shoulder.

We slept like that for two weeks, Lou and I. Well, I say slept, though in reality we drifted in and out of consciousness. Lou really needed that. I was glad I could help, that I could look after him.

I knelt beside Nicky's headstone. The words tumbled out.

"How could you leave him, Nicky? How could you break him down like that? He's not one of the other Factory peacocks. Why did you give up on him? Me maybe, but Lou?"

I took a deep breath, filled my lungs.

I blinked at the memorial stone.

Annie Lennox's *Walking on Broken Glass* came on the workmen's radio across the graveyard. It seemed fitting.

The week before, his picture was on the front page of some of the papers, with the headline "Nicky B tragedy latest". I was on the bus home, and some people had left their newspapers on the seats.

Some of these had fallen onto the floor.

The passengers were walking on them.

Their shoes were wet and dirty, his face was getting muddied. Like when he was a boy.

Kicked around.

I picked one up.

Then another. Before I knew it, I was picking them all up. Frantic. Manic.

I knew they were only used newspapers, but it was his face, Bugs' beautiful, smiling face. I tore the paper right out of this suit's hands, yelling, "You're going to leave him behind like everyone else, like everyone else!" I snatched all the papers, and I jumped off the bus.

The passengers were eyeballing me through the steamed-up windows, but most of them stared ahead, steadfastly ignoring me.

I ran, clutching the papers for two whole stops, until I reached mine.

I sat on the thin bench, a heavy heap.

I remembered those bad movies the Sugar Factory crowd used to watch and laugh at back in the beginning, the film projected on a wall and throwing popcorn at each other.

I was alone in the dark. The streetlight was yellow. The rain let off. A bus drove past me and the wet noise of the tyres roused me from my stupor. I smoothed out every front page with his picture against the top of my thigh, and tried to pull together the pieces where the page had been ripped, to put his smile back together. One by one. I must have had about twenty-five or thirty. Nicky would have stood there and laughed at me, saying "Tam, you are such a freak."

I sat there, with all the pictures on my lap until the drizzle came back. I didn't know why I'd picked them all up, looking at his stupid face, willing my tear ducts to spring. Nothing.

And then, I put all the pictures in the bin beside the stop and walked home.

I knew Nicky would have laughed at me.

"Tam, you are ridiculous."

"You're right, Bugs, I am ridiculous. Sitting here, beside your grave, talking to you in my head. Anyway, I'm thinking about going away. Nana's not ..."

I trailed off. He didn't need to hear about Nana's secrets, Ange's letter. The whereabouts of Ange's parents.

"With Dad and you gone now, there's no reason to stay any more. Ange is never coming back. Not for me."

My knees ached, and my bum was damp from sitting on the grass in the cemetery.

"I'm not needed here anymore. They're all carrying me, and it's horrid with you gone. You're everywhere and nowhere. You won't miss me."

With that, I left.

1976

"That is it. Fuck off! See if I bloody care. You no-good lazy idiots. I gave up everything for you, every fucking thing and you treat this place like a fucking hotel."

I grabbed Nicky's hand and bolted for the front door. I wrenched it open and, without looking back, we raced along the raised walkway, from the front door to the stairwell.

The slam shook the walls.

The smell of cleaning chemicals on cold concrete burned our throats.

We scrambled down the stairs, two by two, school bags spilling with clothes, a favourite book for me and a toy for Nicky.

"Hurry, Nicky, he'll come after us, run!"

A thud. A yelp.

A flight ahead of him. I stopped. Heart pounding. Was it Mick?

I looked back. I couldn't see our father. I couldn't see Nicky.

Gingerly, I took a couple of steps back up.

There he was, crumpled on the ground, his football sticker book lying beside him. I hadn't noticed that he had taken it.

Nicky had missed the last two steps and fallen onto

the landing.

He looked up at me, tears filling his four-year-old's eyes. He bit his lower lip, and picking up the precious book, stood up.

"I'm alright, Tammy. Let's go."

I realised our father was not chasing us. He would have caught up with us then. We slowed to walk down the steps at a brisk pace, though Nicky was limping.

I noticed that he had grazed his left knee, and that it was bleeding below his shorts. We went on down the steps in silence, Nicky clutching his football sticker book. His eyes resolutely fixed, lips thin, chin jutting out in determination. No doubt I wore a similar expression.

We reached the bottom. I stopped. I knelt in front of him. The concrete was cold, hard on my kneecap.

"Let's see your knee, Bugs. It looks fine – a bit sore, just a graze. You've had worse before. It's fine. We'll get it washed up and pop a plaster on it when we get there, alright?"

I stood and took his hand, more gently this time and we walked as quickly as we could along the side of the building, past its corner, and onwards, breathing hard. The last few times we ran away, we went straight to Nana's. We had yelled, "We're running away! We are going to Nana's." Dad had followed. Enraged. Dragging us back by the wrists when he caught up. Demanding Nana stop letting us in.

It wasn't like he ever came to get us when he'd been out.

Only if we had left mid-row.

He would get us soon enough. I knew I could make myself small and take his anger. Nicky would try to stand up to him. It was only a matter of time before we would end up in hospital.

We made a plan to go somewhere else. We were

going to George's.

Mick would not think to look for us there, not in a rage.

We knew George would open the door and smile. That he would give us jam sandwiches, put on the TV. It would be warm and safe. We could stay in his spare room. He would care for us. We had it all planned. He was stronger than Mick too.

We got to the road, looked either way, and waited nervously for a large truck to pass us before crossing. It was only mid-afternoon, and the blustery evening was starting to get dark already.

After crossing, I realised that I had forgotten to grab my jacket, and at the same time, realised that Nicky must be cold too, colder than I was. He was only wearing a simple shirt under his thin coat, and I was all too aware of his skinny pale white legs sticking out from his PE shorts, blood trickling down his left shin. Though he still looked determined, his eyes were glistening, his cheeks were too red.

It was only about a fifteen-minute walk, but at that point, it seemed to be the furthest point in the galaxy from where we stood.

Holding hands, we trotted past the red pillar box, past the flat-roofed pub where Dad would spend so many of his hours and the row of shops, the grocers, the paper shop, the butchers.

"Tam, I wish Mum was still here. She would have made it better. It was good when she was here, Dad was never angry like this before then."

"He was, but you were too young then."

"Do you remember my birthday before Mum left? We had fun."

"That was a good day, wasn't it? We had a picnic at the zoo."

"I liked the penguins best. I like the way they walk."

"I liked the rhinoceros. It was funny, it had a grumpy face, and funny beaky lips."

We chattered about the animals, comparing the best and worst bits of elephants and lions, chimpanzees, and lemurs, which were our favourites and for which reasons: funniest, scariest, bravest, strongest, and so on. Nicky couldn't remember that day, not truly, but I had told him about it countless times when the Ogre had raged and ranted downstairs.

In the telling, I had fused our actual visit with elements of Kipling's' *Just So Stories* and the poem *Albert and the Lion* by Marriott Edgar, in which Mr and Mrs Ramsbottom went to the zoo with their young son Albert. I always said Ramsbottom in a way which made Nicky giggle, and I would often describe how the obnoxious Albert ended up getting munched by the lion.

I only included them when I knew that his amusement would not cost us dearly by attracting our father's attention.

"Tam. I want to go back. Then maybe it would be alright."

"You want to go back? I'm never going back, Bugs."

"No, I wish we could go back to *then*."

We walked on quietly, our footsteps echoing as the light faded. The hedges were overgrown, yet to be trimmed back from their summer growth. Nicky stuck his hand out, dragging his fingers through the browning leaves and branches.

"Tam, I hate it when he does that. Smash smash smash."

He raised his left arm, and brought it down quickly, then his right, then his left, in imitation of our father smashing plates in the kitchen.

"This is not a fucking hotel! You fucking maggots!"

"Nicky, don't say that. We're going away. We'll never

go back, and then we can forget about it all. Don't say what he says!"

On that note, we reached the pillarbox at the top of George's street. Nicky let go of my hand and ran ahead to number 8. He opened the gate into the front garden, ran up the black and red tile path, up the three steps to the door, and poked at the letter box. He was still too short to reach the doorbell.

I closed the gate and latch behind me as George opened the front door. There was an overgrown rosemary bush to the right of it. I associate its distinctive smell with George. The hall light shone out, either side of his tall solid figure. He took in the scene, two cold shivering children, schoolbags on their backs. The girl, barely eight, a sock hanging out from the zip of her bag, red eyes. The boy, a scrawny four-year-old still in school shorts, a bleeding knee, football sticker book in his hand

Without saying a word, George scooped up Nicky and reached for my hand. I remember feeling relief wash over me as soon as we walked into the hall, the door latch clicking shut behind us. The sitting room on the left was warm and welcoming, with a three-bar electric heater and a black-and-white TV in the corner. He took our bags from our backs and set Nicky down on the sofa, then went into the corridor. I sat beside Nicky, put my arm around him. George reappeared quickly with a large white plate.

At the end of the sofa there was a small table, that had only one central leg with three feet at the bottom to balance on. The plate was stacked with thick white sandwiches. Only then did George speak.

"Jam pieces. Eat up."

The sticky sweetness of the jam stuck to the roofs of our mouths. George disappeared upstairs, taking our bags up to the spare room. It would be too cold for us to sleep up there that night as the heating had not been on. When he came back down, he had the bottle of Dettol, a clean white cotton handkerchief and a plaster. He inspected Nicky's knee, and his young patient didn't even stop chewing his sandwich. His trust in that man was absolute.

George was a constant in our lives, especially when we were young. He towered over us like a benevolent giant, smiling indulgently at us, often pulling a hidden toffee out of his pocket, or a clean handkerchief to wipe a snotty nose or teary eyes. That day, once we were fed, watered, and Nicky's wound had been seen to, he lumbered over to his armchair and turned his attention back to the TV. Not to ignore us, but to give us some privacy, because he knew we must have been bad if we had come to his, and that we probably hadn't eaten all day. He pondered the contents of his cupboard and decided that jacket potatoes and baked beans would be a good option for that evening's meal.

He also knew that no good could come out of sending us home to our father that night. He decided to phone Nana, tell her that we were there. That way she wouldn't be caught off guard when Mick appeared in a morose drunken state at her door, demanding to see his children before going through the usual self-castigating rigmarole fretting over us, our wellbeing and his capability as a father.

Those times he dragged us to the flat, he would storm off into the night barely an hour later, leaving us hiding under my bed, holding back the sobs until we heard the door slam. This time, Nicky and I would sleep snuggly on George's living room floor, in front of the three-bar fire, on mattresses made of sofa cushions, under a tent made with a sheet, and wrapped up together, feeling safe.

We munched our sandwiches. Nicky was engrossed

in the film on the television. George had gone to the hall. I heard the dial of the phone click round. I didn't think he would call Mick. Before I could picture somewhere to run to, he was greeting Nana.

"They're here. They're alright. Shaken. They can stay the night."

I exhaled. I hadn't realised I was holding my breath. He lowered his voice. I should not be listening. I should watch the programme. He was asking if there was anything more that he could do or should do. It must have been after 4pm as BBC2 was on. He felt that it wasn't right to interfere in a man's raising of his own children. Nicky squirmed beside me, lying down on his stomach. George said he believed that every family needed a strong disciplinarian, and that though Mick may like a drink, there were plenty of good fathers that did. I sat a little straighter.

"He takes it too far. It isn't right."

I leaned back on the sofa cushion. Our mother was not there to bring softness and cuddles to our lives. Mick was too irascible. Ange had left, but Mick did not compensate for the lack of a mother in his behaviour.

George suggested that we could live with Nana. Mick's temper had grown unmanageable through the years.

Maybe Mick too would have preferred to live alone again? It might have helped him find another wife, get settled again.

I couldn't even pretend to watch the television.

He could try to somehow guide Mick's behaviour. He had known him all his life. It wasn't a father and son relationship, certainly not, but perhaps a more avuncular one that might allow him to speak up. After all, they had worked together for a long while, maybe he could bring it up when they were on site, casually and offhand.

George shook his head, knowing that it was not his place. He said he wasn't even our grandfather. There was no one else to bring it up with, and Mick certainly wasn't the sort of man that you'd ask easily.

He hung up the phone. I focused hard on the screen as he came back into the room. He sat down and sighed.

"George, thank you for the yummy sandwiches."

I collected the plate and mugs and took them through to the kitchen. George could hear me run the hot water to wash the plates with. He called through to me.

"Leave them, toots, I'll get them later."

I didn't though.

I watched the water run into the sink, the steam fogging up the cold windowpane. On the left of the windowsill was a milk bottle filled with rinsed milk bottle tops and to the right a shallow tub in which he grew cress because cress and egg sandwiches were his favourite. I squirted some green washing-up liquid into the water and watched the bubbles form. George's breakfast egg cup, spoon, knife, and plate were still sitting on the sideboard. Bugs was happy watching television with George. It was so nice to be somewhere warm and quiet, my hands in hot soapy water. Wash, wash, washing them clean again.

Nicky had only asked for a sandwich. It had been a heavy weekend for Dad. His team had won a game on Friday night. There were others up late with him. He was back at the pub at opening time on Saturday, and Sunday, without having stopped by at home. Fortunately, there had been some bread, eggs and spam in the flat, so I had cooked up a late breakfast on the first day. But by the time he stumbled in through the door on Sunday afternoon, we had not eaten for over twenty-four hours and there was nothing left. Our father was less than pleased to find the cupboards bare, especially as he had drunk away all the money that he had had in his pocket.

Night had fallen, and the light from the kitchen meant my reflection in the hazy steam was ghostly and distorted, my hair hanging around my pointy pale face, and my eyes dark like a panda's. I pulled a growly face back at myself. My face was the only panda-like thing about me because I was a skinny thing otherwise. Nana always said it was as though I had my Dad's skin and hair on my mother's frame, and that Bugs had Dad's frame with Mum's colouring. We didn't even look related.

※

Social services came once.

I wore my best dress. It was green corduroy, with a big yellow marigold embroidered on the pocket and a wide lace collar. I wiped Nicky's face clean, tucked his shirt in, emptied his pockets.

The kitchen was spotless from my thorough morning clean. I sat him at the table with the crayons and some paper. I gave Mick a second cup of strong coffee and sent him for a shower. I had taken his scruffiest clothes out of the cupboard to wash, so that all he had to wear with his navy jumper and brown trousers. He was bleary eyed, but at least he seemed in a reasonable mood. The fresh baked bread I had brought home first thing had given the room a lovely warm smell.

They stayed for about half an hour. Mick gave all the right answers. I don't think that they noticed the broken pane in the kitchen door. If they did, it had not mattered.

They never came back.

1993

It was late November, one of those occasional sunny mornings, when the pavements sparkle with beautiful but fragile and treacherous frost, and the autumn leaves have all been blown away.

The shops were starting to sell Christmas. Lou and I had taken ownership of a bay window in a pub. The ice cube in my rum and coke had almost finished melting, and there was a scummy foam ring two thirds of the way up on Lou's pint glass. We had been too busy talking to have our drinks.

Our silent glacier thawed and cracked the day before, when another wordless after-dinner wash-up around the kitchen was shattered. The interruption was caused by a plate, dropped, slipping wet from a tea towel, and smashing in two uneven halves on the floor. We both leant down to pick them up, and as we did, we bumped heads. We looked at each other, synchronised as we grabbed our heads. We burst out laughing, hard, hysterically, collapsing down on to the floor. Somehow the laughter became tears, then gulps, Lou made a strange barking walrus sound. Back to laughter until finally we ceased, enough to pull ourselves up again, backs against the cupboards.

As the first wave abated, we looked at each other

once more, and I lifted my half-plate, waving it, pulling a face. Lou erupted again. We sat there roaring with manic laughter, exchanging looks and waving the half-plates, renewing the roll of the hysteria until our sides ached, our cheeks were red and sore, wet from the tears that had forced their way out from our eyelids, desperate to escape by any means.

That strange calmness set in, the one that sometimes sneaks in after such an eruption.

I noticed that Lou's eyes were flecked with gold, and he leant forward, holding my gaze, until we both gently shut our eyes at the last moment possible and he kissed me on the mouth, lips against lips.

Then, I moved my head to his shoulder, and on the cool floor hugging, holding each other we both finally found our tear ducts, no remote control needed. For the first time since the funeral, Lou slept on the sofa that night.

In the morning, Lou made me a cup of coffee, putting it in front of me at the table as I came into the kitchen and greeted me with a solid, "Good morning, did you sleep well?" I had slept, truly slept, and that was an improvement. To say I had slept well would be a stretch.

For a short while we chatted about the quality of sleep, about toast, that my toaster was surely the most unreliable toaster in the northern hemisphere. We talked about the magnets on my fridge, the shelf full of cookery books.

We filled the silence that had numbed the rooms for the last few weeks, words spilling out of us. Yet we avoided anything that could link us to our feelings or to the blonde boy that had left us.

We talked all morning, and exhausted every item that could possibly be discussed, everything that could be invoked without emotion, and so we went out, discussing the importance of wrapping up warmly, the fact that the gritting bins in the street hadn't been filled yet, that the shops looked cheerful with their Christmas decorations up, and while they seemed to put them up earlier and earlier every year they brightened up the streets as the nights drew in.

We walked and talked the daylight away, unable to stop the words from spilling out. I noticed that I was cold, hungry and that the streetlights were starting to seem bright against the fading sky. We were near the 'Arms, which always did have nice pies, and so we went in, still chattering, skin tingling from the day in the cold air.

We ordered, we sat, we talked, we ate, we discussed our food until finally there we were, warm, fed. The words were done.

At last.

Lou's eyes were bright, and his face flushed. I could feel mine was too. He looked better than he had for a long time, even though he was very thin, and his eyes were hooded by weeks of bad sleep and little food. I must have looked like that too. I stubbed out a cigarette in the solid plastic brewery ashtray, grinding out the end on a black misshapen scab were someone else had let their cigarette burnt too long. As I blew out a large puff of smoke, Lou took my hand and looked me in the eyes.

"I loved him. He knew I loved him."

"He did. He loved you too, Lou. He loved you."

1975

"That bitch. She thinks she can walk out. Fucking leave me. Just like that. With the brats."

Standing in the kitchen, Mick ranted at the note on the table, periodically banging his fist off the sideboard.

My brother was only three, and I was seven, and we were tucked away in bed, at this early hour of the morning when he had stumbled back home.

He dragged a chair out and slumped into it, allowing his head to sag down onto the kitchen table, arms hanging limply by his sides. His shoulders started to quiver, to shake. He took a loud breath, held it, and then exhaled. He did this twice more.

With his third exhalation, he bunched his hands into fists, and sat up, letting the air rushing from his lungs become a roar. His fists slammed onto the table, making a thunderous noise. Upstairs, his toddler son whined in his bed, already knowing that crying was not the safest option.

Mick stood up, the chair scraping back, and he stomped out of the kitchen, past the broken pane in the kitchen door, along the hall, grabbing his coat off the hook. He wrenched the door open, stepped out into the pre-dawn chill, and locked the door behind him, without a thought for his two sleeping children.

He locked us in.

He did not think about us for another week.

If he did, he chose not to do anything about the fact that he had abandoned us, alone, motherless, and foodless, locked in the flat.

At least this is how I assume it happened.

※

Nana came to find us three days later and took us back to her house. We stayed there for a while before Dad appeared to find us – maybe a week or two. I'm not sure.

One evening, I heard his voice in the living room. I snuck down the stairs and peered in. There he was. He smiled at me. I hesitated. He looked clean. He had shaved. His clothes smelt fresh. His eyes were red because they were sad, not angry. The only wild thing was his hair. He had not put a hat on when he came here.

He looked at me and gestured me over. I was happy he was there. He pulled me onto his lap and held tight.

I remember his chest starting to shake and it was not long before he was sobbing.

"Tam, my little girl. I am sorry, so sorry. It's all my fault. You and Nicky are going to grow up without a mum. I miss her. I should not have let her leave. She loved me. She did everything she could for me. I pushed her away. I should have done everything to make her stay. She's such a good woman. My angel."

He continued to repeat this until Nana came back and pried me from his arms, saying it was my bedtime. I'm not sure how long he stayed that evening, but it was a few more days until he came back to take us to the flat.

I knew then that Mummy was never going to come back.

I told Nicky an elaborate story.

I said that she was an angel who had come to give us life, but that she had to fly away. I told him that she loved him very much, and that he should be good, because she would know wherever she was. Maybe she might come back if we were good. I added a great many details to the story, like where she was and what she was doing. I told it to him over and over down the years, repeating it often, probably for myself, because that was what I wanted to believe. If he believed, maybe I could too.

For a long time, Nicky spoke of Mum dying. He would tell of how, as a toddler, he had seen his mother for the last ever time in an open coffin, at her wake, her blonde hair arranged over her shoulders, even though I told him she had left us. He would say no, Tammy, no, Mum died. You said she was an angel.

He would draw her, sometimes alive, but mostly as an angel above us. As his skills improved, he drew her in many ways. He drew her in the coffin. That was the memory he polished and carried. I don't think he ever truly believed that she was still alive, though we spoke of her coming back.

Once he asked:

"Did he kill her? Do you think Dad killed her?"

I left that one hanging.

1993

"Nicky, I don't know what to do. What am I doing here, again?"

I was back at my brother's graveside. I had been struggling to sleep since I had found the letter. I could not get my head around it. Any of it.

I looked at the silvery lines on my forearms, the puckered pink marks, the fresh brown scabs.

"Maybe you were right all along. Is Ange dead? You must know, wherever you are? Are the three of you together, happy at last without me?"

I picked at a fresher scab. It was barely enough to pull my focus back. I tried to picture Nicky, Mick and Ange. Together. I could not. The puckered edges of the brown clot. My nerve endings tingled. The letters. Why did Nana have them? Could Mick have sent them to cover up that she was dead? Why would he do that? Maybe Nana had been asking questions. Surely Nana would know her son's handwriting.

I was going crazy.

Ange left because of me.

She was not dead.

I was the hellbaby.

Mick, I mean Dad, told me that more than once. He made sure I knew it. I broke her. He had loved her. He had tried to get her back. To whip her back into shape. It couldn't be done. The perfect girl. Nicky almost fixed her. He was the good baby. He lit her up. He wasn't enough though. He knew that.

"You knew it, didn't you, Nicky? You weren't enough and I was too much. I should have been the one to go. I'm so sorry."

I could feel the sobs squeezing the bottom of my lungs, my ribcage contracting in great gulps, forcing out bellows of poison.

I squeezed my fists tight, the nails digging in. I forced my hands open. My right hand made its way up my left sleeve to pick at the biggest scab. The edges pinched. Pricks of red started to ooze.

The whiteness came over my mind.

The clarity returned.

I sniffed hard. I pulled my right hand back before the feeling took over, and used my sleeve across my nose, my cheek. Nicky chose to go. Ange ran away, from Mick. I knew what he could be like. Mick died of a heart attack, of an abused body.

I took three deep breaths. Steadied myself. I needed to work through these thoughts.

If Mick had killed her, it was true that I would never know. He was dead. I had worn him down. I was too much in the end. Maybe that's why he always called her his "angel" because he knew she was dead. Had he planted the letter to cover it up?

No. He wouldn't, he couldn't, it served no purpose. The writing was definitely hers. Her goodbye note was singed on the inside of my eyeballs.

Could Nicky have written the letters? He was good at imitating handwriting; he was good at anything artistic. But why would he do that? To prove to himself she was dead? To give me comfort? To see if Nana would go to look for her?

No, none of that made any sense at all.

The letters had to be real. And if they were, then Nana had hidden them from us, all this time. Nana who had always been there for us, who knew what Mick could be like. Who had held me when I had sobbed in her arms, wiped Nicky's bleeding nose. Had George, with his homemade jam sandwiches and his hours in the garden, known all along that she had always been lying to us?

Reality wobbled all around me. Nana had known all along that my mother was alive, she knew where she had been, and that she was looking for us.

The realisation detonated in my mind. The flash of a bomb.

The memories I had built exploded. As the debris landed, my mind grasped at the facts.

Nana had given up two children, struggled with the third.

George could not step in. Nana had to raise Mick herself. She did not marry George because she was afraid it would push Mick further away.

In the rubble of my childhood, I saw Ange and Mick, teenagers having fun. Ange abandoned by her parents. I had finally got an answer from Nana. She said it was easier to tell us our maternal grandparents were in Australia than the fact they lived one neighbourhood over. By the time we were old enough to know, Ange had left.

Nana thought she was protecting us by upholding the lie.

Had they ever been curious and come to see us playing in the park? Had I crossed them in the street? Could my grandfather have been the stern old man who grumbled whenever the lady at the duckpond bench gave us sweets? If they were, I did not want to know. They had made their choice.

Ange too had made her choice.

She did not want to know us.

I choked back a sob. The scab on my wrist was bleeding. I knew I should not pick. I thought of the paring knife in the kitchen.

Nana wanted us only if we were neat, tidy, bleached clean by lies.

Nicky had realised this. He had come to the truth in his own way. He thought he could never deserve love.

I looked at Nicky's headstone.

"*visionary*"

Not in the way they all thought.

I needed to find a different way through this.

First, I needed to sift through the debris of memories and rebuild the truth.

1993

I sat across the table from Nana, between us was the china teapot, the one with the broken handle, chipped spout and the crack in the belly that had been mended at least half a dozen times, with glue, with string, and, most recently, with superglue.

It would break again.

George was out, some DIY-based errand that was an excuse to leave Nana and I to talk properly for the first time since Nicky's funeral.

I glossed over some of the facts that Lou had shared with me. Nana knew that Lou had had a special status in Nicky's life, but did not want or need to know the exact nature. She knew well enough that her grandson had not been a quiet boy.

Nana had reached for my hand at that point.

"I thought if I gave him some room, he would settle. I thought maybe he needed to burn off all that young man's energy. Tam, you know what boys are like, they need space to grow."

"Like Dad?"

That had been mean of me. I knew as the words left my mouth that I had cut right to the quick.

"I don't know how we got here. But now it's you and me. And George."

I paused for a moment. Our eyes met. Nana swallowed and nodded for me to go on. She knew I had the shares from the Sugar Factory. I had the means to go.

"Nana! The letters. From Ange, my mother. Why didn't you tell me?"

She glared at me for what felt like forever. I could feel the anger bubble deep down, my jaw clenching. Her eyes bore into mine. I wanted to scream her betrayal in her face.

I stared back.

I was not her Tam in that moment. She was not Nana. She was a thin-lipped old crone, lines around her eyes squeezing into glare, a witch casting a spell.

I knew that look. Dad had worn it. Nicky had worn it. She had made up her mind. She would not tell me about the letters. I could feel the anger boiling up. She would not help me find my mother.

I would not be cowed. Not this time. I fought the urge to make a peace offering. I could not jeopardise whatever it was she might produce. I could not blink. I had to hold fast.

Abruptly, she pushed back her chair and walked out of the kitchen. I reached for my navy leather handbag, flicked the clasp open and took out my pack of cigarettes. I didn't usually smoke in front of Nana, especially not in her house, but this was an exception, like after a funeral. I realised my hand was shaking as I lit up. As I eased my thumb off the gas trigger bit, I heard the drawer of the sitting room desk grumble shut and put the lighter down on the table.

Nana came back into the kitchen, wearing her glasses now. She frowned at the smoke as I exhaled.

Nana put a single sheet of paper on the table in front of me without a word.

I knew that handwriting well. It was the writing of

the note my mother left on the night she gave up. I had read it time after time, stroked it with love and yearning or crumpled it in sorrow and anger, always smoothed and folded before storing it in my hiding place in the hollow bedpost under the loose bed knob until the words had faded and all I had was the memory of her parting words to my father.

For the second time in as many weeks, I had these new words from my mother. Well, not exactly new. The letters were eleven years old, and Nana had obviously read them several times.

I put the cigarette down on my saucer. I noticed Nana come closer out of the corner of my eye. Her face was set and still, the edges of her eyes red. She picked up the cigarette and took a long drag.

With a slight nod, she smoothed down her cardigan and skirt, and walked briskly from the room, breathing out the smoke. I stubbed out the remainder on the tea saucer that Nana had left when she had cleared the table, on purpose, as an ashtray.

Like a diver preparing for a life-changing high dive, I took a deep breath and steeled myself.

Mick,
    I can't do this. I am not coming back. I am not a good mum for Tam and Nicky. Nana does a better job than I ever could. You don't need me. Find someone else. Someone good. I don't deserve them. I don't deserve you.
    Ange

I sat there for a while, holding the letter. It was a different one to the ones I had already found. Nana had decided to keep the others hidden.

I felt the world shake and crumble around me.

I wanted to scream, to bellow across the house, to

chase her with words, chase her with fists and anger and tear it all up.

I could not though. The rage washed over me, through me, but not out of me.

I closed my eyes. Clenched my fists hard.

"What about the other letters, Nana?"

"I'm sorry to say it, Tam, but that is a final farewell note."

After a few deep breaths, I folded the letter back up, and tucked it into the front pocket of my leather handbag. I wanted to scream at her but my voice came out eerily calm.

"You know that isn't true. How could you lie about that? After Nicky. I know you have other letters. I can take time off to look for her. Nana, I'm going to find her, whether or not you want to help."

Resolute silence.

Nana had always known. Through the years. Every time we asked about Ange and she would tell us only distant past. Nothing past her leaving. She never said that our mother was alive. That she still cared. Nana had been there to run to. But she had never tried to fix things. Never given us reassurance. She told me not to ask too many questions. She told Nicky to run along and play.

"Ange, Nana. I need to find her now. She needs to know what happened."

"I don't think that's a good idea, dear. And anyway, I wouldn't know where to start."

My thoughts scattered.

Boys grow straight and strong when properly fed, washed, and given the space. Girls need a firmer hand. Above all else, always understand that it is the girl's fault. Ange should have considered how Mick would feel about her getting a job. A girl should set her face with the shadow of a smile. Ange should have

224

put on lipstick and listened attentively.

Nana had tried to break the mould. It had left her widowed, with two children who called her Aunty. Unable to fully accept love, refusing to let George marry her. Refusing to let us call him Grandpa. She had tried to fit the pieces back together with glue and string, like the teapot.

A family is not made of glue and string.

Nana hid Ange because she could not fit her back into our lives. She hid Davy and Agnes because they didn't fit.

A family has to be held together by love and truth.

I knew what I had to do.

1975

"Nicky is one now, there's no reason why he can't spend the mornings with Nana, and the afternoons with me."

"Suit yourself, Ange. Suit yourself. You always bloody do."

He slammed the door on the way out. I sat on the bottom step and watched Mum smooth her blouse, slip on her coat, and then pat down her hair, carefully tugging her thick fringe over the left-hand side of her forehead, her make-up heavy.

"Now, Tam, honey, I know I've always walked you to school, but you need to be a big girl today. You're seven, and that means that sometimes, especially nice sunny days like today, you can walk with the Ranjeet boys. They'll be here in a minute."

"Mum, I know! You told me twice last night, and I come back from school with them anyway!"

"You're such a clever girl, Tam-tam."

It was the first day of her first "real job", as she called it, as a part-time secretary for Mr Macintyre, a financial adviser. She was fussing about with an excited nervousness that I'd never seen in her before. I was fascinated by it, especially because of her lack of reaction to my father's morning outburst.

"Come here, love. Now, one arm, good girl, and the other? Don't you look smart? My Tammy. Now, let's get your brother. Have you got your school bag? Good girl ... may as well chap the lads out."

She continued to chatter as she laid Nicky in his pram and asked me to open the front door, I stepped out, and she pushed Nicky behind me, turned to close and lock up. She knocked on the Ranjeet family's door, interrupting her stream of words only to kiss me on the forehead, and I could hear her continue talking to my little brother as she pushed him towards the staircase. Kalpesh ran behind her, spinning his arm like he was about to bowl a bouncer at Viv Richards, caught up and picked up the front part of the pram. I could hear her voice drifting back up the stairwell before he got a chance to give her the latest cricket news.

"It's not that we need the money, Mick is such a good provider, but I would like to, you know, bring a bit extra in, and Nana is only down the road, and she is more than happy to look after Nicky. He is such a quiet baby, he rarely ever cries. Mick was right, they do snap out of it once they learn no one is going to come, he is so good with him. Why only the other night ..."

I almost believed her, but even though I was still a girl, I remember that I felt uneasy about her justifications. I was proud of my mum working, but for the few months that she did, somehow, I felt that she would talk a bit too much about it, about how we didn't need the money, about Dad being such a great husband and such a great father, about how it was simply choosing to have a bit more.

Maybe I have now muddled up my memories, but I am certain that it was at this time that we always shared our teabags, ate plain mashed potato, or occasionally boiled carrots, or onion soup. Never any meat, never any pudding, and plain toast for breakfast if we had anything at all. I remember looking forward to break-time at school because the carton of milk would calm my hunger, though sometimes it made me feel sick, especially on the warm days when it was left by the window. I'm sure it was then, because I remember that when Mum left, Dad promised that he would look after us properly, and that he, at least, would feed us right.

He broke that promise too, those first three days that we were by ourselves, locked in.

Halfway through the first day, Nicky started to cry because he was so hungry. I made us both some weak sweet tea. Sweet tea, as there were a couple of tea bags, some sugar, but no milk. There was no food. We didn't eat at all. The two of us were alone. The electricity meter ran out. I pulled Nicky's cot mattress into the living room, and made a tent between the sofa, the wall, and the bookshelf. The same spot that we would eventually call Sofa Toon on our den making days. I brought the pillows and my blankets down from my bed. Later, I also brought the towels down from the bathroom.

At first, I pretended that I was a mummy bird, building a nest for her hatchling. I lined the sofa-nest with the sofa cushions, the bedding, the towels, working up a space for Nicky, and made a space for me to curl myself around him, making it into a story. Every so often, I would kiss my hatchling on the head, and put the kettle on for another cup of sweet weak tea, that we shared. The teabags lost their flavour. The mug was warm and comforting. I helped him to the toilet when he needed to go, but he did have an accident nonetheless. He was only three after all. I carefully cleaned the mess and took the damp sheets to the laundry basket.

There were moments when I could not have been any hungrier, and chewed on one of Nicky's toys, but it didn't help. At least the hunger seemed to fade at times, and I found that drinking water helped, and so I made sure that Nicky had some too. I tried to eat some of the sugar, but it made my mouth feel funny, and I decided that it was better in the tea. I read some of my books to Nicky, but mostly we dozed, cried a bit and I stroked his face. At least it was springtime, and not too cold.

On the third day, I heard the key in the door. I listened carefully, unmoving. No, it wasn't heavy footsteps or slamming doors. I let my breath out. Nana's voice called out, she had come to fetch us. She told me that I had been a good girl, a brave girl. I remember that.

"You'll go home once Dad has had a chance to settle into a pattern," she said.

We stayed with her for about ten days that time.

How could she lie to us all these years?

※

While Mum worked for Mr Macintyre, I would go to Nana's on the way home from school and meet her and Nicky there. Nana would always make something nice for me, like a ham and cheese sandwich, or insist that I eat the leftovers from their lunch. Mum would stroke my hair and say that I had such an appetite for such a skinny runner-bean but would always let me sneak a biscuit or two from the plate on the coffee table into her handbag, for later, after our mashed carrot or whatever she would scrabble together that evening.

I would do my homework on the floor of the living

room at Nana's or at the kitchen table, and then the two of us would walk home, slowly, pushing Nicky's pram. I would sort of hope that Dad would be at home, happy and drowsy, asleep on the sofa or in their room. Often, he wasn't there at all. I nursed that feeling for years, hoping to find it in the spotless calm I tried to create as Mum had every evening back then. Mick did not like mess when he came home.

The week before she had left, Mum had looked more tired than ever. She hadn't been sleeping well, and it made her clumsy, she said. There were red marks, and bright purple bruises, and older bruises fading to yellow on her arms and legs, and rings under her eyes. She had been working for Mr McIntyre, or Mr Mac as she called him, for a couple of years. Or maybe she had only worked there for a few weeks. I do not actually know.

One day, I was upstairs in my room, lying on my tummy reading. I had found a book of Celtic fairy tales in the library and was reading the tale of the Selkies when I heard the door slam. Dad was home early.

"You filthy slut! Where is my money? I know you're stealing my money! I bring home a good paycheque and all I get from you is 'there's none left'."

A low moan, a sob, a thud.

I stopped reading, though I was still staring at the page, I was listening to every word. I'd never heard him be so cruel.

"You fucking bitch, give me my money now."

I lay still in my bed. Was Nicky downstairs? The door slammed again. The Ogre had left. I closed my book, took my blanket and my pillow, and snuck under my bed. I rolled myself into the blanket, and then curled up as best I could. Nicky would be fine. Back then, I knew that the Ogre only ever came after little girls.

The next morning, Mum walked me all the way to school, pushing Nicky in front us in the collapsible nylon pram. She was wearing a pair of trousers and an old jumper, not her usual workwear. She told me she had the day off. She wasn't at Nana's when I got there after school and didn't pick Nicky and I up until after teatime. And the next two days again were the same.

That Saturday morning the house was entirely quiet.

I waited for Mum to get me up once Dad had gone out, which she had taken to doing since he had started going out late on a Friday and feeling poorly on Saturday mornings.

There was not a sound in the house, and I could feel my bladder starting to ache. I opened my bedroom door cautiously and looked towards my parent's bedroom. The door was open, and I could see from the reflection in the cupboard door mirror that the bed was unmade and empty. I snuck out to the toilet, locking it behind me. Once I'd been, I was on my way back to my room, but it was so strangely quiet. I snuck a look from the top of the stairs into the living room. No-one.

I tiptoed down the stairs, and inspected the living room, the kitchen and even the cupboard under the stairs.

On the kitchen table, there was a scrawled note. I picked it up and read it. Time froze.

I stood for a while, holding the note in my hand, and then I put it back on the table. I went to the sink, took a cup from the drying rack, filled it with water, and took three big gulps.

My feet felt cold. I decided to go back to bed. I put the cup down on the sideboard, walked past the table and the note, out of the kitchen, along the hall and up the stairs. I got back into bed. I closed my eyes tight, willing myself back to sleep. Maybe I was still asleep, and I would wake up and the note wouldn't be true. So, I lay very still, squeezing my eyes shut, clenched, every muscle tight.

A clear white pain started to rise from the centre of my palms, where my nails dug in. I focused on it, and it alone, I held on to it tightly, the tops of my fingers exerting themselves. I focused on the points of the pain. Four individual points, like bright stars. I could feel my knuckles strain to white. I grasped tighter. My shoulders, the top of my arms were tense, but my mind was clear, and I could feel my fists start to shake with the effort of holding on to the focus points in my hands. I took a deep breath in, and I realised that I was sobbing.

My face felt hot, and then I let the breath out slowly. I opened my eyes and looked up at the ceiling. There were white pinprick stars, somehow brighter than the white ceiling.

I took another deep breath and uncurled my hands.

My fingers were sore, tight.

I bent my deadened arms up to my face,

I scraped my hair back.

I raked my fingers hard across my scalp.

I rubbed my eyes.

At this point, I noticed a sound, coming through from the next room, a wailing, like an animal.

It was Nicky, he was awake. I listened for a few breaths, feeling myself centre on the sound. Nicky didn't usually cry in the morning, and when he did, Mum was quick to get him to quieten down. And then I realised the truth of it. She wasn't there anymore. Dad wasn't in. Nicky was alone and he needed me. I got out of bed and went next door. He was lying on his back in his crib, which he was far too big for, aged three, and he was surrounded by the wooden bars.

I would need to get him out to help him, but it was too high for me to reach in and down to lift him out. And he was so upset, I wouldn't be able to talk him through climbing out using any sort of step. Perhaps I could make a pile of books?

At that point, I remembered that the front of the crib sort of slipped out, making it into a three-sided bed, because Mum would open it up to put him to bed and tell him stories, before pulling it up at night, presumably so that he wouldn't get out by himself in the mornings.

I cooed at my little brother, reaching in to stroke his arm and face. I told him that I was going to get him out and tried to get him to talk back to me. I fiddled with the latches to loosen them.

All he did was look at me for a moment, and then he started to truly scream, going red in the face, snot and tears streaming, thrashing, and throwing himself about his wooden cage. I looked at him and pulled my arm back. He was a raging animal. I looked towards the door and stood up. I was terrified. Completely overwhelmed. Ready to run away. I took a few steps, and as I put my hand on the handle, the wailing lessened, Nicky gulped, and stifled a sob.

"Tammy."

He said my name. I remember that moment so clearly because I have revisited it so many times in my life. He fought his anger and fear and reached for my name. I wish I could say that I had turned back to help my brother immediately. Maybe this moment is the one that scarred him forever. It could have been me.

It was me.

He needed me.

Nicky pulled himself back to a sitting position and then stood up. He stared at me, his face a bright puce colour.

I wrenched open the bedroom door, ran across the landing and down the stairs, as fast as I could. I grabbed the door handle to the front door and pulled hard on it. Nothing, it was locked. I pulled it again, and then reached into the bowl that sat on the shelf above the hall radiator, under the mirror. The bowl was empty, there were no keys in it. I ran my hand along the shelf, knocking the empty vase over. It rolled off the shelf and somehow only bounced on the door mat without breaking. I turned back to the front door.

I could hear my brother howling upstairs.

I grabbed the handle and heaved on it, willing it to open. I shook it desperately. I pushed my right hand through the letterbox and wiggled my fingers. I wasn't thinking about drawing attention or finding a way to open the door, I needed to get out so badly that somehow that seemed to be the way. The flap was pressing into me. I tried to pull my hand back, but I could feel it dig in to my wrist. The wailing from upstairs continued. I balled my hand into a fist, the edge of the letterbox flap cutting, pressing deeper and harder into my skin.

I started to panic, I seem to remember that I screamed out, but then I focused on the cutting agony in my wrist. I took a deep breath in, then out. I counted, at first fast, but then managed to focus on my breaths and slowed my counting, and talked myself back to a calmer state. I willed my hand open, one finger at a time and then carefully, so as not to trap my left hand, pushed the bronze metal flap open from the inside. The pressure loosened, and I pulled my hand back in, scraping my skin as it came back through. It smarted, the top layer was grazed off, and tiny white peeled bits of skin stuck up. I stared at it. There was a vivid red line where the skin had lifted, and the skin under it looked almost purplish.

Nicky was still crying upstairs. I leaned against the door and sank onto the floor. I stared at the steps. I would have to go up and help him. He couldn't stay there by himself, in his cage of a crib. I kicked the fallen flower vase to the side and it rolled under the radiator. I stood up, took a deep breath, raked my hair back, and went upstairs to help my three-year-old little brother.

I told him stories over the next three days, as many as I could remember or make up, while I was pretending to be his mummy bird. I told him that Mum had always been an angel destined to leave that had to fly away for now and that she would be back soon, with lots of lovely things for us, and not to worry.

At some point over those three days, I took her note from the kitchen table. My bedstead was hollow and one of the bed knobs could unscrew, leaving a tube-shaped space that I used to hide things in, and it was there I secreted away her note. Over the next fifteen years, I read it so often that the paper took on the texture of a frail piece of cloth, and the writing faded to silver filigree, but I knew every word by heart, it was seared into my memory:

> Mick – You win. I can't do this. I am nothing. I can give them nothing. I can't even feed them. I cannot care for them. Nana will help, I'm sure. I am sorry – Ange.

1982

There was a warm smell of cheese and ham that wafted through the house from the kitchen.

A couple of weeks before, in Home Ec, I'd learnt how to make a pasta bake, and with the housekeeping money that Dad now gave me every week, I'd bought the ingredients the previous weekend, knowing they would last until Friday night, and now I made the dish following the instructions precisely. There would be four generous portions, two for Nicky and I that evening and enough left over so that there was another meal, and even a little to snack on.

Finally, I popped it under the grill. Nicky had come into the kitchen, a big smile on his face. He was about nine then, tall for his age, and lanky. Skinny even. He put his drawing book and pencil down on the table, open and showing a battle scene between two heavily plated and bleeding dinosaurs. I thought the background jungle looked rather nice.

"That smells amazing, Tammy."

"Ta, Bugs. Hope you like it."

"Did you know that a blue whale can measure more than one hundred feet and is the biggest ever living animal ever known to have existed. And when it breathes, it spouts water up to thirty-nine feet.

Thirty-nine feet, Tam! That is taller than you and me and Nana and George all together."

I grinned and handed him some cutlery and napkins which he put on the table, and then I filled the jug with tap water, and put a small glass at each place setting. We always liked to lay the table properly when it was the two of us. I picked up the oven gloves that were hanging over the back of the chair, opened the oven door, knelt down and carefully pulled the hot dish out of the oven. Nicky was standing beside me. He made a big show of licking his lips and rubbing his tummy. I put it on a heat mat on the sideboard, a few inches to the right of the cooker, and then I dished up a hearty portion each. It was perfect. It looked almost like the one that Mrs. Langley had made in class.

We both ate and chattered about all sorts of things. Nicky had got a book of facts from the library and was full of information and excitement. We didn't go round to Nana and George's as often now. I was fourteen, and plenty of other girls my age looked after younger siblings on occasion. Not as often as I did. It was easier to stay home, the two of us, no need to explain ourselves with increasingly far-fetched reasons or acknowledge that look Nana gave us when she thought we weren't looking. It was a lot easier still not to have to deal with the drama of coming home to Dad.

At that time Nicky liked to be out and about with some of the slightly older boys who lived in the area. I certainly wasn't going to stop him from going out when he wanted to. It meant that he was out of the way and I could clean the house on Saturday morning. We had fallen into a comfortable pattern, meals together on weekday evenings, homework at the kitchen table. I would shop and cook, Nicky would wash up, take the bins out, and at the weekend we would have lunch together. Dad came and went on his own whim, often leaving before we had even got up, coming back once we'd gone to bed.

Looking back, I remember enjoying those meals when Nicky and I were alone.

That time, as we were finishing up, we heard the keys in the door. We froze and looked at each other. About five seconds elapsed and then I swallowed my mouthful, and winked at Nicky. I urged him to continue:

"So, the sea cucumber?..."

"Hello, my dumplings!"

"Hi Dad!"

I looked up at my father. His eyes were clear. He was clean shaven and not swaying. His clothes were neat. He seemed to be in a good mood and relatively sober. I felt my shoulders relax. Nicky had also picked up on this and loaded his fork again.

"That smells really nice, Tam-tam. Shame I've already eaten. What is it? No, don't get up, pet. I'll wash up, you two go out and play."

I refused his offer with a bright smile and fussed him into the living room. I put his slippers down by his feet as he settled onto the sofa. He insisted that Nicky join him and I listened to my little brother repeat to him some of those facts I'd heard, albeit with considerably less excitement.

After a while, Dad fell sound asleep on the sofa, snoring loudly, and he didn't wake up until after Nicky and I had had a wash and gone to bed. The next morning, though, I got up to find that he had left early and having obviously had a portion of my pasta bake for breakfast, he had left a note that read "TAM – DELICIOUS". I felt a buzz in the pit of my stomach, a pride, a fluttering caged bird of joy. I'd made Dad happy and he was proud of me.

For the next couple of weeks Dad was home more often in the evenings. He was calmer, happier, and more approachable. I decided to make the bake again. Dad had announced on the Thursday night that he would eat with us on Saturday lunch time. He wasn't in that Saturday morning, but I buzzed with excitement nonetheless, sure that he would be back for lunch. He'd never made that promise before, maybe he had finally settled into a pattern. I hoped this was the turning point.

After I had finished tidying up my breakfast – I was always up first – I ran upstairs, had a bath, and washed my hair. Once I was dressed, I got Nicky up and helped him to tidy his room. Then, while Nicky washed, I stripped both of our beds and Dad's. I took three clean sets from the cupboard and made up our beds, and put the sheets in the laundry bag. I emptied the contents of laundry basket into a second one.

Once Nicky was dressed, I gave him the two bags of laundry, the money for the launderette, and enough extra so that he could buy himself a drink or some sweets on his way back. He would spend a few hours with his friends, be back for lunch and then go out again.

I took the cleaning bucket out from under the stairs and went up to clean the bathroom. I put some bleach around the inside of the rim of the toilet, and whilst I left it to work, I scrubbed the bath, the sink and the surfaces, and when I was sure that they were clean, I picked up the toilet brush and scrubbed it too. I cleaned the bedrooms, pushing the furniture out of the way to clean underneath. Once I was done, I went downstairs with the bucket and dusted the living room, and hoovered the carpet, and dusted the radiator shelf. Finally, I cleaned the kitchen. Once I was done, I made a mental note to ask Nicky to take the bin out after lunch.

I had about an hour and a half before I thought Dad might be back. I hoped that he would notice that I worked hard at the cleaning and be happy. Maybe he might stay for the afternoon, and we could go for a walk in the park. It was a nice day, we could stop at Nana's on the way home. She'd give us biscuits and tea, and we could watch a show on the television, all together. The prospect made me buzz with happy anticipation.

I got the ingredients out of the fridge. I hummed as I assembled the bake, remembering to put the oven on to heat up when I was about halfway through the process. I laid the table for three and filled the water jug. The sunlight came in through the window, and it looked perfect.

There had been a stain on the carpet by the stairs, from one of Dad's recent nights out, but last Saturday I spent most of the day scrubbing and bleaching it, and now there was a slightly off-colour patch where it had been. I decided that if Dad did not stay for the afternoon, I would scrub and bleach the rest of the beige carpet. I did not mind that my hands got sore, and red, and that my nails were all short and stubby – it was better than the stain. There were often other marks, scuffs, breakages, and I sorted them all out. Part of me hoped no one noticed at all, because that would mean I had done a good job, but then, I also hoped someone would notice the work that I had done, but only sometimes. Most of all, I hoped that if I could get rid of all the marks, then it would be as though they had never been there at all.

My planning and pondering was interrupted by a ping from the oven timer telling me that the bake was ready. I held it in my ovengloved hands when I heard the front door burst open and slam shut.

My father, unsteady on his feet, filled the hall. He shrugged out of his coat and rocked on his heels and then back to his toes as he tried to hang it on the coat pegs. I stared at him as he tried and failed repeatedly until the tray bake felt hot even through the oven gloves. I placed it on a mat.

"Tammy! Chef Tammy Tam!"

He burst out laughing, and stepped towards me, but he lost his balance, to his right, into the radiator shelf. It would always tip forward at an odd angle after that day. He seemed to bounce off and forward, into the banister. He moved like the flat was a ship in a heavy swell. Right hand to the wall. He reached for the other side of the narrow hall but crumpled as his legs gave way. He swore loudly and floundered to get upright.

"Well don't stare, you silly cow, help me up!"

I moved towards him as though through water, not sure how I should react.

"Dad, are you alright? Are you hurt?"

"I'm fine, get on with it, help me up."

He gripped my arm, so tight that it hurt, and pulled himself up. I almost buckled under his weight. We staggered toward the kitchen, his arm awkwardly around my shoulders, and him limping.

"You left your bloody fucking shoes in the hall again."

By the time we reached the kitchen table, he was gripping my shoulders, so hard that I could feel his fingers on my bones, and when he let go to lower himself into the kitchen chair, I staggered as my feet grounded themselves again. I stumbled up to the counter, breathing deeper now that I was away from him. He smelt stale, of cigarettes, of beer, a hard liquor sweat.

With his left hand he fumbled at his shirt pocket,

rummaged inside it, pulled out a cigarette and put it in his mouth. In his right hand, he held up a lit lighter which wavered back and forth as he tried to focus. After half a dozen attempts, he managed to light up.

He took a deep drag and looked at me hard. He let out a great puff of smoke, like an ancient dragon, and then he ashed on the plate. He had that mean glint in his eyes.

"You like playing mother, don't you? You want to be Ange."

There was something different about his behaviour. He was not angry.

He was not shouting, throwing the words like spears.

He was speaking in a steady low voice, almost growling some of it.

"You can't be my wife."

I would not give him the satisfaction of seeing a reaction, so I turned to stop him from seeing my chin tremble.

I gulped for air twice, and opened the utensil drawer, looking for a serving spoon for the pasta bake. I would ignore what he had said, get out a clean plate for him, and everything would be fine. I told myself to stay calm and started to cut into the bake with the edge of the serving spoon.

Before I knew what was happening, he was out of the chair, fast as a striking snake, and holding my head back by my hair against his chest.

His voice was calm, steel.

"She was pathetic, useless. You are just like her."

He pushed my face forward. Into the bake. Nose. Left cheek. So hot against my skin. My face starting to glow red.

I kept my eyes squeezed shut. Barely managed to hold my head up out of the cheese. Not my chin.

He grabbed my hair hard in his fist. I felt a clump sting. He was going to rip it out. He pulled me back. Swooped his other arm across the sideboard. The bake tray fell off onto the floor. The pasta slopped onto the floor.

"Clear this mess up."

He seemed to float out of the kitchen.

I stood there, hot cheese on my face, dazed. I noticed that his cigarette was lying, still smoking, on the plate. I pulled the kitchen towel from the oven handle where it hung and wiped my face. I have no idea why, but I took a drag from the cigarette. The smoke filled my mouth, but I coughed before I was able to inhale.

My throat was a red-hot poker.

My eyes were stinging with the smoke.

I crushed out the cigarette onto the plate.

I went to the sink, splashed cold water on my face, on my wrists, and then I took the washing-up sponge and put a few drops of green washing-up liquid on it. I ran it under the hot tap and squeezed it a few times to make it bubble. Leaning forward over the sink, I scrubbed my face as hard as I could.

It stung in the soapy liquid. I scrubbed my hands as hard as I could, until they were red and stinging too. Then I leant forward and sipped some water from the tap, which I gargled, and spat out.

I spat it out.

I repeated this several times over, until my mouth felt odd, damp but saliva-less.

I gripped the edge of the sink, and watched the water coming out of the tap for a long while before turning off the tap.

Assessing the bake tray slopped on the floor, I decided that at least two small portions could be rescued from the dish for Nicky and me for lunch. I knew that it was unlikely that Dad would be giving me any housekeeping money that week. He certainly would not be back for at least twenty four hours. I needed to salvage any food that I could. Fortunately, I had taken to carefully budgeting meals every week and putting aside what small change I had. I estimated that we could probably manage for about ten days if we were careful, and we could probably eke that out if we went around to Nana's once or twice. Any more often than that and she'd want us to stay with her. We loved staying with Nana, but she would know why, and then she and George would exchange those looks. They would be disappointed.

I didn't want them to be disappointed.

I didn't want them to feel that they had to put up with us.

1993

"All right all right! I'll tell you! John Major!"

"No, no! NO? really?"

Becky doubled over in hysterics. My cheeks were aching as I gasped for breath.

"With teeny tiny t-rex arms?"

"Yep!"

"That's crazy. And Princess Di?"

We didn't often get stoned. We would go out dancing after pay day, and sometimes to our local pub The Keys, but mostly we stayed at the flat, watching videos on our Radio Rentals TV or studying. I didn't like not being in control. However, smoking pot was something to do at the weekend, and Nicky would come by every so often, and leave us a wee bag.

Becky took a big hit of the joint and passed it over. The cherry fell off the end and I shrieked though it landed on the counter and rolled onto the floor without any damage. Dramatically I poured a whole glass of water on it and we dissolved into hysterical giggles.

The air had cleared from our row.

She had been spending so much time with Steve recently. She had stayed with him while Lou and I shared our grief. I was so glad when she came back, but we had gone to the pub. I had too many pints. I had told her about the letters. About going away. She had held my hair when I threw up but I knew she was hurt.

Two days later it had erupted. Becky had been out with her other friends. I felt like a fish out of water with them and had made excuses. She had slammed the door on her way out. They had only wound her up more. I don't know what we shouted about. We both needed to let it out.

I finally agreed with her that Nana was not all she seemed, could not be trusted. Becky went to have a shower. She came back in her pyjamas, waggling the bag of weed at me.

I grinned and nodded. We needed a distraction. A last night together.

It was time for me to go. I had started to feel like a fish out of water with her too.

)(

The next morning, my head felt like it had been stuffed with cotton, but I finally had the courage. The laughter of the night before was the ballast I needed.

"One way?"

The travel agent repeated it back at me. I nodded.

"Without a visa they won't let you in on a one way."

"How do I get a visa? Aren't there waivers?"

"Not for a one way. No, you'll need a job or a sponsor."

"Fine. Book the cheapest return ticket you can find. I don't care when for."

"Ok. Now would you prefer a morning or an evening flight?"

"Whichever is fine."

"Window or aisle?"

I sighed and answered the questions. The travel agent rolled her eyes. I ignored it. I wanted it done. It was time.

Two days later, Becky waved me off at the airport. We were both hungover and hugged each other tight, the tears dealt with the night before. She would go and tell Nana later.

"You'd better write to me all the fucking time. Don't they say "write me!" over there?"

I grinned and traced the word "me" on her shoulder with my finger. We both grinned but the emotions were bubbling again.

"Go! Go, you silly old bean. This is absolutely what you need. Braw adventures. Go. I'll see you at Christmas."

With a last hug, I turned and made my way towards my gate. Raising my arm above my head I gave her the finger, backwards, just as we always had since we were about fifteen.

I spent that Christmas in San Diego with a naval cadet.

1993

The air seemed to change to heavy yellow as soon as the landing gear dropped. I peered out of the window trying to sight the coastline where only a horizon of buildings stretched out below me. I knew nothing of this city of angels save what I had learnt from the films. It would be almost eight years before I got back on a plane and left the USA.

Though I had a new Walkman, I kept the headphones round my neck while I made my way through passport and visa control, as my ears felt hot and red. My eyeballs were itchy and dry. Even though I knew I had nothing to hide, the Alsatian walking up and down the line of arrivals made me feel nervous. I wriggled my toes in my new trainers. I was self-conscious in my clothes.

Becky and I had been on a big shopping spree the day before my flight. My whole life scraping by, counting every penny, and somehow now I owned a flat and had a steady income from Nicky's art, alongside the money I'd saved working. I insisted on buying a few gifts for Becky and gave her my share of a whole year's rent in advance. All my stuff was new. I felt strange and other.

A lady with an impressive chestnut beehive at

the airport information desk chewed gum as she untangled my clueless questions with sympathy. She gave me the card of a hostel somewhere in the foothills of the city and pointed me in the direction of a taxi rank.

"Always keep a five-dollar bill in your wallet, honey. You never know when you'll need it."

I stared through the taxi window. It was all so alien and so familiar at the same time. The airport palm trees leading onto the freeway. The bleached grey road and pavements, the bright shop fronts, and breeze block walls. The enormity of it. The mountain behind the city. I had seen it all in film, and yet I was so unprepared for Los Angeles.

Over the next few days, I walked down Rodeo Drive, saw Mann's Chinese Theatre, and read the stars on the Walk of Fame. I saw the neon of Capitol Records. I rode the rides in Pacific Park. I hung out on Long Beach and read for hours on the beach walls. I tried tacos. Wandered Little Korea and Little Armenia. Ate a donut from a donut shaped building. Nestled into a corner of Downtown Central Library's marble staircases and pastel murals. Noticed all sorts of different types of streetlamp, and the delicious scent of jasmine in the evening. The light would go pink gold at sunset, and I found a spot where I could eat ice-cream and watch the light twinkle off the sea.

In 1992, there was a tension in Los Angeles. Most people were friendly towards me, the pale translucent stranger from a land of perpetual cloud. They offered advice, recommended places to go. Told me to stay safe. That it was no place for me alone. In between all the "I love your accent" and "are you from Ireland?", there was unease. From the joggers by the beach to the tourist hustlers of the Sunset Boulevard. Go back to the hostel before dark. Always get a taxi. There was trouble coming. The air was wrong. The Rodney King riots had been months before and still loomed large.

I found the jumpiness discombobulating and moved south to San Diego, where I found a hostel I loved. The manager was a particularly nice woman in her late thirties. She organised for me to give English lessons and tours for guests, so I stayed for well over a month. Perched on a beachside wall with my book one day, a shadow darkened my page.

"Excuse me, ma'am, do you have lighter?"

He noticed I was not from the US, and so we got chatting, and chatting became a wander along the promenade, became a soda, and eventually we were dating. He was a naval cadet, from Houston originally, and we settled into a comfortable rhythm. I found a small flat, an apartment. It was easy. Compared to Sacramento, San Diego was a picnic, but after a few months, the sun was too hot, the nights too sticky for me to lie tangled in the cadet's arms. He kept the apartment and I moved on.

There was a lot of fuss about Seattle being the place to go, but it sounded wet and dreich to me. All the music that came from there was angry and frustrated. It certainly didn't sound like a happy place to be.

Somewhere south of San Francisco, near Monterey, I met a librarian who was a poet by night, reading at various gigs and occasionally as a footnote on the bill for an event, and for a fortnight I stayed with him. He wore a fedora when he performed. I'd gone along to a bar with a few folk from the hostel and spotted him after the show, and in an uncharacteristic moment of bravery went up to him and told him I'd liked his set, even though I couldn't genuinely remember it.

FedoraPoet made me laugh. He would jump on benches and recite Burns poems which he learnt for me. His Scottish accent was horrendous. He borrowed a car and we went down to Big Sur, drove the winding roads. He played the Red Hot Chili Peppers in the car over and over.

He came home one evening after I had turned in for the night and he sat up drinking and smoking weed with his friends. I lay in the bed listening for warning signs. He rolled in happy drunk and cuddly.

The next day, I cleaned his "condo". Every surface was gleaming, reorganised. He was not happy about it. I never told him that I had sat in the empty bath crying that day, looking at my wrists, at the kitchen knife, and digging my nails into the tops of my thighs. He told me I was "fucked up".

It was time to pack up and find a new place.

FedoraPoet had spoken a lot about Napa Valley and so I made my way there.

I met a long-haired dude. He was definitely a "dude", some twenty years older than me. He worked in a vineyard as some sort of soil expert, and taught me about wine. I had never thought of it as a delicacy to be enjoyed slowly, and we sat sipping, chatting and whiling the hours away in the evening sun.

I borrowed a straw hat, and my chest got sunburnt, leaving spaghetti strap white stripes to my shoulders.

I relaxed into it. Maybe this was the life I was looking for.

Then he drank whiskey one night, the strong smell reaching me from the glass which I could not take a sip from.

I curled up in a ball. Sobbed. Wailed all night long. Red-eyed when he left for work, clearly puzzled at my ways, taken aback and unsure of what to say or do.

I sat in the empty bath again for a long while, then next day, before packing and leaving without saying goodbye, or even leaving a note, red marks all the way up my arms, and the sides of my thighs.

Since arriving in the USA, I had lived with three different men in three different towns. San Diego, San Fran, and Napa. I had never had a serious boyfriend before. I had just let myself walk straight in and be rescued off the street. I thought I wanted them to want to save me.

I realised I was too freshly arrived. I needed to get more miles under my belt.

)(

I found my way to the Grand Canyon, an incredible place, with its massive sandstone sides scrubbed clean by aeons. I stayed near there for a couple of months, in Flagstaff where the Amtrak pulled in. I got a job of sorts for a while, though I didn't have a work visa and I didn't actually need the money, helping in a library on a youth reading project.

Often, I sat and read in a local diner over a coffee. I found myself stepping in to help serve when Rosie was understaffed, or tired. She was tired often. We had an arrangement for me to stay in her Airstream, parked up on the back lot.

One evening, a German traveller in a tie-dyed shirt, an amber pendant on a thin black string and a scruffy attempt at a goatee came in. We got chatting and he told me that I absolutely had to go to Zion National Park.

"Zion means heavenly city and you will see why they called it that. It is so inspiring!"

Rosie and one of the regulars chimed in, and over the course of the evening I became convinced that if there was anywhere that I would find some peace of mind, this was the place to go. I spent days getting organised with a tent and hiking gear and set off on a Greyhound bus. As soon as I arrived, I was awestruck by the Emerald Pools and soaring red rock mountains.

That first night camping, huddled in my tent, I felt lonelier than ever. The red sandstone made me think of Glasgow. Of how far I was from there. How ill I had fitted in. There or in the States. Unwanted and awkward. I thought of my life. Inconsequential. There was nothing, no one to tether me to earth. The sky was vast and full of stars. I was an infinitesimal speck. Unneeded. Nothing.

I thought about jumping off one of the pinnacles and may well have done so had I found a way up. I spent a day looking at them, considering whether I would go through with it. A more experienced hiker might have managed to climb one. I thought about never leaving the park and hiding in a natural cave, living off the land for the rest of my days. It was too much.

The beauty of it all, the meaningless of me.

I lasted less than a week. The vastness rejected me. I spent the fifth night in a hostel. I had failed somehow. I was defeated. I lay on the bed for a few hours, staring at the sunlight, a line moving across the ceiling. The light changed, so I got into my pyjamas, headed off to find the bathroom. I hadn't eaten all day. My head spun, tiny flashes spreading across my eyes. The corridor flashed, spun, eclipsed.

"Hey girl! Are you OK? We need to call 911."

"Look, her eyes are opening."

"Sit her up. Yeah. Don't look at me like that, I used to faint at high school, get her up, that's it, right, head between your knees. Anyone got anything with sugar?"

"Not me. Isn't there a machine in the reception?"

I had no idea who was speaking around me. There was a hand on my back. They sounded nice.

"Get some water. Give her some space."

I lifted my head from my knees. There were five or six people around me, looking down anxiously. One was holding out a Twinkie bar. I did my best to smile as I reached for it. I opened it and took a bite. The sweet cake filled my mouth. A bottle of water was passed to me, I dutifully took a swig and went back to chewing on the sponge cake. Embarrassment at being helped by these strangers started to fill me. I didn't know what to say to them.

"I'm OK. Thanks."

"Come girl, we'll help you up. Come to the lounge."

I let them guide me.

There was a reception room, behind it was the room they called the canteen where meals were served, and several rounds of cards and chess played, which led through double doors to a sort of informal bar area, itself opening onto an outdoor space. The walls of the bar area went up to the first floor with an open wooden balcony, like an old-timey saloon, but bereft of charm or nostalgia. Some of the doors to the bunk rooms were off this balcony, as was the bathroom. It was there that I'd fainted. They had heard the thud.

I sat with them, answering their questions. They wanted to know my name and where I was from. I said I was a single child. They were friendly and bright. A coke and some fries appeared in front of me, and I confessed that I hadn't eaten since at least breakfast the day before. They teased and joked, and somehow I ended up sitting up half the night chatting to them, and the next morning, I rose and left with them to Montana for the winter season.

I spent a month learning to snowboard on the crisp mountain snow. I enjoyed the après-ski activities, hooking up with each other, and various other people at the resort. I felt like I was part of the gang. I was happy enough to not simply send Becky a postcard, but to actually call.

It was good speak to her.

Until she asked me: "But how are you really?"

The hollow feeling crept back, and I felt quite small.

"I'm fine. It's great here, I've made some nice pals. I've been learning to snowboard. Oh shit. Is that the time? I have to go. There's a party."

"Tam, you should definitely go to all the parties! Have a great time. Love you!"

"Bye! Love you too."

I hoped I had sounded light, happy, untroubled and untroubling.

I spent that evening in my bunk and realised that I did not want to speak to any of my new friends I had made there. They did not know that Nicky had ever existed. I had referred to "my parents" often, never skipping a beat. I did not want them to know. If they did not know the full story of me, then could they truly be my friends?

The next morning, I waved them off to the slopes, claiming bad menstrual cramps and a headache. I was long gone before they got back that evening.

)X(

It all seems such a whirlwind now.

I remember the key characters and plot lines of my US adventure, but it doesn't feel like my life. I know I lived these memories but unlike some of the other ones which I polished like a river polishes stones, they mean nothing, they are just silt. The way I remember characters from TV shows.

I never ran out of funds as Mick's life insurance from the building company and Nicky's money were enough to live off, especially after one of my occasional calls with Becky, about two years in to my travels, when

I told her she could let my room go at last and put my belongings "wherever the fuck she liked". I simply didn't care anymore. She was glad because Steve had moved in at that point, and they were thinking about finding somewhere bigger anyway. She packed up all my stuff, wrapping up my few ornaments, like my porcelain owl from the jumble sale that Nicky had given me one Christmas. In the end, I am glad she did not bin them. She took them back to the flat and left the boxes stacked in my childhood room.

That spring and summer, I hitched my way across Wyoming and Colorado, stopping in various anonymous one-horse and two-truck towns, never in a straight line, winding my way along. I could not believe how utterly like the movies they were, with big pick-up trucks driven by moustachioed men in ten-gallon hats and boots. I was astounded by how many were carrying guns.

I had become bold in walking up to various homes and ranches, knocking on doors and asking if they had a bed or sofa I could stay on for a few dollars. Almost everyone said yes, every wife fretted over such a "pretty little thang" travelling alone across the country and fed me up with steaks, cobblers, and pie, sat me down on porches, by fireplaces, the old dog. A few places I stayed an extra night or two, went to high-school American football matches, learnt about tailgate parties, went line dancing on a couple of Friday nights, and moved on. It was both homely and anonymous. Occasionally misguided, uncomfortable, and dangerous, but I'm not keeping those memories. They were nothing worse than I'd already been through at home, so why hang on to them?

Ж

In New Mexico, I stopped in the local 24/7 for some supplies and found myself chatting to a young cowboy with a big hat and a silver rodeo buckle on his belt. We talked and went our separate ways, but bumped into each other on the main street, where he tipped his hat and winked, and then later again, when he walked into the cantina where I sat with a cup of coffee at the counter. He asked if I might like to join him in the bar that evening, his gaze seeming to lock my eyes in place, so I did. We drank beer from brown bottles. He asked about my travels. I asked about his town. He walked me back to the hostel and took his hat off to kiss me. He said "Good night, ma'am" and I went to my bunk alone.

In the morning, I stood on the edge of town, thumbing for a lift, but the cowboy pulled up in his pick-up truck. His name was Cole. He was nice. He offered to take me to see his ranch before I left. He kissed me again on the front porch. I stayed the day, the night, the week.

I spent the winter with him, on the family ranch which he ran by himself, managing several seasonal workers in the summer, but he was working alone by the late autumn time when we met save for the one ranch hand who seemed to come and go at his own rhythm. His rough calloused hands felt so good on my soft hidden skin, the earthy smell of leather and horse permeated his room even after a long soak in the tub.

Cole wasn't the chatty type, and we fell into a comfortable routine. He would get up long before dawn and tend to the cows and the horses. Unlike when I was young, I enjoyed getting up in a quiet house and organising his breakfast. I knew where he would be. Cole would not be sleeping it off on the couch. There were always ranch jobs for him to do, and I set about deep cleaning every single room, which though tidy, had not been a priority for many years. The days ticked by, the sky was bleached of summer light, the trees lost their leaves.

In the evenings, we sat on the porch by a fire pit or in the house by the hearth, I read books from the local library, and he would study the weather reports and cattle prices. Occasionally he would comment on various political on-goings in the state or the country, I would smile and nod, not feeling the need to discuss it. It wasn't my country or my place. I was just wintering there. He was a kind body to hibernate with.

I came to like the smell of his bourbon whisky, there was something different, something warm about it, it never sent me scuttling. On Friday nights we would go to the bar and listen to a local country band, and on Saturdays we went to the steak house, where Arlene, our regular server, would smile and take me by the arm, telling me to look after Cole, because he was a good country boy.

Towards the very tail end of the winter, I accompanied him to inspect the wood. I was astonished when he got down on one knee by the local creek we had walked to, took off his hat and proposed. I said yes. I didn't know what else to say. I knelt in front of him and ruffled his hair where the hat band had left its mark and kissed him. Two days later, when he was out tending to a cow whose pregnancy had been complicated, I packed up my belongings and left, choosing to take the Greyhound out of town rather than to hitchhike. I had wanted to leave him a note this time, but I didn't know what to write, so I simply left his favourite pie, which I baked, and his grandmother's engagement ring on the scrubbed wooden kitchen table.

He was better off without me.

X

I travelled to Dallas, Houston, Baton Rouge, and New Orleans, up to Memphis, Tennessee, Chattanooga, where they did not cha cha or choo choo, down to Orlando, Miami and back up through the Carolinas, Virginia, Washington. From there northwards, hitchhiking didn't feel quite as safe alone, and neither did knocking on people's doors for lodgings, so I travelled by Greyhound mostly and stayed in hostels, meeting all manner of people, mostly European travellers, though in one hostel there was a Japanese lad who could not speak a word of English and yet knew every single word of every song in U2's back catalogue which he would play on his battered acoustic guitar all evening. We travelled together for over a week. I enjoyed his company. It was uncomplicated, and we parted ways with a hug.

I loved it in New York. My favourite thing to do was to get a bagel and coffee and sit in Central Park and watch the joggers, dog walkers, businesspeople and families going about their days.

Then there was Taylor, a bar waitress with spiky hair and multiple piercings who taught me more about my body than I had ever imagined could be possible. One night, I had too many drinks in a tiny bar and fell asleep in the corner. She woke me, trying to send me home, but I couldn't remember where the hostel was. She took me back to hers, and I vomited. While I had a shower she nipped to the bodega downstairs and bought me a toothbrush. She offered me her bed, I refused to let her sleep on the sofa. I don't know why I kissed her on the lips. Her eyes were green with tiny flecks of gold around the iris. It seemed enough of a reason at that point.

I returned to the hostel the next day but before I knew it, I was staying in Taylor's tiny basement flat share. It was pokey, and cosy, in need of a deep clean.

I never cleaned it for her though. I felt safe hidden away in her arms. I was happy to curl up with a book and let her rub my back while she watched the TV.

One night we ended up in Queens, crashing out on a sofa. In the morning, her pals in the flat bought take out breakfast. I could not believe it. Of all the things that I'd seen across the US, take out breakfast was the one that most surprised me. They had gone the whole way down the four flights of stairs, along the road, past a bodega or two, and a wee store, to buy pre-made pancakes. There were eggs, flour, and milk in the flat. Taylor could have made them fresh in the time it took them.

My girlfriend made the best and fluffiest pancakes anyone ever ate. I would give anything to eat them again.

She knew so much about things, she taught me to name some of my memories. Trauma, narcissist, neglect, abandonment. These were words for a psych project. Not words to mutter across skin and sheets, but they sounded like care.

1996

The bookshop was not a gorgeous, cosy, wooden-shelved empire of worlds tucked away on a street off Central Park. It was as clinical and devoid of character as a bookshop could be. Like a shopping mall Blockbuster franchise. Square neon lights in a suspended ceiling tile grid. The manager was taciturn and aloof. She came in every morning and sat at the till overseeing the shelf checks and new arrivals while she drank her coffee. After that she would go for a meeting and rarely returned until near closing time. The customers were brisk and busy, rarely stopping to browse. They wanted the latest bestseller on the tables, a book to gift. Sometimes they looked for self-help books. I read and reviewed for the shelf cards. I loved it.

One day I came home to find a letter from Lou. He must have got the address from Becky. He had never written to me before. I picked it up, flipped it over a few times, not without admiring his beautiful script, and put it back down on the counter. I wasn't in an "emotional space", as Taylor called it, to read the missive straight away. I ran the sink full of hot bubbly water, pulled on the pink marigolds and set about scrubbing the kitchen clean. I started with the counters, moving all the bits into the corners. I thought about the day in the bookshop.

I swept the floor, filled the bucket, poured in some floor cleaner, setting to mop the floor. I thought about emptying every cupboard and cleaning the inner shelves. I could hear Taylor's voice say "avoidance tactic". I frowned at the mental image of her. I was putting off opening the letter. I wrung out the mop and emptied out the bucket. I made myself a cup of tea, such a faff using a pan for the hot water, sat down at the table and lit a cigarette, though I knew Taylor would complain about me smoking in the kitchen. It was only allowed in the lounge. I finished the cigarette. I opened the envelope and pulled the pages out.

There was a short note on yellow paper that simply read "Tam X Lou", and a photocopied page in Nicky's handwriting, no context to it.

It is so warm.

His whole head feels sweaty and sticky, he is aware of his scalp, the folds of skin on the back of his neck, and at the top of his chest, his lips are dry, and even his ears feel funny. He can hear a noise, other than the breathing behind him, he can hear voices.

He realises that it's the television or the radio coming from another room not his own mind.

Through the redness behind his closed eyes, he can tell that there's daylight in the room that he is in, and his eyes start to blink open.

In front of him, all he can see is the white wall, and the top right corner of the radiator.

The right hand-side of his face feels warm and uncomfortable.

He notices that the pillow smells strange, but he doesn't want to move. Much as he is truly quite uncomfortable, he is happy to lie here a little longer. And he is happy because of the hot weight of the arm that lies over his waist.

He remembers the first time that he woke up with that arm around him. He could only have been about fourteen.

He hadn't expected it at all, but it had felt right even that first time. He'd met HIM some eighteen months before, and even though he didn't understand what it was that he felt around him, it was certainly more than friendship, more than his immense charisma. He felt right when he was in HIS company, like a home returned to. The tree and the soil. The riverbed and the river water. The fire and the hearth. He hoped he knew how to show this like love like rain like sunshine on dewdrops.

I put the letter down on the kitchen table.

I did not know what to make of it. I went out for a walk. To get away from it.

When I came back, Taylor was home. She was agitated and worked up. She marched right up to me. She said I had worried her. She put her hands on my shoulders. She had found the letter. She had cried. She leant her head on me. She didn't know what state I might be in. Whether I would come back at all. She looked me straight in the eyes. Was I alright? The police had not let her file a "missing persons". She kissed me.

I had only been gone a couple of hours.

1989

I sat there, on the steps of the New York Public Library just along from the MoMa. It was the closest I would go to the museum. I hadn't been in and never would. I knew one of Nicky's pieces hung in there somewhere. Lou had done incredible work over the years to build the profile of the Sugar Factory, and Nicky's work had reached an international audience. I had gone looking for him again. This was enough. Close enough. It wasn't the real Nicky anyway. It was Nicky, the artist, the child prodigy, the *enfant terrible*.

If Becky had been there, we would have gone in. She would have made me. Like that time I went to his show in Edinburgh and Mick was meant to come with me and instead had gone to get drunk with "auld pals" in Leith or somewhere even though it wasn't even noon. I had found a payphone and called her. She told me to go and have a browse of a shop or two on Princes Street. She'd meet me in ninety minutes by the Scott Monument.

I had finished my Boots sandwich when she sat herself beside me. She must have run out of the door to make it to the Queen Street train that fast.

"You bought a book, eh? Can't say I'm surprised."

"Well, I'd only brought one for the train and I

finished that, so ..."

She jabbed me cheerfully.

"Just joshin' wi'ya! Come on, let's go. I think we
need to go to the end of Princes Street and then ...
um ..."

We lost ourselves in the map. Then we lost ourselves
in the city. By the Water of Leith. A big bridge, a steep
hill. We found the museum. We found Nicky's show.
We meandered back to a bench in Princes Street
Gardens, a lid of clouds settling above the Castle.

"He'll show up. He'll find his way back like a homing
pigeon. We don't need to wait, you know."

"Yeah, I know. I kinda wish he wouldn't, and I'm OK
with how things are, but I would like to at least care
about where my father is. I don't. I don't want to wait
for him. I just like being in Edinburgh for a change."

"It's OK. He's your father, but he's not really a dad.
He doesn't deserve your worry and that's why you
don't feel it. That's not on you."

"Guess so. What did you think of Nicky's show? I
thought it was ..."

"Interesting?!"

I laughed.

"You can say that again! What was the big pink and
purple ... thing? With the ..."

"Dildos?"

"BECKY! My baby brother made that! It's art!"

We erupted in fits of giggles. Becky made gestures,
obscene and funny. I responded. She laughed harder.
The sillies overtook us, all the way back to the train
station, and by the time we had found seats on the
train, our cheeks and sides were aching. I fell into a
contemplative daze, staring out of the window, ignoring
the books in the Waterstones bag I had carried all day.
Becky was dozing, head back, headphones on, the big
orange foam discs on her ears and metal headband

inhibiting her from leaning to the side. I had always loved Nicky's gorgeous, detailed, realistic drawings, that seemed to capture light and feeling. His abstract work, the things the art critics liked was too weird for me, all bright colours and weird shapes.

I missed Becky. Sometimes.

Standing outside MoMa, I was glad she was not there. I did not want to go in and see Nicky's work on the dichotomies of wealth versus power and inner versus outer experience. I made my way down W53rd St and up 5th Ave to Central Park.

There was a blonde child running to keep up with their parent, maybe five years old. Nothing like Nicky was but something about the light on their hair caught my eye. There was more of my Bugs in that moment than in all of the museums in the world.

It was enough.

Becky would not have understood. If she had been here we would have gone in, found the art piece. I would have been quiet. She would have tried to make me laugh. Then we would have gone to a bar and she would have told me what I was feeling.

The blonde child disappeared into the crowd ahead.

1996

I cried when I left Taylor.

We had gone to look at apartments. It would mean my name on a lease. I liked the idea of our names linked. As we viewed the third place, she said:

"You could fit a great bookcase just there."

In that moment I knew I did not want that. I was not ready for a bookcase. I did not want to own anything other than what I could fit in my bag. I had been with Taylor for over a year, since I arrived in New York late in the summer of '95. I told her the next day before she left for work.

"Let's talk when I get back from work, babe."

I waited until the door clicked shut. I pulled on the rubber gloves. I cleaned the flat and packed my bag, shut the door, and posted the key under it. I would be long gone by the time she got home. Better to leave this way.

I started down the stairs. My eyes prickled. My cheeks felt hot. My chest shuddered.

I stopped.

I let out a sob. I could not leave her like this. I had believed her when she said, "I love you." I believed myself when I said it back to her. I ran back up to the flat, sunk down against the door and cried my heart out.

By the time she came back, I had unpacked a jumper and a book, and curled up with my sleeping bag around me in front of the door. She stood over me. I felt my chin crumple again.

"Babe. How can I even be pissed? Come on."

She opened the door to the apartment.

"I'm not staying. It's just for tonight."

"I always knew you would leave one day. It's OK."

I followed her in, eyes cast down. I felt embarrassed. I should have known that she would take it in her stride. She had expected me to leave after Lou's message had arrived. She was sad I was leaving, but there was no anger in her eyes. She hung up her jacket and got us each a drink from the fridge.

"I thought you might run off on me like you did with Cole, your cowboy! Good thing I hadn't proposed!"

She laughed. The tension eased off. She was the only person I told my life to. We spoke for hours. I promised her I would stop running from my memories of Nicky. We cried together. We got take-out. She was surprised I had stayed with her so long. The plan to get a place together had been a way to allay her fears that one day she would come home and I would be gone. We lit a single candle for Nicky. I told her about the Norackel. She said if she were an oracle she would tell me that my quest had not even started. She lit the candles around the sitting room. We held each other. I told her that my mother had written to Nana. Stroking my hair she told me I had to forgive Nana one day. It mattered more than finding Ange.

"I will find my mother. I need to know what happened."

The following morning, she came to the train station and kissed me goodbye on the platform. I tried to read on the train to Philadelphia. Instead, I watched the countryside, cried, promised myself I would find her

274

again. I knew I wouldn't. I had made the right choice.

I thought about the journey so far.

Mick's death five years before seemed to belong to another life. I let myself picture Nicky as I last saw him. In the bath. It was a static vision, devoid of feeling. Another one of his strange artworks. It had been years now but when I thought of home, I still pictured Nicky there, living his life.

I wondered what Cole would have made of me in New York with Taylor. The grunge dyke, his old plaid shirt tied around my waist. I was a completely different person with her than with him. I was a different person with all of them. The relaxed beach girl in San Diego. In San Fran, I was a bookish librarian. Napa Valley, art sophisticate.

I had been trying on identities like outfits. I had tried to shrug them off when the fit was not perfect without realising that each time, I had outgrown them.

1996-2000

I phoned Becky from a booth at 30th Street Station. She did not respond to my comment that it seemed like a strange name for the principal train station.

"I wondered how long that phase would last. Are you coming home then?"

I felt a surge of anger to hear Taylor described as a "phase" and bit my tongue. I did not want to fall out with Becky on the phone again. I told her I would be home soon and would let her know where I was staying once I had somewhere.

My next phone call was to my bank. I had been living off my wages in New York and a tidy amount had accrued. There was no financial reason to go back. No one to go back for. I decided to travel for a few more months. I kept going for another four years.

I made my way south through New Jersey to Atlantic City listening to Bruce Springsteen on my Discman, and into Baltimore with Nina Simone on my headphones. In Washington, I ate the best chili dogs from a street vendor I ever tasted and looked for Mulder & Scully at the FBI building. I carried on from Maine to Florida.

I visited the big towns and spent days and weeks visiting smaller places, moving on from one to the other. Small town America. I worked in hostels and hotels as I moved, for something to do, to feel grounded. Having a staff room felt safe and cleaner.

After parting with Taylor, I kept my promise to find ways to honour Nicky in every place I stopped. It was hard at first. One day I sat on a park bench with a book of children's stories. One of them was *Theseus and the Minotaur*. He loved that one. He was there beside me in a way. The more I let him back in, the more he seemed to be with me. Good and bad. I spoke to him. With him. Our childhood. My memories.

There were days when thinking about him was a punch to the gut. It was not always enough to dig my nails in. I had a penknife in the bottom of my rucksack. I kept it in a leather pouch. Some days I took it out, wiped it down, thought about releasing pain and blood. Some days I did it. Less and less. I was not needing to do it as often. I did not want to. It did not work anymore. I practised the breathing Taylor had shown me. I went for a walk. I spoke to people I met. I realised that the knife, the nails had never been a release. They had been a distraction. A physical pain to cover the emotional one.

I made of point of finding a more permanent job from early December until at least mid-February. It was easy enough as regular staff often went home for the winter. I realised it was better to be busy around Christmas. Sometimes, like on cold New England nights when I was staying in a guesthouse, I would take a blanket and pillow to sit in a dry bath and read. I read a lot. Good books, bad books, great books, true stories, and pulp fiction. Anything that was circulating on the bookshelves between travellers with road-dusty rucksacks trying to keep the load light and down to one book only, another level of escape within the escape.

I never ran the bath. Sitting in the water in the bath. No. That was not a good thing.

I stayed in a few private houses too, tutored a few children, nannied. It was easy work and enjoyable. Recommended by one family to the next, in my second and third year, I had a good run of spending a month or two in one place and then another. I stayed with nice normal families, with their small rows and tensions. Happy family meals, the occasional slammed door, filled with love. No long quiet hours. Children who spoke back to exasperated mothers. Fathers who went off to mow the lawn in a huff, but came back in ready to talk. Movie nights and mall trips.

I was in Jacksonville, looking after two boys and a girl in a big house in the suburbs. They had two cars, a dog, and a kitchen island. In the bathroom, there was a bottle of expensive red coloured bubble bath. One evening, the youngest boy swirled the bubble bath in. He was excited and called me to see the water turning red. Red bathwater. I recoiled and left the children to clamber in. I ran to my room and packed immediately. I could not stay a moment longer. I was gone before the kids even got out and into their pyjamas. The mum hollered after me in anger, "You won't get your pay cheque! That's the end of your references."

I caught the next greyhound out of town to Virginia Beach. It was easy to blend in with the tourists there. I found a hostel and hung around until a big surfing competition was due to start and hitchhiked to Roanoke Island.

2000

Fall in New England was everything I had expected.

I had made my way there to see the autumn leaves as so many people had told me that they were outstandingly beautiful. The auburn, copper, and flaming hillsides in the clear golden sun of the season did not disappoint. Leaves falling everywhere like golden confetti. It was the week before Columbus Day weekend, and I travelled the Mohawk Trail through Massachusetts to the New Hampshire Lakes.

I found several small guesthouses to stay in along the way, my favourite being an old-fashioned chintzy wooden farmhouse with a wiry, tough, and abrupt landlady, Bren. The skinny poker-faced woman turned out to be, after a glass or two of beer – *bee-yarr,* I thought she said the first time she offered one – a bright and warm woman who made the most delicious apple pie.

I remember the apple pie with absolute clarity, it had a light cinnamon warmth to the melting sweet apple chunks, the whipped cream melting into the crunchy pastry. She'd served up a thick pumpkin soup with crusty bread as the main course. The meal was included with the night, but as I was the only person there that midweek, I joined her and her husband, Jimmy, and the farm help.

Leaf season was prime time, though the summer was also popular with townies from as far as New York, who would come to get away for a weekend. Usually, Bren would serve the guests separately, but it was rare to have one from quite so far away and completely alone. It was a lovely evening.

I went to bed feeling empty and hollow.

It wasn't the searing pain that had been ebbing away over the years, its waves crashing less and less frequently. It was that strange and deep melancholy that can only set in when you are in good and warm company. Sitting with Bren and Jimmy, eating the apple pie, I was hit by a yearning to see Nana, and George, and Becky too. I had spoken to Becky a few times over the eight years that I'd been away. She and Steve were still going strong and had moved to a house with a small back garden. She said I had a room of my own waiting there whenever I needed. I knew that it was only a matter of time before it was a nursery.

Nana was a different matter. I called for high feasts, birthdays, the difficult anniversaries, sent the occasional postcard. We were treading water, though. I hadn't ever said that I knew there were more letters than the one she had shown me. She had been cross that I had left at first. For a while I didn't call regularly, and she started to answer the phone with relief in her voice. We spoke of the immediate only. No mention of Ange between us. She had stopped Ange from coming home. Nicky would still be alive if she hadn't. Wouldn't he?

Suddenly, I wasn't quite so sure.

Jimmy carried my bag down to my rental car the morning I left. I'd only stayed two nights, and yet my stay with them stands out from so many over the years. I felt teary as I drove down the road that led from the farm to the main road but carried on to Lake Winnipesaukee. The reflection of the leaves in the still water was jaw-dropping. I was lucky to be there on a clear day, with a few puffy white clouds in the blue sky. It was entirely picture book perfect, but somehow, even in the warm sun, I did not feel right. I pulled in to a lay-by.

I rummaged down to the bottom of the bag and pulled out my old diary. I locked the car, and walked out along the pebbly beach, finding myself a quiet spot on some rocks that jutted out into the water.

I untied the lace that held the battered old diary together and pulled out my mother's two letters to Nana, well-worn now, and the note that my mother had left my father all those years ago, illegible and flimsy. I stroked them, and folded them back up, and then turned to the page where I had carefully copied out my mother's words back during the first flight to LA all those years ago, and read the words once again. I knew them off by heart and spoke them in my mind as I went back over them.

The tears started to well up. I flicked through the diary.

Every single page was blank.

I knew that.

Not a word jotted down over the years. All I had were my mother's letters.

I had tried to outrun them as I carried them.

The tears came faster as the puffy white clouds shrank in the warming sun.

The spot where I was sat remained in the shadow of the trees. The water around me cooling the air.

I shivered.

My shoulders began to shake.

I dug my nails into my palms, but the soothing

white pain would not come this time.

A morning fish leapt towards a falling leaf, and the water rippled its way to me, lapping the edges of the rock I sat on.

I was the island.

Maybe the water was the answer. Could water hold answers? I read somewhere once that all water had been through the dinosaurs, humans, rock, the sea, the cycle of water the cycle of life. Is this what I needed to do?

Run the bath. Get into the water. Open my mouth and invite the answer in.

Be held by all that came before.

Shoes off, socks off. Slipping in, I could let the lake wash my scars, take me, take me away from it all.

Closing my eyes, ready.

A loud squawk. My eyes sprang open. A heron swept across, vast wings gliding through the air, swooping down, feet dragging briefly on the water. She landed across from me, staring directly at me.

"So whatcha gonna do about it?"

"I was going to ..."

"What? You think that will solve it? What if it all hurts in the next life? What if you don't succeed and your body demands you come back up? Your clothes will be wet. Did ya think about that? And anyway, this is my spot. I don't want you dirtying my fishes."

Deep shuddering breaths.

Getting into water was different to standing in a shower. I had not gone into water since 1992. The heron knew.

I took out a cigarette out but shook and dropped it.

I watched through my tears as it rolled into the water.

I let out a howl.

The heron looked at me in disgust but stayed put.

Another howl.

I balled my fists. I stood up and screamed my lungs out.

The heron shot me a look of disgust and took flight.

I took a deep breath. Silver swoops over the water.

I breathed out and in. Slate feathers circling up to soar over the trees.

I looked around. I was alone. I slumped back on to the rock and took out a cigarette, successfully this time, lit it, and smoked it. I ground it out, and contemplated the still waters of the lake, the cool calm calling to me, promising a soothing embrace.

The heron would be angry. I was losing it. I had a conversation with a bird. It was as good an omen as I could ask for. The bird had warned me and left me to decide for myself.

I had hidden in books and bathtubs and ill fitting lives for long enough.

I pulled my socks and shoes back on. I felt lighter.

✗

It was time to find Ange. I knew it in my heart. I could not outrun it any longer. I phoned Nana from a small hostel payphone. I told her I had to find my mother. She agreed that I needed to.

"Tam, I should have told you sooner. I have more letters from Ange. That might help you."

"I know there are other letters. I found them before I left. Thank you for telling me."

We spoke, properly, at last. She cried. I cried.

She told me she loved me, properly, not a cursory, "love you", but "I love you Tam, I really do". I believed her. I promised to call again. I said I wanted to know more about Ange, the truth. Nana sighed.

"I think we've had enough secrets in this family.

I've told Agnes and Davy, you know, that I'm their mother. I did it three years ago."

"Well done. It was time they knew the truth."

"I'll make copies of the letters and send them to you. On the electronic mail."

I wanted nothing more at that moment than to be back in Nana's kitchen. The distance was at once a breath and an ocean between us. I could not go straight back though.

It was not time yet.

I promised to call again soon, said goodbye, and hung up.

On the Friday of Columbus Weekend of October 2000, I checked my bags in at JFK airport and boarded the next flight to Madrid, Spain.

1980

I remember the day that John Lennon was shot.

We were watching TV at Nana's when the news came on. Nana was talking about "feeding the Christmas cake" which made Nicky, who was seven at the time, giggle at the thought of a cake being fed.

To be from Liverpool but shot in New York seemed glamorous to me. I did not register that he was dead, no, New York captured my thirteen-year-old's imagination, a place of limitless possibility.

I pictured myself going to the airport. I would be an investigative journalist. Go to the murder site and meet the detective. I would be the one to identify the murderer. I would be hailed as a ground-breaking reporter. I would have my own apartment, not a flat, in Manhattan. I would drink coffee and walk in Central Park. I would get a big shaggy mutt. I would have friends who were writers, poets, actors. I would have freedom.

That year at Christmas there was sleet and snow, and the weather was grimly cold. We could not put the heating on. I remember the cold that got right into our bones, our fingers turning purple, teeth set, shoulders hunched, vests on itchy skin. There wasn't much to eat either.

Mick, I mean Dad, had been drinking since the Tuesday before Christmas Day. At the site, they downed tools for ten whole days until the new year rolled round. Ten jovial days enjoying the warm company at the local pub. Dad lost two teeth during that festive season in a pub fight, and though he had once had an athletic build, his face was starting to look wrong. Puffy eyes, sallow skin, he had lines forming around his eyes and thin lips from smoking, a round swollen booze belly taking shape.

George once told Mick that he looked as though he had had "a tough paper round". He seemed to fade in the winter months. I wrote down that description in the diary I kept over that Christmas. It was Nicky's present to me, but I only wrote in it over that holiday. I tried to observe my family, to write factually about our existence, practising for my future life somewhere far away, like London or Paris. I found that I preferred to write out the lyrics to favourite songs, a few rhyming lines that I made up, even some whole poems. Eventually, I would start to write short stories in which I invented mythical heroes like those of Ancient Greece and Rome.

Since school had broken up for the Christmas holidays, we had been mostly at Nana's, even sleeping there. We went to the flat several times, Nana would say that we needed to pick up a scarf or another jumper, though by then we had full sets of clothes in our shared room in her house. Thinking about it now, I'm sure that she needed to check whether her son, my father, was there, both hoping and dreading to find him in equal measure. In fact, he was there a couple of times, once asleep or passed out on the living room floor. I saw his leg, but Nana made us go back out of the flat and wait outside.

Another time, he was sat at the kitchen table, and

stared at us wordlessly. And I remember that the flat was extremely cold, I suppose now that it was because he had not put money in the meter, though I did not think of that then. He had other purchases in mind.

It was cosy at Nana's, and there were always things to do. She had a shelf stacked with boxes of puzzles which we solved on the floor. My favourite was of a painting of a tabby cat with a green collar and a reddish-brown patterned background. Her paw rested on a ball of green yarn, the same shade as the collar. There were shelves full of books and Nicky's box of toys – including his old train set. Nana put the radio on, even though we always asked for the TV. At some point every day, we would wrap up in our coats, scarves, and gloves, and go to the park or trot down to the corner shop. Nana told us it was once a dance bar called La Strada. On the way back we would stop by at the flat. Nana would always have a reason.

"I want to pick up some socks for Nick."

Or –

"Tam, I think you need more hair grips, these ones are getting a bit tangly."

When we stopped by on the morning of Christmas Eve, Mick was asleep on the kitchen table, fully clothed, a cigarette having burnt out in the ashtray leaving a delicate mottled grey tube of ash, a near-finished bottle of whisky by his head, and there was some money on the floor that had fallen from his pocket.

It must have been the sound of the front door being jiggled open and then shut behind us as we came in, or perhaps it was the cold gust down the hall to the kitchen that roused him. He groaned, moved his head, and opened his unfocused eyes in our direction. He was slumped forward in the chair, arms folded on the table, forehead on forearm. He barely moved to vomit over his shoulder, on to the floor. He closed his eyes and slumped there for a while, a dribble running down the side of his face. Nicky and I stood in the kitchen doorway, watching our father.

Suddenly, he scraped the chair back with a horrible screeching as the leg dragged on the linoleum, causing Nicky to jump. Nana was behind us, one hand holding mine, the other on my brother's blonde head.

Mick, I mean Dad, stumbled to the sink, and vomited again, coughing at the end. He rested his head on the cool steel edge of the sink and splashed himself. The sound of the water seemed to bring Nana out of her daydream and she herded us towards the living room and closed the door. We heard her talking to Dad in the kitchen, quietly enough that we couldn't make out her words. There were loud footsteps past the closed living room door and up the stairs.

The door opened, and Nana announced that Daddy was not feeling well, and that we would be going back to hers. She bundled us out. The snowflakes were starting to fall. Big soft feathers. As soon as we got back, had taken off our shoes, hung up our coats and scarves and gloves, Nana said that we were going to bake gingerbread men. The snow was lying. Nicky brought his drawing book in and sat at the table to draw a snowman. We were weighing out the flour when he put down the red colouring pencil and looked up at us.

"Nana, is Daddy going to be alright?"

"I hope he will feel better soon."

"Nana, will Daddy be here for Christmas lunch?"

"Let's hope that he feels up to it."

"Is Daddy going to die?"

At that, the front door opened suddenly, swinging back quite hard on its hinges causing it to bang. Startled, I dropped the bag of flour on the floor.

It opened slowly. It was George, shaking the snow off his jacket, red faced from the cold.

"Sorry! The door got away from me in the wind. Are you all alright?"

Back then, I did not understand why Nana burst into tears. I can see why now.

Christmas Day came and went. Bugs and I sang along to that Christmas number one single *There's No One Quite Like Grandma* on the radio, as loud as we could to Nana. Stockings by the fireplace, all three bars roaring, the tree, the turkey, Christmas pudding. Nicky had an air rifle, and I had a book to read.

I also remember the next day, Boxing Day. I found it and revisited it, more than once, in the bathtubs of America.

I made sure Nicky got washed up and dressed properly. We were going to have a big sit-down breakfast all together. Nana had bought some smoked back bacon, so we were looking forward to a full breakfast of bacon, eggs, grilled tomatoes, toast, and tea. It would be an absolute treat for us.

There was a thumping on the door. We froze in our seats. A key scraped across the lock a few times before it eventually went in, turned, and the door burst open.

Mick stormed into the house, shouting: "Give me my fucking children! It's fucking Christmas Day, for Chrissakes', and I will have my children with me!"

Then he was in the kitchen, towering behind me. He grabbed my shoulders, hard, and started to pull me backwards. Nana said something, but George reached across the table and squeezed her hand.

"My own mother, trying to steal my children. I will have them with me for Christmas! Come on, you two, let's go."

He wrapped an arm under my arms, lifting me up

away from the table. It hurt. My chest, my armpits, a vice squeezing the air from me. His fingers dug into my ribcage. I looked at Nicky. My brother had gone bright red in the face and his chin had crinkled up.

At that point, George stood up calmly and moved around the table, towards Mick, his arms out, palms up, on either side, held low.

"Mick, why don't you sit down with us, let the children eat their breakfast and have a cuppa. There's enough food for you too. Join us for a bacon sandwich?"

Mick punched him.

I couldn't believe it. He had punched George.

George's nose was bleeding. Dripping great big bright red blotches onto the linoleum.

George was standing to my right and I remember watching a drop splat onto the floor, the drip blotching into a messy outline.

No-one moved.

Nana spoke up. There was both steel and a shudder in her voice.

"Now then, Michael. We had an agreement, remember? We had agreed. So, you are going to leave, now. You will leave Tam and Nicky here and come back when you are feeling better."

"I'm feeling fucking perfect, Mum."

I did not know what Nana was talking about, but I could see that my father was ticking, boiling up inside. I could hear my own voice screaming inside me for Nana to stop talking, that it would only make him more upset, that he would take off his belt and whip the back of her thighs, or lock her in one of the kitchen cupboards, or hold her head under the cold tap in the kitchen until she was quiet.

Maybe she did not know that he would do that.

I did, I knew that face.

I knew that he would if she kept on talking.

If she was quiet, and made herself as small as she could, maybe he would swing back and smile, and put the radio on, dance, kick off his shoes.

Just maybe.

I balled up my fist, tight. I could feel my nails digging into the palms of my hands. I could feel the white light of a sharp pain spreading, and the clarity of it focused my mind on what I knew that I had to do.

"It's alright, Daddy, I want to spend Christmas with you too. Nana, it's fine, I will spend Christmas with him."

Nicky piped up.

"But it's not even …"

"Ssh, Bugs. Not now. You can stay here with Nana."

"But it's Boxing Day!"

My father didn't even notice. His eyes had glazed over. I walked to him, taking his hand, the hand that had punched George. I knew that if he thought that it was still Christmas Day, even though it was in fact the day after, then he must have lost the actual day somehow. I would take the full force of it if that would mean the others were spared.

He looked down at me, with bloodshot eyes, and gripped my hand a little too hard. He turned to the door, dragging me behind him, out of the kitchen and along the corridor. With one hand, I managed to grab my coat off the end of the banister, where I'd left it yesterday after the walk that we'd taken to ease off our happy Christmas Day lunch. My mittens were hanging down the sleeves on a string, and my scarf was bundled into it too. As he marched down the path, me stumbling behind him, I heard a wail from behind me. It was Nicky, running after us, in slippers, with no coat.

The snow was falling again. The air was still and quiet.

Nicky's face was red, he was crying, and snotty. He dragged his left sleeve across his face.

"Tammy, don't leave me behind, please, don't go!"

"Come with us, Bugs. Or stay here. We're going."

My little brother shivered the whole way home, holding my other hand, both of us dragged along the snowy pavement by our father as he marched. About halfway we stopped to cross the road, and I remember slipping out of my coat and giving it to Nicky. Mick didn't even notice, and he didn't realise that Nicky was still in his slippers, and that they were soaked through.

A thick cap of white snow sat on top of the pillar box under the streetlamp like a Christmas card.

When we got home, the house was bitterly cold and dark. He dragged us in to the sitting room and sat heavily on the sofa, staring ahead. There was a whisky bottle, probably from his lonely Christmas Eve to Day celebrations lying on its side, empty on the table beside another one that was itself two-thirds empty. The ashtray had overflowed, and cigarette butts and ash lay on the side table itself.

Nicky and I stood between the sofa and the door. My little brother sniffed and wiped his nose on his sleeve again. He was still shivering. A Christmas tree now stood in front of the window that gave on to the main walkway. It looked as though he had dragged it through a pile of tinsel and baubles before being set upright in a scattering of pine needles on the floor. Underneath the tree, there were four haphazardly wrapped presents.

I dropped Nicky's hand and ran upstairs to collect the presents my brother and I had saved up for through the autumn, bought and wrapped for our father, a tie from Nicky and a book about building bridges from me. We had hidden them at the back of the bottom drawer in the dresser in my room. I pulled the drawer open, grabbed my stripy jumper for Bugs, and there they were, two neat packages labelled 'To Daddy – Merry Christmas – xox'.

When I came back down the stairs, Nicky was sitting on Dad's lap on the sofa, and the living room was still dark. Our father was still staring dead ahead, his arms tight in a vice-grip around my brother. Nicky was looking at me, silent tears running down his red face, a terrified look in his eyes. I dropped one of the packages, and Dad turned his head slowly towards me.

"Tam, there you are, my little princess. Come and hug your daddy. It's Christmas, and we should be together, as a family."

I did my best to smile. I bent down and picked up the present that I had dropped and went over to the tree to add our presents to the ones that Dad had put there. Then, I walked over to them. I did this all deliberately because I knew that Mick might switch in an instant. He had eased his grip on Nicky while I moved around the room. As I sat down beside them, I realised that Dad had started crying, mumbling a promise that he would never, ever leave us, that he would never let us go, that he would always be with us.

"It's us three against the world, forever. Always has been. Always will."

Keeping one arm around Nicky, he wrapped the other around my shoulders. I don't know how long he held us like that for, but I remember that later that evening, I was able to see three pink marks on my shoulder where his fingers had dug in to it, and that my shoulder had been sore when we had finally opened the presents.

Nicky had unwrapped a Meccano building set, which accounted for two of the packages, and I was now the owner of plastic baby doll that could apparently wet itself. It certainly wasn't a Rubik's cube, which is what

I really wanted that year.

The other package contained the *Penguin Book of Norse Myths*, and I was genuinely happy with that. Then Dad opened the presents which we had got for him, and teared up again, wiping his eyes awkwardly with the back of his hand.

"I don't deserve you two, you are my angels. You are my reason for everything. Thank you."

After that, he started to show Nicky what to do with his building set and put together a long line of the metal sections, but there was no design, no clear end-product in mind, and eventually he seemed to lose interest and handed the spanner to Bugs, who sat there putting bolts through the holes and making engine noises. Dad sat there for a while staring at the dishevelled tree, and then got up slowly. He leaned down and mussed up our hair and then walked out of the room, taking with him the two-third empty whisky bottle that sat on the table.

We sat on the floor, wrapping paper strewn around us mingled with the mechano-type parts and a bootie from my baby doll, which I had briefly pretended to play with for the sake of peace, by dressing and undressing it. We were listening to the noises in the room above us. First, there was a dull thud and a crash, which was followed by a swear-word. I thought that it was probably the bedside table and the lamp. The loud clunk that followed was probably the sound of a shoe being bounced off a cupboard door. Then came heavy footsteps, and the sound of the bathroom door. We listened to the flush of the toilet, the sound of running water, and the bathroom door opening again. We held our breath, quieter than mice, as quiet as the still furniture in what was left of the fading light on that dull snowy winter afternoon. The footsteps were uneven as they headed back along the corridor to the bedroom.

Everything went quiet upstairs. Minutes expanded like ice, freezing in the cold darkening room. We listened intently, holding our breath until a regular drone started to come and go, the familiar sound of the Ogre upstairs sleeping off the booze. I leant forward to pick up one of the Meccano pieces, and carefully put it into the empty box so as not to make a single noise. Slowly, quietly, we tidied up together, and I carefully smoothed out the wrapping paper and put it neatly on the table. I emptied the ashtray into the rubbish bin in the kitchen and took the empty bottles through. I took a cloth from beside the sink, dampened it with a trickle from the tap, and put a drop of liquid detergent onto it. I went back to the living room and wiped the coffee table. Nicky had curled himself under my coat into the arm of the sofa, the stripy jumper over his knees.

It was dark in the living room when I was done, and we were both hungry as we had neither been allowed to finish our breakfast, nor had any lunch.

"Hey, Bugs, don't go to sleep yet, Bugs."

"Fee Fi Fo Fum, Tam."

It was a code we had between us, to warn each other of the Ogre.

"I know, but it's cold and you got very cold when we came over. Let's build Sofa Toon, and we can snuggle in together. Come on, Bugs."

"Alright, Tammy, but will you tell me a story? One of the Romans and Greeks ones. Not the one with the one-eyed ogre and the wine though."

We made a space behind the sofa, with the sofa cushions on the floor, and curled up together in the blanket that was usually on the chair. We had made Sofa Toon before. Neither of us wanted to go upstairs, and we both knew that the kitchen cupboards would be bare. Nicky's stomach was rumbling, and he was too warm, and sweaty. He didn't want to draw as he often did in this situation, so I told him the story of Jason and the Argonauts, with a few elements of the twelve tasks of Hercules mixed in, and we snuggled in together.

The next morning, it was Nana who woke us up. It wasn't yet properly daylight, but she had come around and let herself in. Mick wasn't anywhere in the house by then. We got our things together and went back to Nana's, and she made us toasted turkey sandwiches for breakfast, followed by Christmas cake. It was rich and moist. The marzipan was still sticky, the royal icing so sweet it made my teeth feel strange.

As far as I know, Dad didn't come back until after New Year, and by then Nicky was better from the fevered cold he had caught on the Boxing Day walk, and we never spoke of that Christmas again, the Meccano set or the baby doll.

X

That Christmas was the first time that I noticed Nicky withdraw into himself. Before, when Mick wasn't around, Nicky was usually quite happy to play with me, maybe to sit and draw, sing and chat. This time, he went off quietly by himself, not doing much. He didn't want to do any of things that he usually enjoyed. He didn't even cry. He went up to his room and closed the door. I didn't think much of it then. Looking back, that was maybe the start of it. I noticed him scratching his left wrist hard, digging his nails in, like I did. Later he would scratch harder, deeper, and once or twice he used a knife. The paring knife. I did nothing about it. I did not stop to think about it. It did not seem that odd to me. I did it too.

It became a part of the things that Nicky did. That I

did. Part of loose memory that I'd somehow overturned and buried under the shiny ones.

Once he drank the vial of Olive Oil from the chemist that we had for our ears. That was probably good for him with hindsight. I told him off because it was expensive. I didn't see a pattern when he drank all the Vicks' Formula 44. He said it was just a silly prank.

I let that stand, and that was not all.

2000

Sat on a low beach wall, the sun on my face. My mind miles away. A sudden bang.

Sharp intake of breath by my shoulder. My head snaps to the left. A sweaty head in a bicycle helmet is inches from my face. I must have looked startled, as he broke into an apologetic sounding jumble of Spanish words. I couldn't understand even one.

His hand gestures told me that he had swerved to avoid a child with a ball, now crying in their mother's arms, and crashed onto the promenade wall where I sat looking out to the sea. He wanted to know if I had been hurt. I smiled and pointed at the photo I held and simply said:

"Mama."

"Mi más sentido pésame."

I could hear the condolence in his voice. I smiled at him, not wanting to contradict the sentiment. He smiled awkwardly and left. I looked back out at the sea. All that water, all those waves, whispering.

※

At first, I would go into a bar or café, wait a while, summoning up the courage, have a drink before I managed to ask whether the other customers I met knew my "long lost aunt" Angela.

After the best part of a week, wasting time on drinks and food I didn't want, I managed to ask a waiter, finding communication between my broken Spanish and his perfect-for-tourists-only English. At the next bar, I didn't take quite as long, almost reassured every time I got a "no, sorry, no". I felt braver as the knowledge that my question was likely to be fruitless permeated my being. I realised I was afraid of finding her. I wasn't ready to meet her. I was only ready to look for her. That was OK.

I started walking in and simply asking.

I filled my map with crossed-off bars and cafés. It was satisfying. It felt like progress.

The first time someone said they recognised Ange, my eyes brimmed over with tears, but my respondent hadn't known her name, and by the end of the conversation, I wasn't even sure that he had the right person. I hoped not, given his salacious comments.

I bought a notebook and scribbled notes, reams of any useful information. Reading it over one evening of the second week, I realised I had nothing, and after a few too many cañas, the crisp cool glass tubes of beer, sobbed snottily on the edge of my bed in a sparse hotel room.

Disappointment. Failure. Anger. Fear.

Disappointed at the lack of progress. Failure as a daughter, a sister, a granddaughter. Angry that I was hurt at all. She'd left me. She hadn't wanted me. Fear that she would push me away.

Why should I even bother looking for her?

Hot tears of frustration ran down my face.

I pictured Bren's New England apple pie. Hot cinnamon apple. Sugary crust. I calmed down.

Retracing the steps that brought me here. Fall in

New England. The heron.

I took deep breaths. I clenched my hands into fists. Tight balls of despair. Dug my nails in hard, leaving four angry red crescent marks. I rubbed my hands together, they were sore.

There was a calming release in that pain.

I focused on the feeling in my palms, and finally fell asleep.

A sore head and itchy palms were all that remained of the previous night's doubt.

I set off, determined to cross off the last expat businesses in the grid that I had marked on my map, despite my tired limbs.

That morning, I unearthed three good leads. A woman who had met a "Greg and Ange", who she described as "hippy types" that she had met at a beach bar party about six years before, in Manacor on the other side of the island.

At a foreign language bookshop, the moustachioed owner told me that Greg, occasionally accompanied by Ange, had been a regular of sorts over the years, ordering and buying a variety of "new-agey books". I felt this fitted well with the picture I had been building up of them. The bookman explained that he didn't think that Greg lived in Palma as he visited about four times a year, about every three months. Though, as it happened, he hadn't been in for at least six months.

A third person, who lived in Manacor, was certain that she'd seen an "American blonde beach bum type and his hippy partner in the photo" in a café there, though it might have been Ibiza. She wasn't sure, and I wondered how much she was saying to be helpful, to please. I jotted it down in my notebook and pondered the fact that it was a second mention of Manacor. I carried on through the afternoon but didn't turn up anything else.

The next morning, I packed up and made my way to the train station. As I left the great bay of Palma inland through Inca, I tried hard to keep my emotions in check.

A part of me almost expected my mother to be waiting at the train station, which I knew was impossible. And silly.

I sat staring out of the window, open book in my hand, planning the next phase of my search, arguing back at the voice that kept saying that maybe she'd got wind of me being there. My first port of call would be the tourist information office, where I would pick up a map, and find somewhere to stay for a night or two. I let my eyes zone out of focus and watched hills of almond trees, lone massive carob trees dotting the landscape, vineyards, and bare dust.

$$\text{X}$$

The train station in Manacor was small enough to be a modest house, and there was no one on the platform waiting for me. Somehow, though I had tried not to have any hope about finding her, I felt winded by the fact that she hadn't magically appeared. Knowing the tears in my eyes to be ridiculous, I found somewhere for a cup of coffee and a bite to eat, and busied myself with the map I picked up from the station office, planning my route around the town.

First things first, I needed a base. I waved the waitress over.

"Hay una pensión cerca?"

My functional Spanish was improving – I fully understood her answer. I wasn't ready to start my quest again. At the very least I needed a shower first, and to get my bearings. The waitress directed me to a family run hotel like a BnB. Clean, basic, nestled in an old honey coloured stone building.

That evening, I went for a walk around the town, picked up some ham, bread and a beautiful orange the size of my face. I ate in my room. It was warm and peaceful. I carefully folded all the breadcrumbs into the towel which I'd spread across my knees and shook them off from the tiny balcony into the night. I knew about Spanish ants.

Thanks to the days, weeks of practice asking around in Palma, I didn't waste time stopping to sit in the pubs, bars and other expat establishments. I walked straight in, up to every counter, clutching my photo and the story of a search for a long-lost aunt. I was efficient and business-like. Each question turned up the same answer, no one knew her, no one had seen her, and no one was sympathetic.

The dark funk that had come over me at the train station had settled in to stay during my few days in Manacor, and by the third morning, I resolved that I would leave on the following day.

That evening, I went down to a bar in the small square overlooked by balconies, sat with a beer, my book, and the photograph of my mother propped up against the serviette holder. The third time the waiter came to my table, with a caña of beer and a small tapa of sizzling chorizo sausages and two thick slices of bread, he picked up the photo. I could not have been more surprised when he said, in broken English:

"Angela? You know she?"

"Yes, she's my aunt. Do you know her?"

"Si. Yes, she live here, before, more years. Angela y Greg. They come here. Before."

I looked up at the waiter in utter astonishment. My mouth probably even popped open. I had not properly looked at him until that point. He was older than I had thought, with a bit of a paunch, hair thinning on top.

305

He would be jowly in a few years' time. My brain was stuck on details as I struggled to process his words.

I tried to ask him for more details, but my questions gushed out, one on top of the other, and he handed back the picture, eyes glazing with a veneer of polite disengagement. He hadn't understood me at all and turned back towards the bar. I pulled out my phrase book, a pen, and one of the serviettes from the holder where I had propped the photo.

The phrase book didn't have the questions I needed to ask, but I pulled them apart, and managed to cobble together, in pidgin Spanish, enough to find out when the waiter came back with a fourth beer that Ange and Greg had been regulars some six to ten years before, but that they moved away from Manacor, where they had, indeed, run a massage and yoga centre. He thought that they had perhaps left the island, but not that they had gone back to the UK. After he left the table, I wrote all this information down very carefully in my notebook.

I felt like I had won the jackpot and downed the end of my glass of beer. I pulled out my purse, and I put more than enough money to cover my drinks, and a generous tip, on the table. I wandered back along the lanes and then into the town, back to the hotel. I had a shower, and got into bed, hugging my legs beneath me, to re-read my notes.

The bubbly feeling that was brewing in my stomach evaporated as fast as it had appeared, as I read it over, realising that though this was all new information, it took me no closer to finding her.

Manacor was a dead end.

I rolled over, tugging the sheet, and reached to switch off the bedside light. There on the wall was a mosquito. I swatted it with my notebook and from the splat, I knew that I had already been bitten. I couldn't sleep. I felt hot and agitated. I got up and paced the room, leaned out of the window. I stripped off my clothes. I showered, I sat down in the shower.

I sat there for most of the night. I could not see where to go next.

In the morning, I returned to the train station with my pack. A train had just left, so I read in the sunshine for almost an hour before the next train. I didn't even think about where I would go next, I wanted to get lost in the story. I was reading Umberto Eco's *Foucault's Pendulum*, and I managed to ensure that it commanded all my attention from the train station, onto the train, to Palma, and back to my attic room in the hotel. I stayed there a few more days, until I finished Eco and another book that I picked up at the guesthouse, Donna Tartt's *Secret History*. I ignored my notebook. I had quick functional showers and read late into the nights until my eyes watered and blurred.

By the time I finished the second book, sitting in cafés and beachside bars, I had decided that I would go to Ibiza next as it was the only other place that had even been mentioned in all my searches.

There, I would continue to ask whether anyone had ever seen her, and maybe, if nothing came up, on to Formentera, and from there, back to the mainland, and then on to the Canary Islands. I knew that I would have to go around all the Spanish islands and follow every lead before I could go back, back to Nana, empty-handed. She would be glad of me home, empty-handed, but I needed to know that I had exhausted every possible lead and clue before that moment came.

1991

Memory is water. You think it is solid. Clear hard fact, immutable. You can hold on tight to it, frozen like ice. When you grasp it in your mind and you try to shape it, it melts, or evaporates. You compare it to someone else's memory, and suddenly it is unfamiliar, slipping through your fingers.

Nicky and I shared so many memories. I suppose I held mine differently, froze them in other shapes.

I remember key events from 1990 and 1991, though if I'm honest I'm not certain any more of the order in which they happened. I was twenty two and twenty three, so I could no longer have been permanently living in the flat, as I stayed at Becky's most weekends and several weeknights. I couldn't get away from it entirely, I was tethered to it by the need to look out for Nicky and the hope that my father might suddenly decide to sober up.

X

Halley's Comet made her second visit of the twentieth century to our solar system, burning bright in the night sky. I attempted to see something, anything through my old broken telescope.

Some entirely irrational part of me hoped that a benevolent race of aliens could be detected within it and that I could ask them to take me away.

One of those nights, Nicky and I lay on the bonnet of a car in the scheme car park that did not belong to anyone, rusting on soft tyres, outdated MOT badges curling in the windscreen. I remember it because, at the time, he rarely came home in the evenings anymore, or even at night, not since Lou had become a permanent fixture in his group of friends. I did not know what to make of Lou. Such an oddball.

It would be one of the rare evenings we spent together, genuinely in each other's company, not merely crossing. Nicky was talking about burning bright and burning out, seizing the day, and using art to foster The Revolution – I could hear the capitalisation of the word in his voice, and chuckled to myself about the Capitalism of revolutionary thought.

In art class, Nicky painted comets with our faces at the centre. He was supposed to be drawing still life compositions of flowers and fruit, jugs, and cups. He failed his end-of-school exams because the pieces were of overflowing ashtrays and empty beer glasses. His portfolio was deemed unacceptable for art school, but I think those are my favourite ones that he ever did.

In any event, at seventeen, Nicky was young for his year and so re-applying would not have done him too much harm. He had plenty time to work on his paintings and drawings and was quickly becoming a darling of the local arts community. I was glad he had included me in this moment of enthusiasm and exhilaration. He asked me to stay at the flat until he finished school, though he was rarely in, and the times that he had been over the last few months, he'd been bleary eyed, grumpy, taciturn. That evening, he had me giggling over silly stories, funny voices, stupid jokes.

He told me about his new friends, at greater length than he ever had. He made it a point to say that Lou made him feel happier than he had ever felt with anyone. It was the first time that I wondered whether there was more than a strong friendship and common interest between them. He was my baby brother and seeing him in any other way made me shy away from the thought. I did not want to press him on it, I didn't know what to ask. My own friendship with Becky was strong, so I tried to liken theirs to ours, reasoning that maybe the lack of a solid family life led us to pour ourselves heart and soul into others. With hindsight I think I misunderstood, but all I remember was that I thought Nicky had a good friend, not a complicated love affair.

X

Lou had somehow set up an art studio in a nearby derelict shoe factory, and he spent his time there, getting high, painting, playing loud music that juddered and blipped. I worried endlessly that they were messing about doing graffiti and drugs, glue-sniffing, and I searched my wee brother's face for tell-tale spots, hoping he'd grow out of it soon. That's what I remember. A wee lost boy, a sister who couldn't find the right thread to lead him out of the maze. I was wrong. I never understood the alchemy of it, their group was much more than a bunch of boys messing around. Lou was a few years older, but he was a nuclear engine.

I was told by the papers how Nicky and Lou were as thick as thieves, the subtext being that they were lovers, and went out clubbing to the straight clubs and the gay clubs, taking party drugs, and getting in to all the right raves and trendy clubs. Nicky and Lou were both good looking boys, with floppy hair, and skinny torn jeans. They had friends who were up and coming models, others who were pioneering a new British sound. I read how a few fanzines and low-readership editors latched on to them, their poster boys. I didn't remember any of that. I remembered a tired and hungover teenage boy sprawled on his bed, still in his clothes, one shoe off and stinking of cigarettes and alcohol, in the shape of his father in the room next door.

The empty spray cans and meaningful slogans, bright clothes, poses and challenging art was not for me.

I was trying to move forward, find a different way.

⋊

It was the year that the first full survey of Loch Ness was completed.

I remember thinking that they had found the floor of the deepest loch, but somehow, I could never find my brother. I wouldn't have known he was a rising star, a scenester, a pet of the culture vultures picking at him.

I couldn't fathom how we'd got to that point: the Chunnel was announced in a flurry of press and shares, linking an island to a continent, Nicky made some sort of debut in concept art, and I moved out of our "city-in-the-sky" two-floor flat, leaving Nicky and my father crossing each other on the rare occasion that they were home at the same time. Mick would stay out days at a time – Dev says he saw him sleeping on a park bench once, and Nicky would stay at "the Sugar Factory", as he called the shoe factory studio in a sort of warped homage to Warhol.

I stayed away.

Mrs Ranjeet told me she'd loved hearing them roar with laughter together, even if it was late and they had woken her by slamming the door on their way in from the pub. She didn't mind that. She hated hearing the door slam in anger as one stormed off, worried either might knock on her door with a black eye, a bloodied nose.

She'd shrug.

My new living arrangements were perfect for me. At the end of the summer, Becky had broken up with Andrew. In the before-last year at school, he had finally wooed her with illicit vodka and a drunken snog after the school disco, and for some years, our small group of friends held them up as the love story of our time. I had known better, that she was biding her time. At school, a boyfriend had some sort of status and pastime value. I did not want a boyfriend. I liked going out dancing though, doing my hair, make up, and so I dutifully snogged my fair share, saw some again and let them put their arm awkwardly around my waist. I slept with some, but mostly they got in the way of reading and keeping the flat tidy.

When Becky and I got jobs at Boots the Chemist, Andrew sort of fell away. Neither of them was genuinely interested in the other once they had grown past days spent making out hidden from parents. They could not even agree on films to watch. One morning, I went over to the Factory to see Nicky, to give him money to do the grocery shopping while I worked, only to discover Andrew entangled with a model daubed the "future face of Britain". I helped Becky to pack up his belongings that evening, pile them up on the pavement, and moved into what had been a small spare room in their flat that same day.

Becky and I worked hard, studying to qualify as pharmacists, and saved as much as we could, only going to the cinema once to see *Robin Hood Prince of Thieves*. We had a small, rented TV. We used to drink boxed wine and watch *The Bill*, *Neighbours* and *Only Fools and Horses*. We filled our flat with posters, pictures, trinkets and drunken late-night chats. We dreamt of getting out into the nicety of suburbia one day.

Most weeks, I would go around to the old flat, hoping to see my Bugs, nervously hoping that my father would be there, in one of his rare quiet moods, sitting on the sofa. At the same time I prayed that he would not be, in case he was any other version of himself. Usually they would both be out, and the flat would be a mess, and so I would set about scrubbing and cleaning, emptying, and re-filling the drawers and cupboards as I went. I still found it to be a soothing endeavour, and in all honesty, I was embarrassed to let loose at the flat with Becky, as she was so much more laid back about it, teasing me, the clean freak perfect flatmate for the undomesticated.

When I was at the old flat, Mrs Ranjeet would pop by and give me a hand, for company I think. She was often in alone. Even when she did not help me with the cleaning, we would catch up on the gossip in the block, have a good natter about the latest news, television, and, sometimes, she would tell me of the latest bust up between my father and brother. There was one occasion when she was especially worked up after she overheard Mick shouting, "I will not have any filthy benders under my roof, I'll beat it out of you!" and she had popped her head out of the door in time to see Nicky stumble down the stairs, his face and nose dripping blood. My brother beaten bloody by his father was not such an unusual sight to her by then, but she wanted to know if Nicky was "*a homosexual*"? She said the word cautiously, wrapping her tongue around the unfamiliarity of it, as though she rarely used it. I suppose she did not. The fact was that I

314

honestly did not know.

Maybe. He might have been. Mostly, I think he wanted people to want him in any way possible.

He enjoyed the attention.

2000

Dear Becky,

Yes – I've got an email address. All is well – I'm still following leads.

What if Ange doesn't want to be found? What if what Nana said was true? I don't really know any more. You know what Mick was like. I'd have run away from him.

I don't know. I've been thinking about it all. Nana always said Mick only got bad after she left. But I remember seeing her with a black eye, I'm sure of it. You know that.

I'll let you know if I turn up anything. Going to have a beach day tomorrow.

Tam

I spent that night sitting in a dry shower again and the next day sleeping on the beach. I would go. I couldn't leave without trying, and I didn't want to be stuck here in limbo.

2000

"Hola!... Hello, erm, good morning. Are you Ange? Sorry, Angela?"

"Yes? Are you looking for a massage, or I can give you the times of the yoga sessions? I'm afraid we don't take walk-ins."

She reached for a leaflet beside a Buddha on a chunky rustic wooden table by the door. I read it as she put it in my outstretched hands. A list of times and levels through the week. I took a deep breath.

"Thank you, I'm not. I am, erm, well, Ange – I am Tam."

The thin greying blonde woman looked straight at me properly for the first time. Her eyes widened as my words sank in.

"Yes. Tam. Of course you are."

She crumpled to the ground. I stood on the threshold clutching my handbag, looking down into the face of my mother, a face that I hadn't seen for twenty-five years, since I was a seven-year-old girl, a face that didn't look like the face I had remembered, but was nonetheless a face I knew well.

She was staring back at me, with the same recognition and the same newness. We were locked there for a long moment, eyes in each other's eyes, and then she took a deep breath in, coming up for air, and as she exhaled again, tears were brimming in her blue grey eyes.

Before I knew it, I was on the floor beside her, around her, holding her, and she was clinging on to my arms, both sobbing.

Great sobs. Gulps of air. Wet faces.

How long we sat there, I'm not sure, though it was long enough for my leg to go numb, and to be aware of the seeping cold of the tiles against the bare skin of my bottom, as my lightweight skirt had crumpled up beneath me.

Reality seeped back into Ange at the same moment, and she pulled her body back, still clutching my upper arms. A strand of her long grey hair fell in front of her eyes, and she pulled her hand back to tuck it behind her ear, and then with the same hand, smoothed the hair on my forehead, and stroked my cheek, still looking into my eyes. She started to mutter:

"My little girl, Tam, my baby."

And, from somewhere deep inside me, a word that had lain unused for years surfaced.

"Mummy."

We smiled at each other, embraced, and kissed each other's faces.

We both stood up, smoothing our skirts automatically in a mirrored action, and I followed her down the cool white hall towards a bright sun-drenched kitchen that gave out to a balcony. The house was on a hillside, so that the back of the house was a storey higher than the front, and therefore the garden was lower than the kitchen.

The smell of coffee was welcoming. I stood dazed. I took the hot mug that she handed me.

The heat in my hands grounded me.

We walked on to the balcony and sat on the metal

chairs by the table, silent. I had no idea where to start, and neither did she. I thought about the search to find her, about Nana, and George, and Nicky, and Mick.

I was unsure of what I would say, but needed to say something to fill the silence. If I am honest, I was surprised to hear myself say:

"You have a beautiful garden, Ange."

"Thank you. It was a bare patch of scrub when we moved here, but we planned it, and investigated the best ways of growing gardens in hot countries. The Arabs have good tricks. For example, you need trees to shade the little plants, and vine type plants growing between them, which provides a sort of canopy, and that holds the moisture in. Like an oasis, you see ... water butts, compost, all that ..."

Her voice trailed off.

"It has certainly paid off. It's lovely."

Another silence stretched between us, not uncomfortable, it was a pause, a bit more time to consider what could or should come next. After a few moments, I knew what I needed to do, and to say.

"Ange. Mum. I would like to stay here in Ibiza for a while, so that I can spend some time with you. I don't want to stay here in your home, I have found somewhere in town, and come to see you as often as you'll have me ..."

"Stay here, we can see each other every day, as long as you like."

I couldn't tell if she meant that, if there was hope or fear in her voice, and maybe it's not always so clear cut. I knew what I wanted.

"No. I think I would prefer to stay where I am, I am comfortable, and Mum, it's been a long time, I think it would be better ... but now we've found each other ..."

I trailed off. My plan was straightforward. I would

stay in town for at least a month, and come to see her during the day, for lunch or coffee – whichever suited her. I might come around for dinner. We had the time to get to know each other.

I could not tell her straight out that she had left us in hell, and that my little Bugs had killed himself.

This was not to spare her feelings.

It was selfish on my behalf.

In those few moments in the warm morning sunshine sitting opposite my mother for the first time in years, I realised that I wanted some time to be me, to bask in the comfort of her presence, before I would have to deal with her reaction – indifference, pain, or guilt. I did not want to have to face my guilt for failing as I spoke to my mother for the first time in twenty-five years.

It was too great a roulette for the first shared moments together.

Nicky had made his choice. He could have been here. Having Ange to myself right now was my reward for sticking it out.

She agreed to the plan, she too thought that it would be for the best that we get to know each other as people before bringing up the past and the questions. We were strangely formal. She and Greg had a Thanksgiving party planned for the next day. I should come to that, stay one night then take our time.

I took her in more fully as we spoke, her long greying hair, the silver feather amulet hanging on the leather thong necklace, a tank top with a pattern of a sun in the middle, a long floating skirt. She understood the notion of taking time to let things happen and unpacking the past slowly.

I finished my coffee and Ange stood up, taking our cups into the kitchen. As she did so, she apologised but had an appointment that would arrive in ten minutes' time. She asked me to stay at the house whilst she did the massage, saying that we could lunch together, but I said no, promising to come back for the party. Though we had barely spent half an hour together and said little, I felt washed out.

She kissed me on both cheeks, and we made our way through the kitchen and down the corridor. She had one arm around my waist, and we held hands across our bodies. We hugged and repeated that we would see each other the next day.

As I walked down the hill towards the town centre, I smiled, hugging my little handbag to my body, though I could feel the leather stick to the skin of my cleavage as I was wearing a strappy top. It had taken over two months, not that long after what seemed like a lifetime seeking answers in the wind, and yet I had found my mother, against all odds.

I realised she hadn't asked about Nicky at all. I felt glad. I wasn't ready for all of it straight away. I had not truly been prepared to find her.

)(

The phone rang in the sitting room. Nana managed to pick it up before it rang out.

"Nana! You won't believe this!"

"Tam! How are you? Where are …"

"I found her, I found Ange, I mean Mum, in Ibiza, I'm in the Canaries. Oh Nana, I can't believe this. I'll put another coin in, there. Goodness this booth is eating up the change. I'm going to stay here a while, maybe a month, I'll call you again soon. I'm about to run out of change! I found Mum. Oh, love to George and you Nana. Bye bye!"

The line went dead.

323

Nana said, "Goodbye, I love you," to the handset before hanging up, stunned. I could tell that she wasn't sure whether to be happy or afraid for me. There was not much she could do though.

She had never thought I would find Ange. She had assumed that the search was part of a process I needed to go through, that I would eventually give up and come back, ready to start my life.

2000

I had been to several Thanksgiving dinners and parties during my time in the States. Some years, I had been to more than one – a dinner on the Thursday, a gathering of friends on the Friday, a party on the Saturday, but I did not know what to expect from this one. Greg, Ange's American partner, had a Thanksgiving gathering every year.

When she invited me, she said that for once, this year, she truly had something to give thanks for, and that being that reason, she wanted me to be there.

I was nervous about it and struggled to settle in myself at all. Ange felt like a wonderful, spiritual but strong distant relative, the sort with whom you might have conversations about the state of the world, broad and impressive catch-all statements about the environment, politics, gender, nothing which amounted to any real information, nothing close or personal. Quicksilver moments that are steady until you try and clutch at them.

As I got ready to go up to the house and spend the night, I knew this was a watershed moment for us. The first time that I would sleep in the same house as my mother for twenty-five years. The first time that I would meet her partner. The first time that anyone else would meet us as a reunited mother and daughter.

X

It didn't seem that long since I had walked into a small café and found Ange. I think I was drawn to this café by a sign that promised tea in pots, though I knew that I would order a coffee when the waiter came over. I was not going there as part of my investigation. I would go back to that after.

After I had finished the coffee, I set my photo of my mother on the table in front of me, searching her blue eyes for some sort of answer that could never come. It was then that the waiter came over to ask me whether I wanted another drink. I looked up and the waiter, an English lad, though by his cinnamon skin and bleach blonde hair, one who had lived here in the sun by the sea for many years, exclaimed:

"Is that a picture of Ange? Let's see."

He whistled low.

"She was quite the looker, wasn't she? Wow. Not that she's aged badly, eh? You visiting her?"

It took me about half a minute to pull my thoughts back together. I blinked at him. My first thought was that he seemed far too young for the way he spoke. It was out of sync. My brain clutched at ideas deciding that maybe he had grown up here. Then the reality of what he said exploded in my mind.

He knew my mother.

"Visiting her?" I repeated dumbly.

He looked puzzled, comically so, and the story I had been telling as I searched started to spill naturally from my mouth again. I had quickly learnt that the tale of maternal abandonment was painful to tell every time, and awkward for all who I told it to.

"Ange is my aunt, but my family lost touch, you

know, after my dad died … I'm here for a few months, to learn Spanish. I thought I'd look her up. D'you know where I can find her?"

He smiled warmly and told me that he wasn't surprised that Ange had visitors who turned up with no address. A lovely woman, perhaps not so good at keeping up with family at a long distance. He winked and smiled, and, in a slightly bewildering fashion, turned and walked away.

I sat there, somewhat befuddled, not knowing what I should do.

I was on the edge of running out of the café when he came back from the bar with a paper flyer, bearing the words "Zen life – yoga and massage – bring a new dawn to your days". There was a Sanskrit symbol underneath it, below which the text read "Let Greg and Ange bring the sun into your life", and an address and phone number in the nearby town of Son Servera.

With hindsight, I have no good reason for not having raced straight there.

I didn't.

I couldn't.

Instead, I took the rest of the afternoon to sit in a beach bar with a book. I had decided to go the next morning, and that I would not rush in, but take my time. I spent that night lying awake, wondering about the following day.

In the dawn light, I put the meeting off by one more day, during which I resolved to take things as slowly as possible when I met her. I reminded myself that while I had been building to this moment for a few months, arguably for years, my appearance on her doorstep would be a complete surprise, and she would not be prepared for me, to be my mother, to answer my questions, and she most certainly would not be equipped to handle the news of Nicky.

It would take a few nights sat in the dry shower tray followed by a few more days of trying to switch off my exhausted brain by lying on the beach, and an attempt to collect my thoughts into an email to Becky. I can't remember now if I sent her anything at all.

I'm starting to doubt whether my memories are reliable at all.

)(

That Thanksgiving, I made my way to the house feeling more daunted than when I had first made my way there to find her. That time I had been excited and unsure of myself, and fixated on what I would say when she opened the door, or if someone else opened it or if it turned out to be yet another dead end.

Thanksgiving was different. I was going to a party. To my mother's party.

I decided to walk up the little hill. It was a beautiful afternoon, and the water in the bay was so calm that it barely sparkled, though the light was clear, like after a heavy rain. I could pick out every detail of the castle. I enjoyed walking up the town streets, the warm fishy smell oddly pleasant, and took my time, partly to ease the butterflies in my stomach.

As I got closer, I started to find the smell of the old streets overpowering and nauseating. I felt that I would retch before I got to the house. I sped up, determined to get there before my nerves got the better of me.

In the States, Taylor had taught me a technique to keep the mind in the here and now, to keep my thoughts from running ahead of me, holding the reins of a galloping heart and bolting brain. In this case, it involved narrating everything around me, the houses, the buildings, and the street as I went along. When I got to the house, I described the windows and door so that I could steel myself to make my presence known. There were geraniums of every colour on every sill and an enormous yucca overgrowing and splitting a massive terracotta pot, so vast I could have curled up and hidden in the womb-like warmth of its dark earthy roots.

With a deep breath, I raised my hand to the doorbell.

I paused. The buzzer was white going yellow in the strong sunshine, with a slightly fading and cracking black rubber washer around it in a rectangular white plastic box that seemed to be surviving the sunlight a little better. It wasn't like the first time. I knew she was there. She had invited me to the party.

I hadn't seen my mother in twenty-five years and she had invited me to a party. I didn't know what to make of this or what to expect.

My finger hovered a long moment before I pressed the buzzer.

2000

The entire evening was a surreal experience. I felt as though I lived it through a glass bowl. Greg had opened the door and immediately enveloped me in a hug before I had even opened my mouth to greet him.

Greg had a tall and lanky build, with a bit of an incongruous potbelly bulging under his fading t-shirt, longish grey hair scooped into a ponytail at the fuzzy nape of his neck, though he was clean-shaven. I stood stock still in his strong embrace with my arms hanging at my side, unsure of how to react. My right fist clenched, and I felt my nails press into the weaker, recently re-healed grooves there. The feeling centred me.

"Hello, erm, good evening, Greg, err, mister, erm … Happy Thanksgiving! Thank you for …"

"At last! We are family, Tam, no formalities, you are my family. Ange is so happy that you reached out to her. It has helped balance her chakras. Of course, we will be complete when Nicky finally comes, but for now, we are a happy family. Come in!"

I gulped when he said the name, my mouth going dry and my mind flapping frantically for a way to set things straight tactfully, however Greg was guiding me by the arm down the hall before I could say a word.

They had set up an outdoor cooking area on the left-hand side of the balcony, with an enormous tagine dish sitting on a paella gas ring, and a barbecue where several stuffed peppers and aubergine steaks sat on the braise. There were two men leaning against the white balustrade by the set-up. On the right, where the living room led straight out onto the balcony, a sofa and low table had been pulled out. The French windows were open, and a sort of relaxed electronic music with an acoustic guitar overtrack floated out. Down the solid cement steps into the garden, there were a few hammocks between the trees, garden chairs, a good dozen people mingling here. There was a woman sat gently bouncing on one of the big silver rubber balls, and I noticed some tall bongos sitting by the wall.

Ange was sitting in the middle of a group. Her head was thrown back in a throaty laugh, her long greying hair puffed out and almost blonde in the light. She was a very good-looking woman and basking in the attention. It was strange to see her like this, completely at odds with the image I had of her.

My deer in the headlights daze passed. Panic raced up my spine. My body readied itself to run back up the stairs, past the chatting men at the barbecue, through the kitchen, back down the hall, out through the door along the street, past the houses and balconies. Every part of me wanted to escape. I started to take a step backwards and bumped into Greg. He chuckled an apology and called out to Ange that I had arrived.

She looked up, and sprung lightly off the bar stool, like a teenage girl might, seeming to glide over to me. She smiled, taking my face in her hands, and kissed both my cheeks.

"Darling Tam, I am so glad that you are here! Let me introduce you to some friends."

In a loud voice she called out for attention and every guest fell silent.

"It is Thanksgiving and I am thankful to share this evening with you. This year especially as I give thanks for the return of my daughter Tam, who has found her way to me at last."

To whoops and cheers all around, she kissed me, a great performance, grabbed my hand, lifting it briefly and triumphantly in the air and led me to the bar area. I saw a flash of Nicky in my mind, that same self-satisfied smile.

Ange made me sit on her bar stool and handed me a drink, waving the occasional nibble of an olive or a crisp or some bread and olive oil in my direction. She introduced me to all her friends, and acquaintances and even a few clients, which she confessed, through a tipsy giggle, to not liking very much. There was no sign of typical American Thanksgiving food.

Each time Ange introduced me as her beautiful daughter Tam, I was kissed on both cheeks, pulled into hugs, bombarded with small talk. Many said they had heard a great deal about me. I wondered if they were being polite or whether Ange had been telling them inventions over the years.

At one point, Greg stood on the steps and gave a speech that was a prayer to Gaia, Mother Earth, welcoming me and thanking me for helping to complete the family. Ange hugged me, and I felt so overwhelmed that I forgot to smile. The guests moved towards the laden table and after standing back for a moment, I followed suit, tucking into an aubergine steak in a pitta wrap, with some of the spiced vegetable stew from the tagine. At least if I were eating, I couldn't be expected to talk, and I felt the attention shift away from me.

Later, the tone of the party changed. Fairy lights

were strung under the vine plants between the trees, and various flame torches and tea lights had been lit. Someone raised the volume of the music from the living room, and a man in a stripey woollen hooded jumper started playing the bongos. I sank to the back of the garden, through the people that had started to dance.

The effect on me at this point was bewildering. I felt like I had stumbled into a world I had no place in.

One of the hammocks was empty, and so I sat down across it, taking in the scene. It was a joyful party, none of the wild desperation I had seen at parties before, loose happy people, moving together like a calm seashore on a bright sunny evening. I could not have felt more out of place if I had been from a different planet.

A jolly middle-aged and slightly drunk woman came and asked to join me on the hammock. She had sat down before I could answer, and we wobbled – bashing into each other as I tried to scoot to the side. She was dressed quite differently, almost Home Counties, with a gold watch and a string of pearls, in a sapphire blue satin t-shirt blouse, slightly damp and clammy looking in patches.

"Now Tam, I know who you are, but I know that in that whirlwind, you've probably forgotten my name, and that's to be expected. You've had to meet everyone, quickly. All of them asking you questions. I'm Margaret, though most people call me Rita here. Short for the Spanish, Margarita, you see. I've been here for years, and when I first came here, I liked being known as Margarita. I'm going to tell you a bit about my time here so that everyone can see that you are in a conversation, and you need to nod every so often. But you don't need to listen, I won't be offended. I like to chat and since my John died, I don't always get to. You need to zone out for a little. I will be your cover, OK?"

I smiled genuinely for the first time that evening. I was grateful to her. She duly chattered on about her first trip to Ibiza in the early '80s. I appreciated that she had named her cat Ariadne. She told me about her younger Spanish lover who worked in a bar. I laughed out loud in surprise when she said:

"He's probably bonking me because I'm so generous to him."

I was rather impressed by her delight in this arrangement, which she described as all the fun with none of the emotional drama, but other than that, I half listened and pondered the party in front of us. Greg was rolling a joint, burning the hash carefully and crumbling it onto a little dish. Ange was back in the bar area, somewhat flirtatiously giggling with a rotund and moustachioed man.

I thought about the warm greeting that I had been given and as I pondered everything that was said to me, I realised that several people had said words to the effect that they were glad that I had finally got in touch, that Ange had been hoping for a long time to hear from me, that it was about time that I came.

I turned this over in my mind. It meant two things. One, that Ange had spoken about me to so many separate people before I had come here, and secondly, that she had expressed the hope of seeing me.

I let these facts sink into my mind, which perhaps, given the amount of beers that I had drunk, took a bit longer than it might otherwise have done.

I had never given that much thought to how Ange felt about me. In my mind, she had always been a distant idealised fairy-tale, benevolent, and detached. I suppose a part of me thought that she would have hidden my existence, and another part felt that perhaps she had always spoken of me, in the way my friends' mothers spoke of them.

I turned to my hammock companion:

"Rita, thank you for this. I really appreciate this time."

"*¡Guapa!* Don't worry about it! Any time. Would you like to go and mingle now?"

"No, I would like to ask you something, but I'm not entirely sure what. I want to know what Ange has said about me. You know, before I came. So many people here said that they had heard of me. I would like to know what she said to people."

"Of course, I understand. Why don't I go and get us a couple of other beers from the bar? No, don't you go, you'll never make it back! I can tell you what I know of you, through Ange. How does that sound?"

"Perfect."

She was back quickly and sat down as she handed me a beer.

She told me what she knew. She had started coming to the studio some twenty years earlier and had quickly become more than a client, a real friend.

Initially, my mother hadn't spoken at all about her previous life, but about a year after Rita had started going to the studio, she had received a bundle of letters, the ones from Nana. After receiving them, she had taken about a month off from teaching without warning, and Rita had been to see her out of concern.

Over the course of several loose-lipped evenings, Ange had told Rita about my father, their life and about leaving us behind. Rita had encouraged her to write, but also told her that as she had opened the door, she should wait, and give us the choice to come to her.

Rita paused in her telling, took a swig of beer, and looked at me:

"I hope I did the right thing? She told me that she had abandoned you and didn't feel she had any right to barge in and claim the role of mother. You know, she always hoped to hear from you. There have been times when ..."

She trailed off.

"... well, I'm sure she wouldn't mind me saying, times when she has cried her heart out about her decision and worse, and times when she has gone to the airport to see if she would see you, or with the intention of flying back to find you. She bought a ticket several times. I'm so glad you came. At last."

Rita went quiet. I didn't know what to say. It had never occurred to me to consider how my mother behaved. I felt a bit guilty. I could have come sooner. At least eight years sooner, when Nana gave me her letter and I ran away to America.

"You know, she'd have been about the age you are now when she first told me about you. I'll be honest. May as well. She was miserable too, back in Glasgow. She was so young when you were born. She was a teenager, caught up in a whirlwind romance that crushed her dreams. She told me she never felt like a mother. It's hard to hear, but often she was glad that she had left you behind, gone to live her life. It did her good to talk about it. I think she felt like her life was over before it started. Anyway, it wasn't my place to say anything other. She always thought that if she'd stayed, she would have done you more damage than anything else."

Rita paused. I gave her a sort of half-smile, trying to encourage her to reach the end of the thought, and not wanting to have to speak. It was a lot to absorb. It hurt. But I needed to hear it.

"She always felt that she had done the right thing by you both. She has suffered enormously. You need to know that."

I leaned back in the hammock. The party was starting to dwindle now, Bongo Man had stopped drumming and was sat cross legged on the ground talking to a younger woman who was wearing a bikini top and a sarong.

I knew from Nana that the first letter had arrived from my mother in 1981, which must have been when she had received the bundle of letters sent to India.

My mind was an insect trapped in amber trying to shatter the orange case, trying to shake itself out. My thoughts were sticky winged things, incoherent and desperate.

The garden seemed to whirl around me.

"Sweetie, you look a little the worse for wear. Why don't I show you to the spare room, and you can call it a night. We'll say goodnight to Ange and Greg on the way."

I nodded and let her lead me by the hand through the party. I must have looked drunk or stoned, though I was neither, the smiling faces swirled before me as they called out goodnight.

Beside the spare room, there was a small, shared shower and toilet on the top floor above the kitchen, with Greg and Ange's bedroom across the hall, and a fourth door off the landing with the sign "Sshh, therapy in session".

I thanked Rita and gave her a hug.

The first one that I had given with any sort of real emotion the entire evening. My overnight bag was already on the bed, and I pulled out the large t-shirt which I slept in, and my toothbrush and toothpaste. In the bathroom, I brushed my teeth then washed my face.

When I looked up at myself in the mirror, seeing my face was like looking at an oddly familiar stranger, the beads of water dripping, and a lock of hair plastered to the side. I leant forward and drank greedily from the tap. I hadn't realised how thirsty I had been. I towelled my face dry, and then went back to the room. Despite the chatter from the garden, I think I was asleep before my head hit the pillow.

The next day, late in the morning, I woke up. The heavy-duty Spanish style blinds, that I hadn't noticed the night before, had kept out the morning light, and I woke up feeling thirsty, relaxed and slightly disorientated. If I wasn't in the guesthouse, then … my mind whirred into gear, then, in the still complete darkness of the room, it all came back.

My gut lurched and I threw up in the toilet. I cleaned up, and got into the shower, still in my t-shirt and pants and sat under the running water.

I stayed there for a good half hour, thinking over everything that Rita had told me. Nothing was as linear as I remembered.

I peeled off my sodden t-shirt and washed properly, dried off and crept back into bed, naked, ready to be born again as the real me, reformed.

※

Light flooded the bedroom when I opened the blinds, and I had to blink a few times because it was so bright. My eyes adjusted, and I looked around. It was tidy except for my bag spilling its guts all over the floor, nothing that could not quickly be set right.

I picked up the bag, put it on the bed, and took out my clothes for the day, a pair of lightweight cotton trousers and a strappy top. The door to Greg and Ange's bedroom was ajar, and I could see that the bed was made. I nipped to the bathroom and retrieved my overnight t-shirt and pants from the shower curtain rail and scooted back to the room. Once I was dressed, I left my overnight bag neatly repacked and zipped up on the tightly made bed and made my way downstairs. My flip-flops clip clopped on the steps.

Ange was sitting on the kitchen counter, crossed-legged and sipping a steaming greenish liquid from a thick glass.

"I thought we could do my morning sun salutations together. I'll talk you through it."

"OK."

I was relieved any big talk could wait until the sun had been properly greeted in her fashion.

Our yoga practice was genuinely enjoyable and peaceful, in the garden under the vines. Fortunately, I had done a little yoga in the States and could almost keep up with my mother, even if I wasn't anywhere close to her flexibility. She had a toned and lithe frame and executed all the movements with practiced confidence.

When we were done, we went back up the steps to find that Greg had set out lunch, a light salad of fresh tomatoes sprinkled with basil, sliced cucumber with mint and green peppers, a plate of Can Caus goat's cheese, a light green leaf salad and some fresh bread. We chatted about the party the night before, and I said that I had enjoyed meeting all their friends, and mentioned Rita's kindness. Ange declared that she just loved her. I wondered when she would ask about Bugs. She seemed to be avoiding any meaningful conversation.

After the plates had been cleared, I told them that I was expected back at the guesthouse. They were both disappointed that I would not stay with them. I knew that before that happened, there was a lot I needed to tell Ange. It boiled down to the fact that I could not spend another night in my mother's house knowing that her son was dead when she didn't.

Greg must have picked up on something, because when the post coffee quiet settled, he announced that he needed to go and run some errands in town. We cleared the table, and though it was another beautiful day outside, Ange and I went to sit in the cool shade of the living room. I think she sensed I had something to tell.

Side by side on the sofa, I started from the morning after she left.

)(

"Ange ... Mum ... I ... OK. That Saturday morning, when you left, the house was completely silent. I was sleeping. I waited for you to come and wake me up. You didn't, and I needed a wee. I snuck out to the toilet, and then I tiptoed down the stairs. There on the kitchen table, was your note. I picked it up and read it."

I recited the letter to her:

> "Mick – You win. I can't do this. I am nothing. I can give them nothing. I can't even feed them. I cannot care for them. Nana will help, I'm sure. I am sorry – Ange."

Ange blanched.

She had tears in her eyes. She blinked and I nodded. I had to go on.

I told her Dad had not been there to feed Nicky that morning, nor would he be for many mornings, or evenings, or even lunches ...

I told her it was the first time that I had dug my

341

nails in to clear the pain.

I showed her the silver crescents in my palms, the marks on my arms.

She needed to know.

I told her about dinners with Mrs Ranjeet, details of things I remembered, about the Norackel, the Wild Boys, the Sugar Factory and Lou. I told her about Mick drinking, and disappearing for days. I told her he had collapsed in the hallway many times, and that one morning I found him there, dead.

I paused and looked at her. She swallowed hard but sat motionless.

She said nothing. I could hear Greg padding around the kitchen.

He knocked on the door as he opened it and looked us both up and down.

"Ladies, you have been talking for a long time, and you both look washed out. You should have a break. Come and stretch, have a drink, have some food."

I almost blurted out that Nicky had died by suicide, if not for any other reason than not keeping it from her any longer, I looked at her face, and she needed some time to process all this new information, and to talk it over with him.

"Thanks, Greg. I could do with a bite. Come on, Mum."

I had been calling her Mum since I had found her as a kindness, as a wish maybe, but it felt right, something for us both to cling to.

We ate on the balcony in silence. At the end of the meal I hugged them both, and told Ange to call me at the BnB when she was ready to hear the rest.

As I walked away, I felt like the land drinking up the light after a long winter.

It was five days before I heard from her.

2000 / 1975

It was almost Christmas.

My hosts hung threadbare tinsel garlands and a sign that said "*Feliz Navidad, Mery Christmas*". An ornate and detailed nativity scene with a still empty manger had pride of place in the sitting room.

It was late when Ange called me, asking to meet the following morning. That night, I decided not to sit in the shower. I lay on my bed with the thin curtains open, letting the streetlight flood over me.

I could not sleep.

Nonetheless, I was ready bright and early and came out to find Ange waiting in her battered Suzuki four-wheel drive in front of the guesthouse. Where once there should have been a spare wheel on the back, the long industrial size screws jutted out. The grey plastic dashboard was faded, with a few deep scratches and marks. I climbed into the passenger seat on the right-hand side and leaned over the gear stick to hug her and planted a kiss on her cheek.

She nodded.

"I thought we might take a drive up the coast, and maybe go for a walk to one of the secret beaches. I've brought some bits and pieces for lunch."

"That sounds lovely, Mum."

The word "Mum" still felt awkward, but I wanted to call her that, and she seemed to take comfort in the implied affection of it.

We headed west past the airport, we turned inland, but in the small town of Sant Josep de Sa Talaia we turned back towards the coast. We drove through an area of larger houses, but soon the landscape turned to farms and then to a pine forest, the rich warm scent filling the car. Eventually we turned off and started down a steep track. It occurred to me that not only had I not even considered that Greg and Ange might have a car, I had never seen my mother drive, nor had I known whether she could drive at all. It struck me that I hardly knew her. The real Ange was not as I had constructed her in my memories.

We drove in silence for most of the way, with Ange only interjecting the occasional fact, such as the name of a place, or pointing out a house where a friend might live. I commented that there didn't seem to be many lights or decorations for Christmas yet. She spoke of Christmas in Spain. I wondered why she hadn't asked about Nicky at all. She had not asked me about anyone. Maybe she knew already. Had it made the papers here? Did she even get the papers? He wasn't well known outside of the UK until after his death, and his celebrity might not have seeped out of the art magazines here. It was entirely possible that she did not. She and Greg did not watch television. After everything I had told her about our childhood, the most probable explanation was that she was giving me time to tell her.

The track petered out, but there was a space to leave the car. We got out, stretching our legs, and she pulled a rucksack from behind her seat by leaning in to the open back of the jeep. Resting it on the wheel guard inside the boot area, she unzipped the bag and pulled out a litre and a half plastic bottle of water and took a swig from it. She then held it out to me, across the open space of the back of the car. I took it from her hands and took a swig too. I hadn't realised until that point how thirsty the dust from the track had made me. The way the hills and the jagged coastline plunged straight into the sea reminded me of the Californian coast.

I walked around the car, took the cap from her hand, and screwed it back on to the bottle, and then put it into the bag which she was holding open. As she zipped it back up, I put an arm around her shoulders and gave her a light squeeze.

"Right, Mum, where to?"

I followed her across the parking area towards what looked like the edge of a cliff, but was the start of the path. I knew at once that this was her expedition, her story-telling day, and just as I had felt only a few days previously, she had geared herself up for it – I knew that once we were on the path she would start.

I was ready.

"For a long time, I told people that I left home to see the world on my twenty-fifth birthday. But I never used to say that I also left my husband, or that I had left my seven-year-old daughter and my three-year-old son behind. They would not have understood."

She missed a step in her walking, her right foot coming down a bit more abruptly but without stumbling she carried on, a step ahead of me.

"Your father, Mick, was a few years above me at school. There must have been a lad a few years older than you that all the girls liked at your school, right? Mick was that lad. I wanted to be the girl in my class that went out with him. I didn't want to get married and have a family. Sure, I daydreamed it might happen eventually but not before I had finished

345

my last year. I wanted to dance with him. Kiss him. Maybe... well I was just seventeen. I hadn't thought about it all. It's not like it was easy to find out how sex worked back then. It was all whispered information. Then I fell pregnant."

She pulled her hair back into a tight ponytail.

"My parents, I mean your grandparents ... They were Christians, heavily involved in their church. It always came first. All the commandments. The Bible says this, the Minister says that. It wasn't for me. I didn't believe, I didn't want to be good. There was too much out there for me to do."

She paused and cast about for the words.

"They were old fashioned. They did not approve of me being pregnant. Back then, girls got in trouble and got sent to homes. They let me get married. I didn't have to disappear. But they did not want to have anything to do with it. After the wedding, they disowned me. They went to church and prayed for complete strangers, but they had no prayers or forgiveness for me."

"Nana always said they were in Australia."

"Oh Tam! I used to tell you that when you were little. It was just easier than trying to explain to a four-year-old that her grandparents didn't want to have anything to do with her."

That was as much as she was going to say about them. I felt the door close on the subject as heavily as a coffin lid.

Ange answered my unspoken question.

"Tam, in those days, abortions weren't legal, back-alley ones, well, they were hard to arrange. I'm sorry but the truth is if I'd had the option, I would have done it. Mick too. We didn't have many options. He could have abandoned me too. I would have been sent to a single mother's home if he hadn't married me. You would have gone into the adoption system. He tried his best for us to be a family, and I tried too. We really did. We were both so unhappy."

She stopped on the path and swung her bag off her shoulder, pulled out the water bottle and handed it to me.

"We had huge rows, and yes he did hit me a few times, but that wasn't so unusual back then ... and I wasn't a great wife. The makeup sex was brilliant. Sorry, you don't want to know that. We were young, we didn't know what we were doing."

It was a dry day, and we were both flushed, a sheen of sweat on our foreheads, and dust on our faces. I could see that tears had carved a small pink streak beneath each eye on her dusty cheeks.

"I really didn't want to be a mother. I was angry at him all the time. Tam, the neighbours, the folk I'd grown up with, they talked about me being pregnant so young. I didn't want you tainted with it. If I left, you would have sympathy and kindness. With me as your mother you would have been tainted for life."

I knew the story I had told myself and this didn't quite fit with the fairy tale girl I had pictured. I had filled in the blanks so many times before but I had never imagined this. She had been a headstrong young woman.

She skipped ahead to the night that she left us.

One night, Mick had gone back out, and she had gone to Mrs Ranjeet. I hadn't known that Ange and Mrs R had had such a close sympathy for each other. Whenever she needed to knock on the door for help, the older lady had always let her in, washed and tended to any wounds, sat quietly as my mother had allowed the tears to flow.

That had been the fourth time that she had been truly afraid for her life.

"He really went for it. My left arm was popped out of its socket. It took me a long time for it to be strong again."

She rolled her left shoulder but did not turn to look at me.

"I knew he would never hurt you or Nicholas. I had tried to be your mother but I hated it. I loved you. I knew you could all be happier if I just disappeared."

She had barely been able to swallow because her throat was so sore from where my own father had almost crushed it flat.

"You need to know. I pushed him. I hated the pretend happy family life he was trying to build. I didn't want it. You're grown now and I'm glad to know you, but I wanted to get out of it all so badly, I didn't care how."

She had struggled with Nicky's tantrums and my introspection, hated laundering nappies. She was confounded by preparing meals that my father would eat with false cheer.

She told me that she cried in the kitchen because she couldn't cope with two children, that she was not fit to be a mother, that we were hard work. That she hated having to care for us, the endless demands, her puffy eyes and all the things that she was missing while she was stuck at home. The soul-crushing loneliness without ever having a moment to herself.

I felt my temper flare. That wasn't our fault.

I bit my tongue and clenched my fists and it hurt just enough to focus again.

I needed to let her continue. She thought someone else would do a better job. She had hoped Nana would step in and take us away. Nana was always popping round with comments on everything Ange was doing wrong. Taking over.

Every morning Ange woke wishing we had vanished.

I stopped, took off my shoe and pretended to shake out a stone. She halted. We were completely silent. I didn't want her to stop, but I needed a moment. She took a few more steps along the path.

"Not far now. Almost there."

She seemed to find it easier to talk as she walked ahead, always a step away from me. I put my shoe back on and we set off again.

"I convinced Nana that I needed to go to London for a few days, to get some rest. That's where my friends Babs and Jane were living. I got the train. From the moment I left the flat I felt lighter, better. I slept the whole way there on the train. Spent the whole weekend out having fun. I felt like I was me again. Coming back, I just couldn't face it. Being a mother. I told Mick we should look at putting you up for adoption. We could go our separate ways. Nana was having none of it. She said we would always regret it."

I thought of Davy and Agnes growing up in the Ayr countryside. They had happy childhoods on the farm. Mick however …

"Mick would always listen to her. That's when we had the fight. He wanted me to stay."

I tried to focus on how she would have felt, screamed at, beaten, afraid for her life, for wanting to leave. For admitting that she could not cope alone.

"I went to Mrs Ranjeet. When I came back, I packed and left. I thought Mick was home. Tam, I need you to know I did not think that you were alone in the flat."

"So you thought it was OK to leave us with a passed out drunk?"

"No, it's not like that. It's …"

"Ange, it is what it is. We were alone for three days."

She turned to look at me.

"I am truly sorry for that. I am."

349

"OK."

It wasn't alright at all, but I needed to know the rest of the story.

"I snuck out and got the first train to London. I called him once. I was only going to spend a week with Babs and Jane. I told him I was going to come back, get my own place, work for Mr McIntyre. You know. Get myself sorted and then we would work out what to do with you. Mick wasn't happy, he said that if I ever came back, then I should be ready to be a mum, to throw myself into family life with him, to stop wishing I was somewhere else. He said it was all three of you or nothing at all."

She wiped her brow.

"I almost did come back. I hated being a mother, I really did. I missed you. I missed you both. I packed up to come back a couple of times. But I called Nana and she told me how happy you were. One time she came to pick me up from the train station when I arrived. She asked me if I really wanted to be a mother, be Mick's wife. The truth was, I did not. I wanted to be free. She bought me the return to London then and there. I never even left the station."

It was like glass shattering around me, every carefully constructed memory being smashed.

"I knew then you were fine. Nana was looking out for you. Mick was a good father. I believed it. I am so sorry that I was wrong. I spent the last five days thinking of everything you told me. I had not thought for a moment you would be unhappy. With me gone, you would be fine. Free of my mistake. All of us. So, I decided to make the most of everything London had to offer."

She drifted into telling me what the UK was like at the time, with surprising detail. It crossed my mind that maybe, like me, she had revisited the time in her mind, polishing the memories like a window to peer through.

It was 1975, and Harold Wilson was Prime Minister, and Margaret Thatcher had become head of the Tory opposition. Unemployment soared, the IRA were active and inflation was huge. There were also several high-profile murder and rape cases, the clear majority being of women at the hands of their partners. She had let Babs and Jane convince her that she could end up being one of those blurry front-page pictures.

"It gave me a good excuse to stay with them, to play the part."

Babs and Jane had become obsessed with these terrifying headlines in the press. She added that her personal fixation with the stories was probably linked to some sort of depression. She was persuaded by the narrative. If she went back to Mick she would end up that way.

I was amazed by the level of detail Ange had retained as she recounted the kidnap and murder of teenage heiress Lesley Whittle, who was discovered strangled on a ledge in the drains below Bathpool Park near Kidsgrove in Staffordshire. She remembered almost every detail of Lord Lucan's conviction for the murder of nanny Sandra Rivett. Then there were three women attacked with a hammer in West Yorkshire, in the alleyways of their towns. She shook her head as she told me that one of the victims, Tracy Brown, was only fourteen.

She had clung to these terrible events as a sort of mantra that justified her flight. She had made them part of her personal life memories. They were surely as much a part of her as the time I fell off a wall, cut my knee and carried a jaggy scar.

"Things were changing a lot for women just then. Second-wave feminism was coming over from the States. We could imagine beyond marriage and babies. I felt I was a living embodiment of it."

We had reached the end of the track, which opened into a small cove. The sand was fine, and the sea was calm. It was idyllic, like a movie location. While she had yet to ask me about Nicky it was clear that we had tacitly reached a point where we would take a break.

Ange and I fell silent as we spread a couple of sarongs on the beach to sit on. I pulled some sunscreen out, and smeared it on my arms, legs, and face, which were all starting to feel a little burnt. There were a few stinging scratches on my limbs which I hadn't noticed while we'd hiked down. We unpacked the food and sat for a while, slowly eating in a deep ponderous silence in the hot sunshine.

Ange pulled out a Tupperware box of grapes. She snapped off the lid and held the box out to me. As I took one, she said:

"That year, Hampstead broke highest ever rainfall records."

"What? Ange, how do you remember that?!"

"I remember so many things from that year. Before and after can be a little hazy."

She chuckled.

She went back to telling me her story, by saying that "George Davis is innocent" was sprayed on every wall all over the country.

"London in the '70s was crazy. I wanted to seize every opportunity. I hadn't run all that way just to work and spend weekends cleaning the flat. I wanted to have as much fun as I could. I did too."

Winding through the release of *Bohemian Rhapsody*, the rise of Roxy Music and the omnipresence of Supertramp, Ange eventually got to telling me about the key event in her move to Goa. Babs was working for Atlantic Records and had managed to get backstage passes to all five of Led Zeppelin's sold-out shows at Earl's Court.

Together with Jane, the three had gone along. Ange did not go into a great amount of detail, but it was clear to me that they had been groupies. Babs got them in to all sorts of aftershow parties, and they clearly made themselves very welcome.

Ange went on to explain that somehow, through this network, it was arranged for the three of them to head out to Goa for a month, to spend time with another band. They had felt it would be a free holiday, and that for the most part they would just be having a nice time.

She loved Goa, and when it was suggested that they stay on into the New Year, they agreed to see in 1976 in the sunshine.

"It was actually a lot more innocent than you'd think. Mostly it was groups of friends having a lovely time together. Maybe getting a little high. None of those sex orgies, not really anyway. Usually one girl was going steady with one of the guys and sure the rest of us would enjoy a few dates. Casual flirting."

I almost choked on a grape. "Sex orgy" is not something you expect your mother to say, no matter the context. She was smiling to herself, her gaze distant, lost in a memory, and didn't notice.

It was February '76 when Babs and Jane headed back, but Ange felt that she was finally finding some "headspace" as she called it, some inner strength, and she needed to build herself up before she would think about coming back. She found a small hotel – practically a B&B – and stayed there for about a month. It was this address that Babs had taken back to Nana, though my mother would not get the letters for several years. Because she never received any news, Ange went on to build the assumption that she was not needed or wanted, let alone missed.

"I felt completely free. It was a wonderful time."

Once again, I tried to tell myself that she wasn't indulging in wild fun, that she had been very broken and mistreated, but that story was becoming unstuck. I was struggling to keep inner anger from bubbling out. I wanted to shout at her. How dare she be having the time of her life when her own children were abandoned, left to fend for themselves with a dangerous drunkard? I clenched my fists and felt my nails dig into my palms and focused on that.

"I knew your father would be a wonderful dad to you. Do you know, when I got home from the week in hospital when you were born, it was maybe a bit silly because I wasn't fully healed, but I was young and went out to meet the gang, and your father, he sat all night cradling you, even when you cried, and it was him who managed to get you to take a bottle. He adored you. And Nicky."

My head was spinning. I thought he was the one who had gone out drinking for days. I sat in stunned silence as she carried on.

Having met a group of travelling "artists and freethinkers" as she put it, she moved on up the coast, where they went on to set up a community and retreat. I knew the broad-brush strokes of this part of the story, from the letter that she had eventually sent to Nana many years later. I listened to her tell it, adding detail to what I knew of the years in Goa, her passion for art, her yoga practice, meeting Greg and letting her wild nature settle a little.

X

When Ange finished talking, I closed my eyes and focused on the red tinge inside my eyelids. Without saying a word, I got up, meandered directionless around the cove, and decided to go for a swim. She was lying on the hot beach, dozing, or pretending to.

My mind was whirring. I wanted to scream. To cry. To run.

I went to the water, my toes curling up at the fresh waves, and I strode in, standing waist deep. There were tiny fishes in the clear water. An old plastic bag too, which I fished out and took back to the shore, intending to take it back up the path later. I went back in, and swum the length of the cove a few times, the movement of my body in the water helping me to find my centre again.

I breathed deeply and found a jot of calm compassion. I knew we weren't finished. I was carrying a secret too.

I was the one who had tracked her down out of the blue. She hadn't asked how Nicky was yet. I did not think she knew. I had appeared on her doorstep. We had both been so stunned neither of us had thought beyond the moment. At the Thanksgiving party there wasn't a chance. The next day I had told her about our childhood. Today was her turn. I wanted to scream at her. I could almost hear Taylor's voice telling me to let the emotions out. I ignored her. I resolved that if Ange asked, I would tell her. I would not lie. I would not volunteer the emotion yet. I was not ready to bring it out into the open and deal with her reaction. I did not know her well enough.

I got out of the water and slowly made my way back to our camp.

We lay back in the sand in silence, eventually dozing in the sun for a long while.

I asked a few more details here and there. I wanted to challenge her on all of it. But she had shared her story, she had made her confession, and I did not feel that I was able to tell her that it wasn't fair to abandon us. Memories of my father were creeping back, not the Ogre, but the daddy who taught me to ride a bike, and then Nicky, holding us under our arms and running back and forth until we were ready to shout "Daddy, let go" and squeal "No Daddy, help", catching us again, laughing with joy, out of breath as we managed to cycle ahead, one hand on the small of his back. Nana sounding out our letters to us and Daddy applauding when we pieced the sounds into words. Doing a jigsaw together on the sitting room floor. Proudly framing Nicky's first "proper" picture. Details I had forgotten.

As the sun started to make its afternoon descent, we paddled in the lapping sea, enjoying the feel of the sand under our feet, and the cool of the water. We shook down our sarongs from where we had been sitting, packed up and silently made our way back up the track, back to the car, back towards town.

The whole walk back up the hill and the drive was strangely comfortable despite all I had learned.

The truth was out.

Indeed, I'd perhaps only felt this depth of calm companionship with a few other people in my life, Bugs, Becky and, on occasion, Lou. Unlike previous times though, this feeling lasted. As we pulled up outside my B&B, I felt compelled to ask Ange if I could stay at her house. She nodded in agreement, and I picked up my belongings.

However, I had yet to tell her about Nicky. I had been basking in our little bubble of shared truths, knowing all along that I had not been entirely honest.

Ange was not a delicate perfect being who had fled in fear for her life.

She was a disillusioned young woman who had ran away from harm, possibly with undiagnosed postnatal depression. She had been lost with no way back. She had built herself a new contented life. She did not want to step into a role she felt was not ever hers.

Dad, he was a man. Flawed but human.

Nana had taken us in, given us love, been there for every scraped knee, every broken promise. There to teach us our letters, there to feed us fresh bread and jam. She loved her boy, she loved us. For better or worse, she had tried to protect us.

I had to tell her the final part.

2000

"A black coffee, thank you."

The coffee machine whirred, a modern steam engine, the type that had powered the '90s coffee house revolution. I stared at the barista in a daze. It had been an early start and a short flight, and I was back on the mainland, with a few hours before my next and final flight.

"Miss, please, 250 pesetas."

It seemed expensive compared to the cafes of the last few weeks, but we were in the airport. I handed over a two-euro coin, newly in currency.

"Gracias. Keep the change."

Rita hadn't been as effusive on the drive to the airport, though she did try to be kind nonetheless.

"She'll get better. Greg will take care of her. Maybe, one day, you'll be able to come and visit."

The statement hung in the air. I thought about the day before.

I had joined Ange in her morning yoga practice, and when we finished I told her everything. About Bugs, about his smile, his enthusiasm, his tantrums. About Lou and Nicky's 'deep moods'. She sat silent, statue still. I told her about his dalliances. I had told her about the 'Lost Boys', about the drugs, about his anger, about the day I had realised his trousers were no longer mud-stained in the laundry basket and smelt of nicotine and tar. I told her about his periodic disappearances.

"He did inherit my character then."

I stopped and looked hard at her for a minute. She was right. How had I not noticed before. I had been so caught up in the idea of her as a delicate creature made of porcelain. She was not that person at all. She sighed.

"You're like your father. Kind and gentle, intelligent, strong, thoughtful. Except when he would drink. It was the '70s though. Everyone drank all the time. Every day. Never stood a chance, did he?"

I decided to ignore that. Maybe it was Nana I took after.

"Mum, one morning, about nine years ago now, Lou called me. Early. Nicky was missing. Really missing."

I felt the locks break. I couldn't pause for breath. I couldn't stop the flood of words to let her breathe and take it all in, Nicky's death, the years alone in the USA spilled out of me. The misery in the bathtubs and all the misguided, hurtful relationships. My own suicidal thoughts, and the attempts. The self-harm.

I told her about Bree's apple pie.

"Apple pie? You're telling me about apple pie?"

"Mum, I didn't know how to say it."

"Don't call me Mum."

Her face seemed to have changed. All the softness had dissipated. She looked hard.

"I never have been Mum or Mummy, and I've let you call me that too long now. I'm Ange."

She paused.

"Ange, I'm sorry. I didn't mean not to tell you for so long. I didn't know how."

She shifted in her seat.

"Tam, it's been good having you here. I thought you'd come out of curiosity, I didn't expect much else. I'm still not ready to be a mum. I don't think I ever was meant to be. What Nicky did ... it does hurt, but I can see you're carrying this pain. I gave birth to him, but I didn't know him. I don't really know what you want me to say."

I stared at her. I had expected, maybe even hoped that after the shock she would hug me. I did not know how to react to this.

"There's a reason so many religions consider suicide to be the ultimate act of transgression, it causes so much hurt. It is a sin in the primal sense. You didn't owe it to me to come and tell me. I thank you, I suppose, for feeling you had to."

"I didn't. I thought maybe ... you should know."

She laughed, bitterly. I saw her face clearly. I had been seeing her wrong all along.

"Look, we can be friends. Maybe like an aunt or a big sister. That would be nice, wouldn't it?"

I closed my eyes, trying to clutch at straws of thought.

"Oh, and Nana called the other day. It was so strange to speak to her after all these years. Apparently, Becky tracked down the studio number on the internet. She's wondering how you are and if you'll be back soon. She's missing you, you know. She's done a great job helping to raise you."

I nodded, but it was a mechanical response.

She went back into the house.

I sat alone in the garden for a long time. After a while, I made my way into the house, and let myself out into the hot early afternoon, walked in a washed-out daze back to the BnB, down the street, as though shockwaves were reverberating and pushing me away. The notion they were from the detonation of my own meticulously forged memories crossed my mind.

I didn't have my belongings with me and the family were surprised to see me back, but the room hadn't been taken, and they lent me a clean t-shirt and toothbrush the next day.

)(

I spent the night sitting in the shower holding a sharp meat knife from the kitchen that I did not remember taking. I did nothing with it. I did not intend to. I simply held the handle tightly until I dozed off and dropped it, the clatter rousing me from my daze.

In the morning it was still there, a stark reminder in the shower tray. I picked it up, wiped it down and replaced it in the kitchen drawer when I went down for breakfast.

In the morning, I knew I had to go back. I was nervous, but I did not want to run away and leave her without knowing where I had gone.

I made my way back to Ange's and let myself in. They had given me a key. Greg was doing a headstand in the garden. I went up to her room. The blinds were shut. She was lying there, in the dark. She looked small, tired, and frail, unmoving.

"Mum? Ange?"

No response.

I bent over and placed a kiss on her forehead. I stroked her hand. Then I left the room. Greg was in the kitchen when I came back down. He smiled kindly.

"Tam, I'm sorry to hear about your father. I'm even more sorry about Nicholas. But I think it's time for you to leave. I mean leave the island. First thing tomorrow. She has a migraine. It happens sometimes. I just think you're looking for something she can't give you. She doesn't owe you. I don't mean that you're not welcome. I just think you both need a bit of space."

I swallowed down a dull feeling.

"It's OK, Greg, I think you're right. I have a few things upstairs in the spare room. I'll just go pack."

I didn't know what else to say.

Greg went upstairs with a cup of fresh mint tea for Ange. I waited a moment, until I heard the bedroom door click shut, and followed him up.

I went into the spare room, which now felt entirely cold – like it too wanted to spit me out into the world. I hadn't expected this. I had certainly not dared to hope that she might soothe me; but perhaps we could have helped each other, held each other, got through it together.

I packed my belongings – books, swimsuit, shorts, a sarong, a few knickknacks I had accumulated. It didn't take that long, though I felt as though I moved as slowly as a bug caught in sap. I didn't look back as I walked down the stairs, along the corridor, and opened the door to let myself out.

I took the key out of my pocket and put it on the hall table.

I felt a sob rise at the back of my throat and tears prickling my eyes. I gripped the door handle as hard as I could, until the clear white sensation was strong enough to focus on. I held it for a moment longer. I heard a noise; Greg clearing his throat on the landing upstairs. He had seen me and was waiting for me to leave.

Everything that needed to be said had been.

2000

I closed the door gently, waiting for the latch to click.

Only then I looked properly, taking in the front of the little Spanish townhouse. My mother's house, with its cheerful riot of geraniums, an overgrown jasmine, heady scents filling my nose. I bent and stroked the rough earthenware edge of the yucca's enormous terracotta pot, shattered and split when the plant had tried to put down its roots. My mother's vessel had not been strong enough to hold the tree, to take its needs and look after it. I looked up. The tree was thriving, but it needed a new place to grow if it was to ever spread its branches, fronds reaching into the deep blue sky.

I made my way to the town centre and found a café, but my head felt fuzzy, as though it was still early in the day. I decided to go back to the BnB to pick up my book and head to the beach. It was like I was moving in slow motion, every movement pushing against the tide. I lay down on the bed and shut my eyes for a moment.

The next thing I knew I was waking in the dark of night, the world outside still and silent. I pulled the covers over me, cocooned, and slept until the dawn sun had well and truly risen. I had never slept twenty-two hours straight before. It had been a deep dreamless sleep, nothing like my usual tossing and turning. I felt refreshed, light.

I washed, got dressed and packed up for the final time.

I stripped the bed and made a neat pile of sheets and towels on the bathroom floor.

I was ready to go home.

)(

When I left the BnB, I was surprised to find Rita sitting by her car, perched on a wall, eyes closed, face turned up to the morning sun. She called out as brightly as she could muster.

"Morning, Tam! Do you need a ride to the airport?"

"Good morning, Rita, thank you, that's kind, but I am happy to get the bus or a taxi."

"Nonsense. I'll take you."

I wondered if Greg was ensuring my prompt departure. I didn't mind. With that, I put my bag in the back seat of Rita's car. As soon as my seat belt was done up, she started the car, and we set off, Rita intently staring at the road ahead over the steering wheel.

"Tam, Greg told me some of it, he's truly sad for you. I'm so sorry, I feel like I built up your expectations. You're a grown woman, I suppose I never thought you were also still a child looking for your mum. I thought maybe it was curiosity."

"It's fine. I'm glad I met her. You know, I do have family back home. George and Nana, and Becky. I'm looking forward to getting back to them."

"Good. Maybe you'll come back for a nice visit sometime?"

After she dropped me at the airport, I found my

way through security. There was a café built in to the cavernous hall in a traditional syle with wooden beams and painted tiles.

I adjusted the strap of my navy handbag on my shoulder. I also had a rucksack, into which the handbag would fit. It was already heavy with my in-flight entertainment. A thick book, a couple of magazines, my CD player, and a few favourite CDs in a yellow and black case. I picked my coffee up from the stainless-steel bar and made my way to the little table.

The warm steam had set me thinking to breakfasts in the little café by the BnB, simple toast and grated tomato with a coffee and fresh orange juice, then to breakfast made by Greg, chopped fruit, yogurt, nuts. My thoughts wandered back to Ange. Maybe it was the journey ahead, maybe I was weary, and this felt like my first sip of decent coffee for what seemed like a million days, but something was shifting in me in the anonymity of the Ibiza airport. Although one side of the waiting lounge had large floor-to-ceiling windows, little sunshine penetrated under the suspended tile ceilings creating a surreal timelessness. A man in a blue cap pushed a large polishing machine across the ceramic floor.

I had always thought that my mother was but a girl when she met my father. I had assumed her to be a lost teenager in love with a bad apple, then her parents had left for Australia, believing her happily settled. It was not that clear cut. She had been a young woman, a little wild, still finding herself. In some ways, she still was. I thought about her in this new light. I felt more mature than her. She was right about something though; our relationship would never be that of mother and daughter. I did not need that now.

I toyed with running away again, New Zealand perhaps. I was done, though. Unlike Ange, I was ready to go home. Ready to go back to my family there. Life was not that broken. It was life; messy and imperfect. And mine.

I wryly congratulated myself on being so calm, settled and pragmatic about it all.

Gate Fifteen. My lucky number.

I smiled to myself, feeling the passport and boarding card in my back pocket. I knew why I was going back. I felt positive. Ange was not the angel that I had believed her to be. She was just my mother. She was never 'Mum'. Beautiful and imperfect, broken and mended into a shape that could not hold me. Simply reaching for a life. I understood that.

But what was I reaching for now?

Across the concourse from the café are the security gates which I had come through. I squint a little and picture them there. Greg with one arm around Ange, smiling, face creased and holding back tears, a little to their right, Nicky, shouting something no doubt slightly rude with a great big grin, his blonde hair a bit overlong, and Mick looking slightly embarrassed but waving his arm. All happy, well and sending me off. Like the end of that awful *Star Wars* movie *Return of the Jedi* Bugs had so loved. I imagine that, smile and wave back.

I think I'll keep this as a memory. They can stay behind.

I turn and head to my flight.

Epilogue: 2001

I look out of the window over the tenement parking lot.

The rain has stopped, and a beam of sunshine sparks off the puddles, a golden path towards me filled with warmth. The world is clean.

And now, everything is different. This is not home. Not now.

When I had arrived from the airport, Nana was there to welcome me with a hug, looking older now, softer somehow. She had held me tight and cried on my shoulder. She apologised for hiding things. I had forgiven her already. She knew that I would not have come back otherwise.

The flat had stood empty for the best part of a decade. It was time to let it go. The sale had been quick; people now wanted to live in these blocks. There were new families moving in every day.

I said my goodbyes to the neighbours. I would see them again, but it was still the right thing to do. Mrs Ranjeet had got her daughter-in-law to make me the biggest pile of samosas to take with me. I could not say no. Seumas, one of Nicky's 'Lost Boys' had fished a bottle of whisky out of his cupboard. It had already been started but he said I was to have a dram on the first night at my new place. Morna gave me a box of Walkers shortbread, and Neil handed me a lump of coal. I wondered where he had got it from and quipped that it was not Hogmanay. He chuckled.

"Well, if ye need a tall dark stranger to grace yer doorway, ye ken where I am!"

Hugs, cards, and well wishes now filled the bag which I slung over my shoulder.

The flat is pristine. There is a new kitchen and a modern bathroom. Lou took the bath and had it installed at the Sugar Factory. I don't need to understand why. That's his thing. There's a big double-sized shower now, with a rain effect overhead and a separate movable one. The bedrooms walls have been replastered, sanded, repainted, the carpets changed, all the skirting has also had due attention.

I walk down the hall. Nicky no longer sits at the top of the stairs, his grazed knees poking out from his shorts, peering at me through a thatch of hair. My father's coat hasn't hung musty in the hall. My mother's empty, weather-beaten flowerpots have finally been taken from the windowsill. Nana won't pull and jiggle the key in the door ever again. I don't need rescued from here anymore.

The front door has been repainted red, the lock fixed, complete with a new brass number. The hall shelf has been replaced. The broken pane in the kitchen door has been mended. All those years it had stood witness to our family, broken in a fight. I had waited for Mick to fix it, for Ange to come back and repair it. For Nana, or George with his tool kit. In the end, it was me who got it sorted. It was odd being able to look through it without the cracks making everything look disjointed and out of place.

We spent a week gutting the flat before the workmen came. I kept the picture of Dad and Mum on their wedding day, the one with me on my bike. Us all on the hospital bed the day Nicky was born. There were a couple of Nicky and I through the years that I liked too. I would have one framed. I kept Nicky's sketch book. I wrapped the paring knife from the kitchen in a forgotten silk scarf of Mum's. I put them all in a memory box, which I left in my old bedroom until today. Nana and I had thrown everything else out. We could speak freely now. As we cleared each room in turn, she helped me turn over my memories, light them differently, fresh shadows, new angles. The flat was unrecognisable.

Balancing the box, I pulled the door closed behind me, locked it, and posted the keys through the letterbox. I headed along the walkway. I noticed that the lift had now been fixed but had no idea when that had happened. It didn't seem recent. Maybe while I had been away. I walked down the stairs. They had been cleaned and the walls painted. I smiled at my younger self reading in the stairwell. Things were moving on and changing. I tucked my memories under my arm and set off to my new home across town.

There's a sign in the car park.
NOTICE: WORKS TO START 01.03.01
GREEN SPACES INITIATIVE
REMOVAL OF CAR PARK
CONSTRUCTION OF PLAY PARK AND PUBLIC SPACE

I hope a tree or two might be planted, maybe one that has outgrown its pot.

Acknowledgements

I am fortunate to have many wonderful people who have cheered and championed me in my journey to publication. Each and every one of you has played a vital role, and I am immeasurably grateful.

Here I am just going to thank my publisher – Peter, Ambrose and Josh – for all their work and my husband and children for their support at home – "Mummy is writing."